Praise f

"Lane has per
Consistently st
Lane's is one of the best."

—*Booklist*

"Shades of *Miss Congeniality* lend a rosy hue to this frisky romance. . . . [Lane's] use of comically protracted sentences will make some readers feel as if they've just run a marathon, but in the end, they will be glad they did."

—*Publishers Weekly*

Reinventing Romeo

"The story is a fireworks decathlon . . . technical details, romance and opportunities for sabotage should light readers' fuses."

—*The Akron Beacon Journal*

"One of those rare novels that manages to combine suspense, humor, and romance believably in one package. Not many new authors can pull off this feat, but Connie Lane does it successfully. . . . *Reinventing Romeo* balances suspense with sexual tension to create a page-turning tale of adventure and romance. It's an engaging ride well worth the price of admission."

—*Milwaukee Journal Sentinel*

Romancing Riley

"Sassy and stylish. . . . With its fresh, feisty characters and diverse settings, this past-meets-present tale will help Lane win over a younger generation of romance readers."

—*Publishers Weekly*

"Lane's fast-paced story is a lot of fun, and the electricity between Riley and Zap crackles."

—*Booklist*

Also by Connie Lane

The Viscount's Bawdy Bargain

Published by Pocket Books

CONNIE LANE

THE Duke's Scandalous Secret

POCKET BOOKS
New York London Toronto Sydney

This book is a work of fiction. Names, characters, places and incidents are products of the author's imagination or are used fictitiously. Any resemblance to actual events or locales or persons, living or dead, is entirely coincidental.

An *Original* Publication of POCKET BOOKS

POCKET BOOKS, a division of Simon & Schuster, Inc.
1230 Avenue of the Americas, New York, NY 10020

ISBN: 0-7434-6287-4

First Pocket Books printing September 2004

10 9 8 7 6 5 4 3 2 1

Lettering by David Gatti. Illustration by Alan Ayers.

Manufactured in the United States of America

For information regarding special discounts for bulk purchases, please contact Simon & Schuster Special Sales at 1-800-456-6798 or business@simonandschuster.com

4zorro

The Duke's Scandalous Secret

1

Lynnette Overton was a pink of Society. It had been remarked among those who knew her that she was as merry as a cricket, and more than one gentleman of her acquaintance thought her quite taking in her own, straightforward fashion. No one had ever accused her of being a cabbagehead. Nor had it ever been said that she was so timid as to not say boo to a goose.

Yet even she was not one to take foolish chances.

Before she climbed into bed that night with a cup of chocolate and a copy of Mrs. Mordefi's newest sensational gothic novel, Lynnette locked her door. She was too taken by the glittering light of a full moon to pull her draperies shut but even she was not so blinded by the sparkle as to let it beguile her. So she also made sure that the French windows that looked onto a wide veranda, and from there over the gardens, were fastened tight.

It was a good thing she did, she told herself, settling down with her book. The happenings at Greystone Castle were enough to curl her liver.

The noise came from outside my window, a low, inhuman moan that seemed at one moment to come from the wind and the next to shiver in the air all around the ancient castle walls. My heart beat like a marching army, the sound so loud in my ears I wondered that my father, or my dear governess, Madame Bretaigne, or any of our servants who were asleep in their own chambers, did not hear the uproar and come to my aid.

Except for my own rough breathing and the sound outside that seemed nothing less than the exhalation of hell, Greystone Castle was quiet, its inhabitants blessedly and soundly asleep at this late hour, insensible to the terror that coursed through the air like the reverberation of thunder.

A frisson like icy fingers touched Lynnette's shoulders and she burrowed farther under her blankets. She fluffed her pillow and tilted the book to make the most of the single candle that burned beside her bed. Her heart pounded, nearly as unmercifully as that of poor Clarice, the besieged heroine in this, the latest tome from the wildly popular Mrs. Mordefi.

Pounding heart and icy shivers aside, Lynnette could no more have stopped reading than she could keep herself from taking another breath. Mrs. Mordefi had long been her favorite author and *Greystone Castle* was all that Lynnette had hoped for. And more.

* * *

I do not remember pushing back the blankets under which I was huddled, weak and shivering with fright. I do not remember my bare feet touching the icy flagstone floor. I cannot recall, though I have tried mightily in the long years since that most haunting of nights, when I took into my hands the candle that was lit beside my bed. I know only that I carried it with me, its light around me like a nimbus in the black void. The flame did not shiver; my hands did not tremble. Nor did my feet falter. They carried me relentlessly nearer and nearer, step by inexorable step, to the window and to the horrific sound that shuddered in the air just outside.

A small scraping sound interrupted Lynnette's reading and she gasped and sat up, automatically looking around her bedchamber.

"Looby!" She scolded herself instantly for being so suggestible as to let Clarice's plight affect her own pleasurable pastime. Yet it was not so easy to convince herself that what she'd heard wasn't the sound of her doorknob turning.

Though she knew full well that her housekeeper had been abed for hours and was not inclined to move about the house at night, Lynnette called to her in any case. "Mrs. Wilcox?"

There was no answer.

"Of course." She clicked her tongue, a reminder not to be so fanciful. Ready to settle down again, she positioned the pillow behind her in a more comfortable fashion. When she did, her hand brushed against the paper that was tucked beneath it. Just as it was tucked there every night.

Suddenly, in spite of the reasoning that told her otherwise, the sound she'd heard outside her door did not seem so unlikely.

Lynnette swallowed the dry-as-sand taste that filled her mouth. She did not need to remind herself that while she was visiting Brighton recently and out to tea with friends, someone had slipped into her lodgings. When she'd returned, she found chaos. Her bedchamber had been turned upside down. Her desk had been emptied. Even her wardrobe had been thoroughly searched.

She knew this single sheet of paper was exactly what the intruder had been looking for.

"No use kicking up a dust," she reminded herself. "You're home now at Plumley Terrace and no one can get to it here." It was good advice, but it did not keep her from propping herself on one elbow to look across her well-appointed room and toward the doorway again.

"No one. Nothing." She let the words escape on the end of a sigh and forced the tension out of her shoulders. It was not as easy to untwist the knot in her stomach so she reached for her cup of chocolate and sipped. She closed her eyes, savoring the taste and the heat that poured through her and eased her jangled nerves.

Soothed, she went back to her reading.

* * *

I remember nothing at all until the moment I found myself at the window. I could see little beyond my own reflection, my pupils wide and dark, my hair loose around my shoulders like an ebon shawl. I knew that beyond the glass was naught but the vista of lonely countryside that extended for miles around our home. There was no balcony outside my chamber. No foothold of any kind at all in the sheer rocky face of Greystone Castle. Far below, glistening in the moonlight, was the moat that ringed our walls, and below and to my right, the medieval drawbridge that was never raised because Father believed it to be only for ceremonial purposes, those occasions when someone of importance came to call. In our isolation, we did not often have visitors.

For one heartbeat, then two, nothing happened and I realized that the sound that had disturbed my sleep and brought me from my bed had stopped. The quiet pressed against me, as real as the darkness that surrounded me. I shook my head, certain that the noise and the shudder of fear that rode on the air with it had been nothing more than a dream, that I had imagined both the sound and the chill that crawled along my skin like the frosty fingers of death.

"Sleepwalking." My own whispered word echoed back at me from the stillness like a prayer.

I was sleepwalking. Certainly that was what was happening. Thus, all was explained. The sound was not real. It was nothing but a figment of my too fanciful imagination.

If I dreamed the sound then perhaps I was asleep still. I must certainly be. For as I stood there, endeavoring to see beyond the blackness that wrapped our castle like a shroud, a face appeared outside my window. A pale face, with eyes as yellow as a rodent's, and as hot as flame.

Lynnette bolted upright, as startled by the appearance of the face at the window of Greystone Castle as was poor Clarice. It was a few moments before her pounding heart finally slowed and the blood did not rush so fast in her ears, and it wasn't until then that she heard a faint sound on the other side of her room. Like Clarice, she was not prone to fits of imagination. Like Clarice, she did not need to be. The sound was real enough.

"Mrs. Wilcox?" Lynnette's voice was small in her ears. It echoed back at her in the dark. "Mrs. Wilcox?" she called again, yet even as she did, she knew the noise she heard could not have been made by her housekeeper. Mrs. Wilcox was elderly and as plump as a Christmas goose. She was not adventuresome, nor was she the type who would risk a walk in the moonlight, fearing as much a case of the vapors as she did an encounter with ruffians.

It certainly meant Mrs. Wilcox was not on the broad veranda outside Lynnette's window.

And that is surely where the sound originated.

Lynnette hesitated. But only for a moment. She had yet to find a mystery that did not leave her so curious that she simply had to investigate and she had never been one to back down from a challenge. Taking her candle into one hand, she padded across the room to the French doors.

Her head still filled with the fabulous pictures Mrs. Mordefi painted with her words, it took a minute for Lynnette to realize that because of the candle, she could see little beyond her own reflection staring back at her from the glass. Her eyes were wide, and because they were a shade of gray she had always thought unremarkable, they looked to be no more than a reflection of the moonlight. Her hair, streaked with mahogany in good light, was inky in the darkness. Anna, her maid, had carefully brushed it before Lynnette climbed into bed, and it was loose around her shoulders. Rather than look at herself—and think of Clarice—she blew out the flame.

Outside, moonlight tipped the garden with silver and threw the magnificent grounds of Plumley Terrace into a jumble of light and shadow. It was a soft early spring night with little breeze and there were no trees growing near Lynnette's spacious second-floor room.

"And nothing to account for the noise," she told herself, and just to prove it, she bent at the waist and tilted her head first one way and then the other to see as far to either side of the veranda as she could.

Nothing.

No sign of what might have caused the noise. No sign of movement. No sign of anything at all but—

Out of nowhere, a man appeared on the other side of the glass, just inches from Lynnette. Her heart stopped. Her breath caught. Frozen by surprise, she could do nothing more than stare.

He was tall and broad, swathed in dark clothing from

head to toe. Against the black cloth, his face was as pale as fish scales.

The moment of paralysis evaporated in a rush of fear. She cried out just as the intruder jiggled the knob on the door. Finding it locked, his eyes narrowed and he shot her a look of such venom that she stepped back. Her feet tangled and her nightdress twisted around her knees. Panic closed around her and before she could brace herself, Lynnette hit the floor. By the time she pushed the hair out of her eyes and regained her senses—as well as her breath—the man was gone.

She stared through the blackness toward the window, expecting to see the shadowy form again, and when she did not—for one minute, then two, then longer—she pulled herself to her feet and scurried back to her bed. She had no intention of closing her eyes, but she tunneled beneath the blankets and pulled them up to her chin, taking comfort in the familiar, lavender smell and the feel of the finely woven linen against her skin.

It wasn't until then that her hand brushed the leather cover of *Greystone Castle.* Lynnette pulled the book out from under the blankets. She removed the paper from beneath her pillow and tucked it into the pages of the book. She shook, not from fright so much as from relief. If it wasn't for Mrs. Mordefi and the tremors of fear the woman's books shot through her, Lynnette would not have locked her door or her window before she went to bed.

That meant that Mrs. Mordefi—bless her!—was

responsible for saving the single, precious piece of paper that had once belonged to Lynnette's mother.

And possibly Lynnette's life, as well.

"So then Varclay, he says . . ." Across the dining-room table from Lynnette, Arthur Hexam was laughing so heartily, he nearly choked on the biscuit he was eating. He took a sip of claret and pounded his chest.

Never one to be outdone, Roger Palliston, who was sitting to Lynnette's left, saw his opportunity. He took over the telling of the story. "Varclay says, and in that high-pitched voice of his that always sounds as if he's talking through his nose, he says—"

"What do you mean, no wager?" Deware Clifton, the young Duke of Latimer, was a far better actor than anyone might have expected. He popped out of his chair and, as if by magic, the expression on his face changed, as did his demeanor and his voice. Polished one second, he was nervous and twitchy the next. Just as James Varclay had been nervous and twitchy the last time Lynnette happened across him. The imitation was so perfect, everyone gathered around the dining room table of Somerton House laughed and applauded.

Fearing she would betray herself if she did anything else, Lynnette applauded, too.

No one there could have guessed how little she felt like joining in the merriment.

In spite of the candles that flickered all around, the delicious food, and the very good company, a shiver skittered over her shoulders. Ever since the night before when the man appeared outside her window, every noise made Lynnette start, every movement just out of the line of her vision brought her spinning around.

Just to be sure she was safe.

She was safe here.

Reminding herself of the fact, Lynnette pushed down her terror. She looked around the table at the people who were so dear to her and some of the tension that had her insides tied into knots eased. Across the table, her cousin Nick, the Viscount Somerton, was sitting side by side with his darling wife, Willie. Just a few weeks earlier, they had announced that before the turn of the year, the viscount would have an heir. Now, husband and wife looked lovingly into each other's eyes, their hands entwined, their laughter mingled as easily as their smiles.

It was a good thing Nick was so preoccupied. He had always had an unsettling way of reading Lynnette's moods and that would not do. At least not yet. Before Willie settled him with her great good sense and in a love match the likes of which the *ton* had not seen in ages, Nick was known to be overzealous. For now, the news of the intruder and of the sheet of paper Lynnette had taken the precaution to sew into the hem of her dress for safekeeping was best kept secret. Lest Nick should do something rash before Lynnette had time to work through the puzzle for herself.

Another burst of laughter from the people around the table brought Lynnette out of her brown study. She was just in time to see Latimer slip easily into playing Varclay again. His nose in the air, his voice as high as the ceiling, he looked around at the small assemblage. "There must be a wager! The Blades and the Dashers have been wagering since damned Hector was a brassy pup!"

"I own, it is most exactly what Varclay said," Hexam added, his pudgy face split with a smile.

"Exactly!" Palliston concurred. "And then Willie—"

"Then Willie did what any sensible woman would do." They had stepped onto what was clearly his domain, and Nick took over the telling of the tale. "She reminded Varclay that my wagering days are over. The poor man hardly knew what to say."

So that she might look to be as fully engrossed in the narration as they were, it seemed the right time for Lynnette to say something. "Are the Blades so desperate for amusement that they have to come to the Dashers to find it? What sort of wager did they have in mind?"

"That is the true wonder of the thing," Nick said, his blue eyes twinkling in the candlelight. A platter of the biscuits Willie called kaju badam—she'd learned the recipe during her early years in India with her missionary family—went round the table and Lynnette helped herself to one. She had eaten little since the night before but she knew that if she picked at this as she had at most of tonight's dinner, Nick and Willie would surely take note. She nibbled the biscuit.

"If you can believe it," Nick said, "they want us—the Dashers—"

"To help them—the Blades—" Latimer added.

"To discover a secret," Hexam put forward.

"A secret . . ." Palliston was as much of an actor as Latimer. He let the drama build before he leaned closer to Lynnette, his florid complexion redder than ever thanks to the candlelight and an evening awash in claret. "A secret about the Duke of Ravensfield!"

If Lynnette needed something to distract her, they could not have found a better subject than Thomas Flander.

She swallowed hard and took a moment to school the sudden flare of emotion that threatened to betray her interest. "I cannot imagine there is any man in London who has fewer secrets than Ravensfield," she said. "He is quite the blood and always a subject for the gossips. The *ton* talks incessantly about his sense of style and how much of a go-as-you-please he is to always dress in black, day or night. They speak of his carriages and how much they cost. They talk about his many homes."

"Adzooks! She's as right as rain about that." Hexam rolled his eyes. "Even if he should try not to hear it or pretend not to care, a man cannot but go to a ball or a garden party and not hear who the Duke of Ravensfield is currently bedding."

The very thought was enough to make heat flood into Lynnette's cheeks. She took a sip of wine.

"Be that as it may," Nick said, getting up to refill her glass when he saw that it was empty, "the Blades are convinced that Ravensfield is keeping something from them. It's pure fustian, of course. The Season has yet to start in earnest and the Blades are blue-deviled. They need something to spark their spirits and so they've concocted this story and the wager to go along with it. The man's gone to the country. It's as simple as that."

"Except that he hasn't been seen for two whole months." Willie's expression was as mild as the spring night but her eyes glittered with mischief when she looked at her husband. "The Blades have gone to call on Ravensfield," she said, telling this part of the story to Lynnette. "And he has turned them away at the door."

"They've written to him," Latimer added, "and their letters have been returned."

"They even went so far as to send a special emissary to Broadworth Hall, that new country home Ravensfield built in Berkshire. His favorite ladybird." Palliston winked. "Word has it she returned to town in a fit of the dismals. Seems his grace took one look at her, turned her right around, and sent her back to London. Never once let her through the front door of Broadworth!"

"That is remarkable." Lynnette tipped her head, considering. "And why did the Blades think the Dashers might know something about all this? What did they want you to do?"

"What they wanted us to do is to find out what the man is up to," Nick explained. "You know, spy on him, learn what secret it is that keeps him rusticated. They said if we could discover the duke's secret before any of them did, they would pay us an amount of one thousand pounds."

When Willie pushed back from the table, Lynnette did, too. Seeing that the ladies were going to stand, the men rose to their feet. Lynnette accepted Palliston's arm when he offered it.

"The Blades must indeed be moped," Lynnette commented. "I can't see why they care so much. They should leave the man in peace."

"But the Season is starting." Hexam scurried ahead and opened the door into the salon where the men would spend the rest of the evening playing whist while Lynnette and Willie put their heads together for a long chat. "The Blades say that things are deadly dull here in London without Ravensfield."

"What they mean . . ." Nick led Willie into the room and, with a kiss on her cheek, deposited her on the sofa near the fire that sparkled in the grate. "Ravensfield has the deepest pockets. Without him in town, the Blades aren't nearly as free in their spending."

"Or as likely to attract the handsomest women!" Latimer laughed. "He brings them in like honey draws flies."

"Like a magnet pulls metal," Palliston put in.

"Like—" Realizing the plate of kaju badam had been left on the table, Hexam hurried back for it. "Like Willie's biscuits attract me!" he said, returning just as quickly as he left. They all laughed.

Except for Lynnette. She was too busy thinking. She smoothed a hand over the skirt of her silvery sarcenet dress. "I have been considering a trip to the country," she said, and when the others of their company looked at her in wonder, she added, "Mr. Hexam is right, the Season has not started in earnest and things here in town are dreadfully dull. A trip to the country might be just the thing."

Nick's gaze was a bit too probing. "If it's a trip to the country you're looking for, you no doubt will be heading for Oxfordshire. You have a home there, after all."

"Indeed." Lynnette smiled smoothly. She had a home there, right enough, and she loved Watersmill Manor as much as she loved anything. Still, if she left town and headed there, the man who had followed her to Brighton and had been so bold as to appear at the door of her bedchamber was sure to catch wind of it.

Yet if she traveled somewhere a bit more unexpected . . . Somewhere where she might have a chance to collect her thoughts and decide what her next move should be in regard to the message her mother had written so long ago . . .

If she went, perhaps, to Berkshire . . .

She broached the idea carefully so as not to arouse suspicion. "Watersmill will be no more exciting than London is this time of year. I was thinking of something with a bit more spirit. If the Dashers are looking for someone to play the spy with Ravensfield—"

Nick put an end to the fancy with one stern look. "Absolutely not! I have already delivered our answer to the Blades. We will not participate in this or any other wager. I neither know nor care what Ravensfield is doing in the country." He plunked down in a chair at the card table. "The man is insufferable."

"And very handsome!" Willie's voice sparkled with good humor. "If you gentlemen are not interested in Ravensfield's doings, you must at least admit that the women of the *ton* are eager to find out what's going on."

"That's right." Lynnette offered Willie a smile in thanks for bolstering her argument. "Ravensfield may have turned away his friends but, surely, if a woman arrived on his doorstep—"

"You heard what Palliston said," Nick reminded her. "A woman has already arrived on his doorstep."

Lynnette tisk-tisked away the very idea. "Not that kind of woman. I mean a gentlewoman. If she arrived unexpectedly. Perhaps seeking help. If she was in some sort of distress. With a broken carriage wheel, let's say, or—"

"Bah!" Nick had only just picked up the deck of cards. He slapped it on the table. "Surely, Lynnette, you have better things to do than go chasing after a scoundrel like Ravensfield."

Lynnette refused to be put off. "Oh, pooh! The duke cannot be so much of a rogue as is rumored. He knows you, Nick. He knows our family. If I happened to arrive in the neighborhood, if I happened to be in need of assistance, if I happened to appear at his door, he would have no choice but to welcome me into his home. And while I'm there—"

"What might happen while you're there is exactly what worries me." Apparently deciding the conversation was over, Nick picked up the cards and shuffled.

He forgot that stubbornness was a family trait.

"Well, I wouldn't go alone." The very idea was caper-witted and Lynnette dismissed it with a shake of her head. "So you see, you needn't worry about my virtue. I would have my maid with me, of course, and my coachman and—"

"Are you so in need of money, then, that you would take the Blades' one thousand?" Nick asked her.

It was on the tip of Lynnette's tongue to tell them all. If she explained—about the coded entry in her mother, Madelaine's, missing diary, about the paper she carried with her now that interpreted the code and, perhaps, identified the person who was responsible for her mother's banishment from Society—she knew they would understand.

Then again, she remembered that nine years earlier, Madelaine had thought her own friends would understand her plight, too. When they did not, when all except a few loyal souls turned away from her after she was accused of an infamous jewel theft, Lynnette remembered how her mother's reputation was left in ruins, and how Madelaine had died, her spirit—and her heart—broken.

Before Lynnette was willing to open her mother's life to new scrutiny, she needed answers. She would never find them if the thief who must surely have Madelaine's diary succeeded in recovering the key to the code, as well.

"It is not the Blades' money I am after," she said. "It's a bit of excitement. If I arrive at the duke's home looking like a paragon— "

"You could not look otherwise, Miss Lynnette," Hexam told her, snatching her hand and bowing over it.

She thanked him with a quick smile. "If I wear my new Hungarian wrap, the one that is lined with pink silk—"

"Pink silk would surely bring out the pretty color in your cheeks," Latimer said, sending her a smile along with a wink that told her that while he was sincere, he did not mean the comment to be overly personal.

She smiled at him, too, and got back to the matter at hand. "If I wear my Caledonian cap, the one with the black feathers that I have been told looks all the kick . . ." She stopped and gave Palliston his chance to break in, and when he only grinned in agreement, she breezed on. "Even a man such as the duke could not turn away so respectable a woman."

"Especially one who would, no doubt, look so very delicious." Nick's comment was as airy as the way he dealt the cards out on the table. The way he dealt the cards out on the table told her that the subject was closed.

She gave up without a fight.

Or so it seemed.

For even as Lynnette joined Willie on the sofa and fell into deep conversation with her, even as they chatted about baby names and the latest gossip, Lynnette's mind was already on the road to Berkshire.

It was the most logical plan, she reminded herself, for it would keep her person—and the paper that had been written by her mother—safe.

What she did not admit—even to herself—was that there was another motive behind her scheme.

For though she had met him only once and he had—no doubt—promptly forgotten her, it was a fact that she had been, ever since the day she first clapped eyes on him over the rim of a glass of ratafia, head over heels in love with the Duke of Ravensfield.

2

Thunder rippled through the night air like the growl of a wild beast. Its vibration traveled along my spine and burrowed beneath my skin until my bones shivered with the sound, so like a death knell. No sooner had the reverberation died in my ears than the coal-black sky split with a firebolt so fierce, I could see the entire countryside, as if by some sorcerer's magic. The forest around me lit, as dazzling as day, and for one moment, my outlook brightened along with it. With even a hint of light, I might find my way out of the tangle of trees and brush that had me so turned around even here on my father's own lands that I did not know one direction from another.

As quickly as the light flickered, it died. My hopes perished along with it. With no path at my feet and no sign of where I was or how I might make my way back to the sheltering walls of Greystone, I stood, frozen. When the icy pellets of rain began in earnest and beat against my cheeks, I could do no more than stand and tremble, all too aware that behind me, somewhere in the dark, He waited for me to make another wrong turn.

"Damnation!"

Lynnette was not often inclined to curse. Yet this time, she could hardly help herself. It was late and long past nightfall and her carriage was well and truly stuck in the soft ground left from two days of rain. Recalling the passage of *Greystone Castle* that she had read before they veered off the road did little to cheer her.

Especially when she found herself in much the same predicament as poor Clarice.

As if to emphasize the point, thunder rattled in the sky overhead. Lightning flickered in the night air, throwing the landscape around her into a mix of light and shadow.

"At least it isn't raining," Lynnette consoled herself, but no sooner were the words out of her mouth than she heard the first drops hit the roof of the carriage.

"Hell and damnation!" she muttered, peering out the window. The road they were traveling was heavily forested on either side, and when her coachman, Garvey, started out in search of assistance, he had assured her that he knew exactly where they were.

"Broadworth Hall can be no more than a bit of a jaunt that way," he'd said, stabbing one gnarled finger into the dark. "You just sit tight, Miss Lynnette, and I'll be back quicker than a lamb can shake its tail."

But that was a good long time ago and Lynnette was certain that Garvey himself was lost somewhere in the forest. Her maid had been taken ill outside Silchester and left there at an inn until someone from Plumley Terrace could come around to collect her. Lynnette was alone. She knew they would have no assistance this night unless she found it herself. Pulling her Hungarian wrap closer around her, she stepped out of the carriage.

The rain beat harder. The black feathers atop her Caledonian cap drooped into her eyes and she pursed her lips and blew at them. To no avail. They were as wet as her newest pumps were muddy thanks to the soggy ground, and as soaked as her mulberry muslin gown was in a matter of moments. Pity, for she had worn the gown because the color brought out the highlights in her hair.

When another thunderbolt crashed overhead, Lynnette jumped. She cursed her luck as well as her sense of direction. She knew she was somewhere in Berkshire. She knew she was somewhere in the vicinity of Broadworth Hall. She was certain that the *somewhere* in question was the middle of nowhere, and that there was no sign of Garvey and nothing around her but trees, their leaves so heavy from the rain that they bent low to the ground and dripped down on her.

Until she was wetter than ever.

Undaunted, even if she was drenched, Lynnette continued on her way. Her shoe caught on a tree root and she nearly lost her footing. Startled, she squealed and instantly regretted it. The last thing she needed was to remind herself that she was alone and helpless.

"Helpless, indeed!" She was indignant at the very thought. Another peal of thunder crawled through the sky and, though it shivered the leaves on the trees directly over her head, she forced herself to keep still. A flash of lightning was sure to follow and, this time when it did, she would pay close attention. She might see a path. Or a landmark. She might catch a glimpse of a rooftop. Or a road.

Just as she expected, the lightning flashed, as bright as a Catherine Wheel. What she did not expect to see along with it was a man swathed head to toe in black. He was standing motionless some twenty feet or so to her right.

By the time Lynnette sucked in a small noise of surprise and jumped back, startled, the forest was once again plunged into darkness and she'd convinced herself she was imagining things.

The figure was too tall to be Garvey. Too broad. Too dark. And Garvey, she told herself, was the only one fool enough to be out wandering in weather such as this. In the middle of the night. In the middle of a storm. In the middle of a forest. No one but a jinglebrains would simply be standing, as rigid as a stone, in the full rage of the storm.

Like some black sentinel of the unrelenting night.

She shook the fantasy from her head along with the words that sounded as if they had been lifted, to the letter, from Mrs. Mordefi. It didn't make it any easier to banish the memory of the figure who had appeared on her veranda back in London as if he had been spawned by the night itself.

"No one knows you were coming to Berkshire," she reminded herself. "Not even Nick and Willie. No one knows you're here."

It may have brought her some small comfort if she didn't consider that it also meant that should she be trapped too long in the storm, no one would know where to look for her body.

The cold reality that seeped into her bones was enough to get her moving again. As carefully as she could, considering that both her dress and her wrap were weighted down with water, she stepped over a fallen log that lay across what there was of a path. No sooner was she on the other side of it than she swore she saw a movement to her right. Like a shifting in the night air.

In the next flash of lightning, the man in black materialized out of the rain no more than an arm's length away. He made her a deep, showy bow.

The next second, the forest was plunged once again into darkness. But though she could no longer see the man, she could still feel him there. As if the lightning that slashed the sky overhead were somehow made flesh. The air around her sizzled. A hand touched her sleeve.

And Lynnette didn't dare wait to see what might happen next.

Her footsteps fueled with fear, she turned and ran.

Behind her, she heard the man's voice rumble. Or perhaps it was just another crash of thunder. Lynnette wasn't sure and she hardly cared. Mud sucked at her shoes. A prickly shrub plucked at her Hungarian wrap. A low-hanging branch loomed suddenly in front of her nose and she ducked under it and lost her footing. She went down on one knee and a shot of pain stabbed her ankle.

Even that was not enough to stop her. Not when she knew that the man was still somewhere behind her in the dark.

Lynnette pulled herself to her feet. When she put her weight on her left foot, she bit back a cry of pain and moved on. Panic blinded her and she took one step toward what looked like a turn in the path. Too late, she realized that the ground there fell sharply. She scrambled to regain her footing but with the pain in her ankle and the disobliging slew of mud, it was impossible. Before she could brace herself for the fall, she was already on her backside. The water and mud picked her up and carried her and because she could do nothing else, Lynnette went along for the ride.

Fortunately, the hill was not steep. Nor was it too tall.

Unfortunately, there was a large puddle of water at the bottom of it. At the same time she splashed into it, a crack of thunder boomed directly overhead and a bolt of white-hot lightning sizzled in the air. She shrieked and landed nose down against something that did not feel at all like the muddy earth she expected.

In fact, it felt like the toe of a man's boot.

Shaking the surprise from her head and finding herself with a face full of feathers for her effort, Lynnette raised herself on her elbows and looked up. Another crack of thunder shuddered the air. Another bolt of lightning flashed and fire outlined the black hulking shape of a large man.

It was the last thing she saw before she fainted dead away.

"Infernal . . . Damnable . . . Beastly . . . Worthy!"

His eyes narrowed against the water cascading like a cataract off his hat and into his eyes and from there onto Lynnette Overton who was cradled in his arms, Thomas Flander, the Duke of Ravensfield, bellowed for his valet. When the man did not appear instantly—as all good valets should when they are bellowed for—he raised his voice until it rang from the rafters to the cellars of Broadworth Hall.

"Worthy! Where the devil—"

"Here, your grace." Worthy scurried out from the direction of the kitchen where, now that Ravensfield thought of it, he'd instructed the man to wait with the rest of the staff and one shivering and wet-to-the-gills coachman while he went in search of the young woman who was supposed to have the brains and the good sense to be waiting for rescue in her carriage.

Ravensfield wasted a sneer on Lynnette, who was still in a swoon and, as such, completely unaware of the epic proportions of the expression.

"We've got to do something with her." Ravensfield caught himself in the act of handing over the young lady to Worthy's care. Force of habit. In addition to acting as his valet, Worthy was also his secretary, his right-hand man, and his confidant. Not only was he used to foisting problems on Worthy, he depended on it.

And right now, Lynnette Overton was a problem.

Still . . .

Ravensfield pulled Lynnette closer and adjusted his hold, the better to keep a safe grip on the wet, muddy, and very slippery Miss Overton. It wasn't as if she were much of a burden. She was as light as a feather, and she lay in Ravensfield's arms as if she'd been made to occupy the spot.

The thought crawled along his skin, warming the places he could have sworn were soaked through with rainwater.

And the fact that he was thinking it as he stood in the grand entryway dripping on the Axminster and leaving a trail of mud behind him, only served to remind Ravensfield that he needed to get the young lady in question mopped up, dried off, and back on her way to wherever it was she'd been headed when she'd so dampishly ended up on his front doorstep.

He didn't need a guest. Not any guest. Not now. More precisely, he didn't need a woman hanging about the house because women were too often too talkative, too frequently too demanding, and too many times, too much of a distraction to allow a man the kind of peace and quiet he so desperately needed.

"We've got to get her dried off and cleaned up and . . ." Ravensfield chanced another look at the woman in his arms. She was a pretty enough thing, even if she did look a bit like a cat that had been dragged from the gutter. Her skin was porcelain. Her face, though free of the paints so many women used to enhance what beauty the good Lord had seen fit to bestow, was well made. She had a small nose, turned up slightly at the end, ruler-straight brows that were the same dark color as her hair, lips that were bowed, as if designed for kissing. Smeared with mud and soaked with rainwater, she looked more like a doxy than a diamond of the first water yet even smeared with mud and soaked with rainwater, she was far from unattractive.

If she were one of the bits of muslin Ravensfield knew from town, he would gladly have warmed her body with his own. But this was Nick Pryce's cousin, damn it, and as such, one of those proper women with proper reputations and the morals to match.

Ravensfield turned about, swinging Lynnette in his arms as he did. "Devil take it, Worthy. What the bloody hell am I supposed to do with the baggage?"

"Upstairs, your grace." Mrs. Beatrice Brickhaven, known to one and all simply as Mrs. B, was as much the paragon of housekeepers as Worthy was the non-such of valets. Her head high, her shoulders back, and a deliciously dry and warm-looking blanket draped over one arm, she rounded the corner like a frigate heading to dock. She never stopped but went to the staircase and sailed right up. "Thinking that the young lady was bound to show up here sooner or later, we've readied a room for her, your grace. If you'd follow me, sir."

When he saw that the room prepared for Miss Overton was near his own, Ravensfield did not comment. Though he had never made a secret of the fact that he valued his privacy, he had never specifically forbidden the use of any of the rooms on the second floor for guests. Then again, as far as he could remember, in the year since Broadworth Hall had been completed, Lynnette Overton was the first guest he had ever had.

The thought raced through his head while he watched Mrs. B open the door of the room just across the passageway from his study. It was just for a few hours, he told himself, tamping down a sudden spurt of panic. Once she was changed into dry clothing and had something nice and hot ladled into her, Lynnette Overton would be on her way.

And he could have his precious privacy back.

Adjusting his stance to walk into the room sideways so as not to damage either Lynnette's head or the wall with her muddy shoes, Ravensfield stepped into the room. He stopped short of laying Lynnette on the bed.

"I suppose we should . . ." He turned to look toward where Mrs. B waited near the door. "I mean, there's no use putting her on the bed. Not in her wet clothes. I suppose that means we should—"

"Jenny will be here in a moment, your grace," Mrs. B

said, referring to one of the younger maids. The housekeeper crossed the room and busied herself laying the blanket on the floor next to the bed. "She will help. If only . . ."

It didn't take a genius to read between the lines and through the silent insinuation of Mrs. B's sentence. "If only I am not here. Yes. Of course." It was not propriety Mrs. B was worried about. It was Jenny, and Ravensfield knew it.

Most of the Broadworth staff had come to Ravensfield from London. As a matter of fact, most had once been employed by Nick Pryce. They had deserted the Viscount Somerton en masse thanks to the scandal that ensued when a lark resulted in the kidnapping of the woman who later became Somerton's wife. Of course, the ungodly wages Ravensfield offered them had something to do with their exodus, too.

Jenny was not one of them. She was a local girl, and like some of the other young and uneducated servants who had lived all their lives in the villages that surrounded the Hall, Jenny was particularly nervous when her master was around. It was no secret why. The lesser classes did like a good rumor and the rumors that swirled around Ravensfield were as plentiful as the trees that grew on the seven thousand acres that surrounded Broadworth Hall. There was a time such idle talk would have rankled him. Now, it meant that the servants as well as the folk from the villages gave him wide berth. The maids refused to talk too loudly when he was in the house. The footmen thought twice about making themselves conspicuous. And that was just fine with Ravensfield. It meant they left him alone.

Holding tight to the thought, he bent and gently settled Lynnette on the blanket. Just as he did, her eyes fluttered open.

They were gray and soft. The color like moonlight.

The ridiculous notion stuck in Ravensfield's head, and as much as he tried to dislodge it, he found he could not. Her gaze flickered over his face. A smile touched her lips. And before he knew it, she was asleep again.

"Devil take it!" He stood up and backed away. "Did you see that, Mrs. B? Did you see the way the girl perked up there for a bit? Why didn't she stay awake? Why did she have to—"

"I'm sure it was quite an adventure for a young lady of good breeding, sir. Out there in the night with the storm raging all around. As it was for yourself." Mrs. B looked down at Ravensfield's mud-coated Wellingtons and the puddle that was collecting around him on the carpet. "Perhaps you'll want to get cleaned up yourself. While we settle Miss Overton."

"Settle?" Ravensfield didn't like the sound of the word. "You mean settle as in 'for the night'? You're not going to let her stay, are you?"

Mrs. B folded her hands at her waist. "It is not for me to say who stays here at Broadworth and who does not, your grace. It is your home, after all. Yet it would be less than honest of me not to point out the facts. The young lady's carriage is some distance away. Stuck in the mud if her coachman is to be believed. It is quite late and Miss Overton walked a great distance. She is wet and cold and I am told, of your acquaintance."

"Not really," Ravensfield answered. "I know her people, of course. They're—"

"Respectable. Yes, your grace. One look at the girl and I can tell that much. Far be it from me to tell you how to conduct yourself, your grace . . ." Mrs. B didn't need to finish the sentence. Anyone who knew the old girl knew exactly what she *wasn't* saying. Offering an opinion might be far from Mrs. B's bailiwick but that had never stopped her before and it wouldn't stop her this time.

"You cannot send her away," she said, glancing over her shoulder at him while she busied herself unfastening the clasp that held Lynnette's cloak. "It looks to me as if she's in need of a hero."

"A hero?" There was nothing funny about it but Ravensfield barked out a laugh nonetheless. "If that's what she's after, then she has come calling at the wrong place. If it's heroes the girl wants, then she best read a good book."

"Yes, your grace." As soon as the spotty-faced dumpling named Jenny entered the room, Mrs. B handed her Lynnette's wrap. She gave the door a pointed look. "Now if you'll excuse us, your grace."

More often than not, it would have irritated the hell out of Ravensfield to be dismissed so blatantly by a servant. This time, anxious to make the best of what was left of the night and eager to make sure that everything was ready for Miss Overton's departure in the morning, he was only too grateful to oblige.

"Of course," he said, and being sure to give Jenny a wicked smile as he left (just to keep the rumors flying), he headed out into the passageway and straight for his study. He locked the door behind him, poured two drinks in quick succession, and drank them even quicker before he sat down in the chair behind his desk.

"Devil take women for being so much of an inconvenience," he mumbled, and just so the thought could not occupy him for longer than it deserved, he reached for a blank sheet of paper and pulled it in front of him. He dipped his pen in the silver inkwell near his right hand, sucked in a long breath, and sat with his hand poised above the paper.

It wasn't until a small puddle of ink had dripped onto the paper that he realized he was still thinking about Lynnette Overton.

"Damnation!" he grumbled. He crumpled the piece of paper and hurled it across the room. But that did not stop him from thinking about how pretty Lynnette was or how, even though she was wet through and covered with mud, the scent of lavender still lingered around her, like a springtime cloud. It didn't keep him from thinking that the few curls that escaped from her ridiculous bonnet and were plastered to her face reminded him of the color of mahogany. Or how the feel of her body against his made him think that two months was far too long to be away from society and the pleasures of town.

Like all women, Lynnette Overton could be a distraction right enough.

All the more reason he needed to be rid of her.

3

That night, I dreamed again of the man with the fiery eyes. It was not a terrifying dream. Or perhaps it would be more truthful to say that it was not terrifying in the same way as so many of the fantasies that tumbled through my mind of late. Those dreams left my stomach cold. This dream was different, yet just as disturbing. I tossed and turned beneath my blankets all night long, and even once I awoke, I could not put the memory of it from my mind. Nor could I ignore the way it made me feel.

It left me trembling.

She had just begun to read, but Lynnette laid her book on the blanket that was spread over her lap. She tipped her head, thinking. How odd that Clarice should dream of a man whose eyes enflamed her and whose very presence made her feel as if the earth were not quite stable under her feet.

Lynnette had had much the same dream herself.

Even as the thought formed, there was a knock on her door, and before she could bid her caller to enter, the Duke of Ravensfield was already in the room.

Though it was early in the day, he was dressed completely in black. Except, that is, for his blindingly white linen and a neckcloth tied so skillfully and with so much panache, it was no wonder he was the envy of every gallant in London.

It was no surprise that he had captured female hearts from one end of the kingdom to the other, either.

Lynnette took a deep breath, trying her best to force her own suddenly galloping heartbeat into some semblance of control.

It didn't work.

In spite of her best laid plans and her own good advice to herself that when she arrived in Berkshire and came face-to-face with the duke, she would be a pattern card of grace and sophistication, a paragon of wit and intelligence, an example of all that was best in womankind so that he could not help but fall under her spell . . .

In spite of it all, she found herself tongue-tied and feeling more like a peagoose than a grown woman who should have known better than to let her good intentions—and her heart—be assaulted so easily and breached so quickly.

Yet how could she help herself? From the top of his coal-dark hair to the tips of boots that had been shined to perfection, Thomas Flander, the Duke of Ravensfield, was every bit as handsome as she remembered.

As if it had been chipped from stone, his chin was firm and square, and though Lynnette had heard more than one woman of the *ton* whisper behind her fan that it was simply a reflection of the duke's stubbornness, she thought instead that it was a sign of that certain, admirable personality that took to command as easily as to breathing. The notion was fostered further by the apparent fact that the duke's nose had been broken a time or two. Thomas Flander was not a man to back down from a fight.

Lynnette sat up as much as she was able considering that beneath the blanket, she was stretched out on the sofa, her left leg propped on a pillow so as to ease the swelling in her ankle. She leaned forward, hoping for a better look at the man. The way she remembered it, the duke's eyes were as black as his morning coat. She might have been able to confirm the memory if he wasn't so busy looking at everything in the room.

Everything but her.

It was a pleasant morning and the breeze that wafted through the open windows was warm and scented with early roses. Still, the duke chafed his hands together as if to be rid of a chill.

"Good morning," he said, addressing the pleasantry to the dressing table that stood against the far wall. "I trust you are well this morning, Miss Overton. I am happy to see that you are up and about."

"Except that I am not, your grace." Lynnette looked down at the sofa and up at the duke but still she could not catch his eye. He paced a fitful little pattern just inside the door. "Up and about, that is. I am awake, certainly, but—"

"Just a figure of speech!" A noise rolled up from deep in his throat, one that reminded her of the thunder that had growled through the forest the night before. "What I mean, of course, is that I'm glad to see you're awake and ready to be off. After what you went through last night, it must be quite a relief to know you are well and able to continue your journey."

"Indeed." The frost of his words touched Lynnette's insides. She had a paisley shawl draped over the back of the sofa and she reached for it and pulled it onto her shoulders. "I would think, your grace, that you might at least offer me breakfast before you shoo me out with the chickens."

"Breakfast?" For the first time since he entered the room, the duke looked directly at Lynnette, his eyes wide with mortification. "I do beg your pardon, Miss Overton. Has no one offered you—"

"I have had my breakfast, your grace," she told him, but only because when he looked so contrite, she could not bear to taunt him further. "It is, after all, quite late. Nearly eleven if my clock is to be believed. If I had waited this long to eat, I daresay I may have found myself in a swoon again."

"Of course. So . . ." He began to pace anew. "You're ready to head off to . . . I hope I am not being too forward to ask but I do not often have visitors here at Broadworth. Where was it you were headed, Miss

Overton, when you found yourself lost in my forest?"

"Bath," she told him, the lie so effortless, it surprised even her. "My dear friend Susan Grimsey is feeling poorly and I was headed there to cheer her spirits. We have not had a fortunate journey." This much of the story was, at least, the truth, and she breezed through it with little compunction. "My abigail, Anna, was taken ill. Then, of course, we had the bad luck to get stuck in Broadworth mud."

A smile flickered in his eyes. "I apologize for my mud," he said, and he made her a formal bow that sparked a memory.

"You!" Lynnette sat up as straight as she was able, the impact of the duke's smile forgotten beneath the epiphany. "You're the one who was in the forest last night. You chased me."

"Chased?" Ravensfield considered the possibility. But only for a second. The next instant, he slashed one hand through the air, as if to banish the very idea from the atmosphere. "Balderdash! I was not chasing you," he said, glaring down at her. "I was trying to corral you. Though heaven help me, you made that far more difficult than you needed to. Had you had the good sense to realize I was there to help you, you might not have run away. Then again, if you had any sense at all, you would have waited with the carriage, as I am told your coachman instructed you."

"I did wait." Lynnette lifted her chin and met the fierce look in the duke's eyes. "Until I tired of waiting."

"Then perhaps you might have at least stayed in the

vicinity of your carriage so that you were easier to locate."

"I would have gladly stayed with the carriage. If I wasn't worried about Garvey's safety. I am told he made it through the adventure unscathed."

"Which is more than can be said for the rest of us. It may take my greatcoat a month of Sundays to dry. And my Wellingtons . . ." A shiver snaked over Ravensfield's broad shoulders. "The stable boy has been busy all morning scraping away the mud."

She should have apologized. It was, after all, her fault that the duke had been forced to leave the comfort of Broadworth and go out into the storm. She would have apologized. If not for the fact that in his pacing, Ravensfield closed in on her. He took one look at the book that lay atop the blanket on her lap and barked out a laugh.

"No wonder you acted so much a cabbagehead!" He pointed an accusatory finger at the book. "Reading claptrap such as that!"

Lynnette's spine stiffened along with her resolve. Feeling too defensive in her current repose, she swung her legs off the sofa and gingerly settled both feet on the floor. She pulled back her shoulders and pinned the duke with a look that, had he been paying attention, he would have recognized as being similar to one he'd seen from her cousin Nick on more than one occasion. If stubbornness was a family trait, so was a certain blind and uncompromising loyalty to friends.

"I have never met Mrs. Mordefi," she told him, flattening one hand protectively against the cover of *Greystone Castle.* "Nor am I ever likely to, for word has it that she is something of a recluse whose poetic sensibilities are too agitated by the noise of the city and the overwrought admiration of her throngs of readers. Still, for the hours of pleasure her stories have given me, I consider the woman a bosom-bow. As long as we are being plain with each other, sir, you should also know that I consider my own taste above reproach. And certainly beyond ridicule. *Greystone Castle* is not claptrap. It is adventure. Wonderful, romantic adventure."

He made a disparaging noise. "That's all well and good for a certain sort of readership that is able to distinguish real life from what happens in the pages of a book. But when romantic adventures addle a woman's brain . . ." He grumbled a word under his breath. "Going off in pursuit of things that go bump in the night! Exploring ancient ruins! Bravely facing the most terrifying demons of hell!" The duke pressed one hand to his heart in an exaggerated dramatic gesture. "Just the kind of rubbish that makes a woman think she's capable—"

"Of exactly all the things of which she is capable."

Ravensfield pulled in a long breath and let it out slowly, schooling his voice along with his emotions. "I was going to say that it makes a woman think that instead of staying put and waiting for rescue, she can head out on her own and obtain help for herself."

"Which, might I remind you, I did."

"Which, might I remind you, you should not have done. If I had not—"

"Terrified me?" As much as she hated to admit it, Lynnette thought it only fair to let him know that his actions were unaccountable. Her fingers played over the leather binding of *Greystone Castle.* Before she left London, she'd slit the inside cover of the book and inserted her mother's note into it. On one hand, she was grateful that the man she'd encountered in the forest was the duke and not the second-story man who had threatened her peace, her quiet, and her precious possession back in town. On the other hand, remembering how frightened she'd been when she thought she had been pursued from London only made her feel foolish.

She stifled her chagrin under an icy layer of outrage. "You might have identified yourself."

"You might have kept still so that I had the chance."

"You could hardly expect me to stand there like a clunch so that you might swoop down on me and—"

"I do not swoop! I never swoop!" Ravensfield's voice boomed against the luxurious appointments of the spacious room. He controlled himself with an effort that was nearly palpable, straightening his morning coat and running a hand over his neckcloth as if checking to see that each crease and fold was exactly in place. A muscle twitched at the base of his jaw, and watching it, Lynnette realized she'd been mistaken about him.

Was it a sign of his commanding character she thought she detected in the duke's iron jaw?

The women of the *ton* certainly knew better.

They knew pigheadedness when they saw it.

A new emotion overtook Lynnette, rushing heat into her cheeks. La, but she did like a challenge! Making the duke fall in love with her was going to be more of an endeavor than she thought. Which meant the reward of his affection would be all the sweeter.

She was already smiling, ready to make the first foray, when Ravensfield cut her short.

"Your carriage is ready. Your things are packed. I trust you will be back on your way to Bath soon enough."

No!

It was on the tip of Lynnette's tongue to cry her protest, to tell him that it was too soon for her to leave. After all, she had only just arrived and he had not had nearly the time he needed to get to know her. How was he supposed to fall as madly in love with her as she had been with him since the fateful day when they were first introduced?

She controlled her objection but only because she remembered the signs of his stubbornness. A man as strong-willed as Ravensfield could not have his mind turned so easily. Not with arguments or with logic.

But womanly wiles . . .

She controlled the smile that threatened to betray her.

Womanly wiles were something else altogether.

Lynnette propped her book in the crook of her arm and prepared to stand, testing the strength of her ankle as she did. As she expected, it pained her enough for her to be aware of it. But not so much as to incapacitate her.

"I am sorry to have inconvenienced you, your grace," she told him, the better to catch him off guard. "I will most surely be leaving, just as you wish. I would like you to know how grateful I am for your hospitality and—"

The rest of her apology was lost in a most convincing shriek of pain. As gracefully as a dancer, as persuasively as any upon the Drury Lane stage, she crumpled to the floor.

"Damnation!" Ravensfield was at her side in an instant. He scooped her into his arms and, as carefully as if she were made of porcelain, he lifted her and settled her back on the sofa. "Why didn't you tell me you were hurt?"

"I didn't . . ." Lynnette winced and touched a finger to her ankle. "I thought—"

"You thought you could take care of it yourself. Yes, I have no doubt of that." Ravensfield grabbed for the pillow and propped it under her left ankle. "Don't you know that twisted ankles can be devilishly inconvenient things?"

"I do. I mean, I did. I only thought that—"

"To get away from here as quickly as you could." An emotion she could not read shimmered in the duke's dark eyes and the expression on his face softened. "I have no doubt of that, either," he said, "for I'm certain I made you feel as wanted as a flea in a pack of hounds.

I have kept myself here in the country for a good long while and I'm afraid my town manners are not as polished as they should be." He knelt on the floor next to the sofa so that they were eye to eye and took one of her hands in his. "I do hope, Miss Overton, that you will find it in your heart to understand. You must certainly rest for the balance of the day. Please . . ."

One corner of his mouth quirked as if he were in as much pain as she pretended to be. "Please consider yourself a guest here at Broadworth Hall."

They were not exactly the ardent words of admiration she hoped to someday hear from his lips.

But they would do.

At least for now.

Just thinking of all she hoped to accomplish caused heat to flood through Lynnette in a rush that made her feel as if all the air had been suddenly sucked from the room. Her cheeks colored, certainly, for she could feel the warmth there. It was that heat—overmastering and disquieting—that cascaded through her like liquid fire. The same fire she felt in Ravensfield's touch.

"You are too kind." The duke was on his knees next to the couch, and she took the opportunity to practice the sort of breathless, wide-eyed look she had seen so many Society toasts use to their advantage. "If I could rest but a bit, I'm sure my injured limb will be recovered enough to—" Lynnette adjusted her position and winced. "Do not worry, your grace. It isn't painful. Not too painful."

"No, I can see that." Ravensfield's smile was begrudging.

Still, at such close range, it was nothing short of devastating.

He glanced at the pillow and the hem of her gown where it hid her injured ankle. "We must send for a doctor. That will certainly help. A doctor will know what to do and you'll be up and about in no time at all and then you can—"

"No." His offer was so fervent, she had no choice but to stop it, one hand on his arm. "We must not inconvenience some kindly country physician who surely has more important things to do. My little injury isn't nearly bad enough."

"I will be the judge of that." He was not the kind of man who asked permission. Lynnette knew that. Yet she hardly expected that he would be so forward as to lean closer. That he would nudge the hem of her dress just enough so that he might have a look at her ankle.

Because she had been resting and had not thought anyone would notice, she had not put on her stockings. Her legs were bare and the feel of Ravensfield's hand brushing her skin was disquieting and intimate. It slammed into Lynnette with all the force of a fast-moving curricle. It made her tremble.

Ravensfield looked down at the pretty little embroidered slipper on Lynnette's foot and from there to the body part in question.

It was only an ankle, he reminded himself, and not so different—except that it was swollen and bruised, of course—from other ankles he had seen in his time. Slim. Well turned. Shapely. Naked limbs were nothing new to a man of his experience. Especially when those naked limbs belonged to a woman with a fetching face, an appealing figure, and the boldness to stretch herself out and allow him the indulgence of a leisurely appraisal and the luxury of skin against skin.

Except that Lynnette was not like other women.

The thought caught Ravensfield unawares and he turned it over in his mind at the same time he savored its effects. One glimpse of Lynnette's bare limbs impacted him as no amount of naked flesh ever had. He tightened like a watchspring and his gut caught fire. He wondered what it might be like to kiss her.

He was not a man who let himself stay curious overlong.

"You don't do things halfway, do you, Miss Overton?" He leaned closer still, touching a finger gently to the spot near her bone where the skin was the same color as the bishop's blue in her shawl. "When you twist an ankle, you do it most thoroughly. Does it . . ." He pressed a finger to the spot that was puffed and too pink, and when Lynnette flinched, he softened his touch, but he did not move his hand away. He straightened, the better to see the outside of her ankle, which was against the back of the sofa.

"Not as bad here," he said, gliding one finger over the bone. "Does this hurt?"

"No." Was it his imagination, or did Lynnette need to gulp a breath before she was able to answer?

He slipped his hand up a little farther, past the area that was swollen. "And this?"

"No."

"But here . . ." Ravensfield slid a finger again to her ankle at the same time he cupped it, willing the warmth of his hand to ease the pain. He looked into her eyes. Last night, he'd thought they were the color of moonlight, but the sunshine streaming through the windows made them rival starlight sparkling on water. They were flecked with a color that reminded him of a twilight sky. And so unwavering, Ravensfield could not help but feel emboldened.

"I see"—he glided his hand back and forth along her leg—"you were right. You cannot leave Broadworth. Not when you are in such a condition. I simply won't allow it."

Her tongue flickered across her lips. "Forgive me for being so forward, your grace, but not long ago, you were ready to bundle me yourself and toss me into the first passing carriage."

"I was." A smile tugged at the corners of his mouth. He couldn't say why. It was hell hearing the truth from her and it should have irritated him no end. "That was before I knew you were . . ." He allowed himself the luxury of another look at her ankle and the slim strip of bare leg exposed at the hem of her gown. "Before I knew you were injured," he told her and himself. "You're not angry at me?"

"For wanting me gone?" She tipped her head as if considering, an action that made her look dewy-eyed and all the more delicious for it. "I must say, your grace, it does make a woman curious. In town, they say you are the most amiable of hosts. Yet here in the country—"

"Here in the country, I value my seclusion." It was as much of the truth as he was willing to tell her, and before she could make a to-do about it, he decided to change the subject. He leaned closer still, until he saw her glance down to the place where his mouth was in dangerous proximity to hers. "Miss Overton, you are most remarkable. You are unscathed by your adventure in the rain. You are undaunted by an injury that would have laid any other woman low. Is there nothing that can shake you?"

"Oh, yes, your grace." Her words disappeared on the end of a sigh that vibrated against his lips. "I do think I could be shaken quite thoroughly."

And he was just the man to do it.

It was a truth that had bolstered Ravensfield's self-esteem for as long as he could remember, which was exactly why it was a damned inconvenient time for his own words to come recoiling back at him.

Lynnette was not like other women.

That was as true as could be.

Certainly she was not like the women he usually bedded.

Lynnette was a Society miss. Her background, her upbringing, and her reputation were spotless. Compromising a woman of such character was too unscrupulous. Even for him.

It was also too dangerous.

For such a dalliance would lead nowhere except to the parson's mousetrap.

And no kiss was worth the price of his freedom.

The reminder was like the cold slap of an icy wave and Ravensfield backed away. "Excellent!" He pulled himself to his feet, putting as much distance as he politely could between the enticing Miss Overton and his own ungovernable longings. "Then you'll stay. For the day," he added, just in case she should misunderstand and think the invitation for longer. "And by tomorrow you'll be feeling chipper and you can be on your way. To . . . Wherever!"

Still smiling a smile that strained the corners of his mouth, still hoping to sound as hale and as hearty as a man could when he was all but setting his guest out by the side of the road, he hurried out of the room. In the passageway with the door to Lynnette's chamber closed behind him and his own unaccountable attraction to her as firmly locked away (or so he hoped), he breathed a sigh of relief.

"That went well," Ravensfield told himself, and he went about his business as ready to believe it as a man could be.

Then again, he had always had a remarkable facility for lying to himself.

4

Lynnette was certain that playing the invalid was the quickest way to Ravensfield's heart. After all, he could not fall in love with her if they didn't become better acquainted. And they could not become better acquainted if she did not stay at Broadworth. At least for some time.

Though she was certain her cousin Nick, his friends, the Dashers, and possibly even Willie would not agree if they knew where she was and what she was about, she was certain in her own mind that she was not a complete looby. She understood full well that there was something that kept Ravensfield here in the country, some secret he was reluctant to reveal. It was why, of course, on that first morning, he had been so anxious to see her on her way.

But he had also nearly kissed her.

The memory of the moment still sang through Lynnette's veins and thinking about it made her nothing if not more determined. If the only thing that would keep her from leaving Broadworth and its master was her infirmity, then she would not—she could not—recover. Not until she had a chance to learn the workings of Ravensfield's heart.

Unfortunately, pretending to an injury did not afford her the access to him that she expected. The duke insisted that she would not fully recuperate unless she was left undisturbed. On his orders, her door was kept shut so that she might have absolute quiet. The maids who assisted her were instructed not to prattle so that she might have peace. Her meals were brought up to her on a tray.

The rest of Broadworth went about its business as if she had never arrived. And Lynnette?

Lynnette was incredibly bored.

There was only so much reading she could do. Mrs. Mordefi's newest story was both clever and satisfying—not to mention deliciously frightening—but even *Greystone Castle* was not enough to fill hour after lonely hour.

She drummed her fingers against the window ledge.

After two days, even the magnificent Berkshire countryside had lost its appeal. After three days and a morning filled with lowering clouds and a mizzling rain that fogged the windows and left her chilled to the bone, she had had enough.

If she moved very quickly and very quietly, she decided, she could leave the house and be back before tea time. Until then, no one would look in on her.

Her mind made up, she dug through her trunks. She found her half-boots, slipped them on, and laced them up the front. She located a cloak that was warmer than her Hungarian wrap (even if it was not as stylish) and threw it over her shoulders. To cheer her spirits, she chose a pretty little Dutch bonnet. Though she sincerely hoped she would not happen upon Ravensfield, she reached for the ebony walking stick with the ivory head, the one he had presented her the day after her ignominious arrival so that it might aid her in exercising her injured limb. She'd take it with her just in case she might need it to prove her infirmity.

A stroll in the garden would help dispel the energy that bunched inside her, she told herself. A walk to the stables would do her even more good. And a gallop through the countryside?

She forced herself to put the thought out of her head. For now, she would be satisfied with a bit of fresh air.

Lynnette poked her head out into the passageway and looked around. As always, the door to the room directly across from hers was closed. There was no sign of the servants and none of her host. For the first time, she was grateful. It would not do to run into Ravensfield.

Closing the door behind her, she slipped down the stairs and from there, it was easy enough to steal out of the house. Before long, she was in the back garden. She paused beneath the spreading arms of an oak tree and breathed in deeply, enjoying the heavy, wet scent of spring flowers and the smell of cut grass.

The hint of freedom made Lynnette heady with excitement and she kept walking. She came to a hedge in which there was a gate and, pausing only long enough to make sure there was no one about, she pushed open the gate and stepped onto a neatly tended stone path.

This close to the house, the landscape was tame and though her ankle smarted a bit as if to remind her that her injury was not a complete sham, she was not about to let such a small inconvenience stop her. Swinging the walking stick in one hand, she followed the path through a glade where lilac bushes stood shoulder to shoulder upon her left and a river ran briskly to her right. A little ahead, the path split. The well-kept part of it continued on beside the river. Another portion, its stones thick with moss and grass growing over their edges, veered to the left and disappeared into the living wall of lilacs.

There was never any question which path she would follow.

Lynnette sidestepped her way between two massive lilacs. Behind them, the river's sound was muted and the vegetation was so closely packed, the ground was nearly dry. It was more gray and gloomy here than it was out on the path and she paused for a moment, letting her eyes adjust to the dim light. When they did, she saw a stone wall up ahead.

It was, for the most part, taller than Lynnette. Here and there, the stones had come down in a tumble and where she could see over them, she spied what looked to be an entire field of standing stones.

"A graveyard!" And a very old one, too, by the looks

of things. Fascinated, Lynnette moved through a space in the wall that must have once contained a gate.

Had the sun been shining, the cemetery might have been a pleasant enough place. The grass was tidy, and here and there violets pushed through the soil. But the sun was not shining and a chill wind blew. Lynnette held her cloak closer about her.

The cemetery was not large. The fifty or so stones in it were set close together and the path between them was twisted and pinched. Many of the gravestones were crusted with moss and some were so ancient that they leaned like old men. Along the far wall was a mausoleum but though it may once have been grander than the final resting places for more common folk, even that small building looked sad and forlorn. Its door sat closed but on a tilt and trees and bracken grew close around it, as if in an eternal embrace.

It was very quiet. Lynnette did not even realize it until she was aware of the sound of her own heartbeat. There were no birds singing here as there were out on the path. Not even the burbling of the river penetrated the walls or the vegetation.

Except when she was reading and more than willing to give herself over to a writer's imagination, Lynnette was not a fanciful woman. Yet she thought that if there were ghosts anywhere in the world, she would find them here.

"Looby!" Her voice muffled by the damp air and the trees that ringed the graveyard from every side, she discarded the thought with a twitch of her shoulders. "You are safer here, certainly, than you would be back in London. For there, the man in black might appear out of nowhere intent on burglary. The dead can do no such thing. And everyone here is most certainly dead."

Everyone, that is, but the man she saw that very instant as he stepped out of the mausoleum. His back was to her and she was certain he had not caught sight of her. He was too busy trying to close the mausoleum door on its rusted hinges. It was the perfect opportunity for her to slip away unnoticed, yet Lynnette could not run.

She was rooted to the spot, her breath suddenly gone, a lump of terror in her throat that made it difficult to breathe. When he turned, the lump dissolved and Lynnette's breath whooshed out of her on the end of a sigh of relief.

Pity the Duke of Ravensfield did not seem as pleased to see her as she was to encounter him.

His eyes flashing, Ravensfield stalked across the graveyard. "Miss Overton, what the devil are you doing here?"

She was so relieved at seeing the duke rather than one of the ghosts her imagination had envisioned, she grinned. "I felt the need for air," she said and because it was not a lie, she dared to meet his look of unmitigated annoyance. "I have been in the house all these days and—"

"And how the devil did you get here?" He looked all around as if that might help shed light on the question. "If one of my stableboys allowed you a mount—"

"They did not and you mustn't think it."

"Then if one of my coachmen gave you a carriage—"

"They are innocent as well."

"If Mrs. B is so lax in her care of you that—"

"Please, your grace!" Lynnette could not stand the thought of one of Ravensfield's servants taking the blame. "Mrs. B has no idea that I have left the house. Your coachmen were not coaxed to do anything they shouldn't have done and I assure you, your stableboys are not to blame. I am, myself, responsible. I walked here."

"Did you?" He glanced from the top of her bonnet to the tips of her boots and back up again. "I thought you were hobbled."

In her surprise at seeing him here, Lynnette had almost forgotten. She leaned heavily on the walking stick. "It was . . ." She adjusted her stance enough to make it clear—or so she hoped—that she was in some small amount of pain. "It was difficult."

"Then why did you do it?"

"It is just as I said, your grace. Days in the house with not a breath of fresh air. Hours with nothing to do and no one to talk to."

"So you came to talk to me?"

The very idea was preposterous and she tossed her head. "Don't be ridiculous. How was I to know that you were here? And what are you doing here, at any rate?"

Ravensfield grumbled. He looked away, back over his shoulder toward the tomb she'd seen him walk out of. "I might ask you the same thing," he said, swinging his gaze back in her direction. "Certainly, there is nothing in a graveyard that can interest a gentlewoman such as yourself. Dirty, old stones. Nasty gaps in the pathway. You'll be lucky if you don't turn an ankle again. Come."

It would have been a kindness to say he offered his assistance. Rather, he grabbed her elbow and hauled her back toward the break in the wall where she'd come in. He might have been successful if Lynnette was in the mood to be put off. But while the prospect of walking back to Broadworth Hall with Ravensfield held some allure, the chance of staying here a while longer—and having him all to herself—was even more appealing.

She untangled herself from his grip. "I think these dirty, old stones are quite interesting," she said and just to prove it, she bent to read the inscription on the nearest one. It was old and nearly worn away. She could make out little more than a name, *Benjamin*, and a family name that began with the letter *S*.

"Graveyards tell a village's history," she said, giving up on Benjamin and moving to the next grave. "They are repositories of art and sculpture."

"Not this one." Ravensfield barked a laugh. "In case you have not noticed, Miss Overton, this graveyard has long been forgotten."

"And there is no church." The realization hit her suddenly and she glanced all around, as if to verify the assertion. "How very odd. Are customs different here in Berkshire, then, that their dead are not buried in hallowed ground?"

"Not these dead." Again he took her elbow and made an attempt to pilot her out of the graveyard.

Again, Lynnette resisted. "Look." She pointed at the nearest grave. "This woman's name is Clarice. Isn't that odd? That is the name of the heroine in *Greystone Castle*."

He was not impressed. "There are hundreds of women named Clarice," Ravensfield said. "I myself have an aunt named Clarice."

She had already moved on to the next grave and bent to read the inscription. She gave him a sidelong look. "You are teasing, surely."

He glanced toward the stone wall and the opening that led out to the path. "I could tell you all about her on our way back to the Hall."

Lynnette stood. The nearest grave was hewn from stone and shaped like a sarcophagus. She was not weary but she leaned back against it nonetheless, the better to look as if she needed the support. "Tell me now," she said.

"About Aunt Clarice?" The noise that rose up from Ravensfield's throat was not quite a laugh. "Frightful old thing. I would tell you all about her. If we had more time."

"Are we late for something?"

"We are—" He hesitated and it was that more than anything else that made Lynnette suspicious. Ravensfield was not the sort of man who wavered. Not about anything. Eager to find out what had him so turned about and making sure to limp just a little, she walked along the track that led closer to the mausoleum—and farther from the path back to the Hall.

"If you do not wish to talk about your Aunt Clarice, then tell me about someone else," she suggested. "Here." She pointed to the nearest stone. "Here is a man named James Whitcomb." A memory prodded her and Lynnette backed away from the stone in wonder. "How odd, there is a hero in one of Mrs. Mordefi's books. I believe it is *The Beast of Carnaby Hall.* His name is James Whitcomb."

"Not so odd. I was up at Oxford with a James Whitcomb." He stepped back, the gesture clearly designed to signal the fact that their visit to the graveyard was at an end. "Curiously enough, he had a cousin by the same name. Perhaps your Mrs. Mordefi knows the family."

"Perhaps." Lynnette tipped her head. "Perhaps you might tell me, your grace, why you're so anxious to be gone from this place."

He was not used to being challenged. Certainly not by a woman. If Ravensfield had been any less of a gentleman, he may have pointed it out. As it was, he gave Lynnette the kind of look she had always thought the disdainful reserved for those they considered puddenheaded.

"You don't want to know."

"I would not have asked if I didn't want to know."

"But really, Miss Overton, I think it simply better if we leave before we discuss this. There is less chance . . ." He glanced around and though Lynnette was certain there was no one about and thus no one who might overhear, she found herself looking around, too. Ravensfield leaned nearer and lowered his voice. "Less chance of them hearing."

"Them?" Though she could not say why, the single word sent a shiver up Lynnette's spine. She tugged her cloak closer around herself and did her best to maintain her composure. If she intended Ravensfield to fall in love with her, the last thing she needed was for him to think her simple-minded. "Whatever do you mean?"

He shook his head, reluctant even now to tell her more.

It was that, more than anything, that piqued her curiosity. "Do you mean—"

"Haunted."

His voice was so low, the word so ominous, a tingle raced through Lynnette. It left her breathless. Even before she knew she was doing it, she found herself glancing again at the mossy stones. "It can't be true," she said, more to comfort herself than for any other reason. "Such things happen only in the pages of a book."

"Do they?" Ravensfield's eyes lit. "Why do you think there is a graveyard here with no church to consecrate it?" He did not give her time to answer. It was just as well, for Lynnette did not know what to say. The duke took her by the shoulders and turned her so that she was facing the mausoleum. He leaned over her shoulder, his voice a rumble close to her ear.

"Suicide," he said.

Lynnette gasped. "You mean—"

"It happened a hundred years ago. Long before the

property came into my family. They say he was a baron."

"He? Is he the one who is buried—"

"There?" Ravensfield looked toward the moldering tomb and shook his head. "No. The baron has his proper place in the churchyard. This is the tomb of the woman he loved."

Lynnette swallowed hard. "And she—"

"Hanging."

She must have turned pale for her cheeks suddenly felt cold and Ravensfield looked at her closely. "Have I frightened you, Miss Overton? You must forgive me. Certainly, I never intended to do such. I just thought you should know—"

"If he loved her, why did she kill herself?"

For just a moment, Ravensfield seemed as surprised at hearing the question as Lynnette was to have asked it.

"You said she was the woman he loved. Yet if she was so loved, it seems unlikely that she would take her own life. When a man and a woman are in love . . ." She took the opportunity to look into his eyes. "I would think they would both be very happy."

"You would think that, wouldn't you?" As if the force of her look was a physical thing, Ravensfield backed up a step. "It's just that . . ." Living in these parts, he must have known the story as well as he knew his own name. The fact that he seemed reluctant to impart the details told Lynnette that it must be sad in the least, and possibly scandalous.

The truth dawned and though Lynnette did not even

know her name, she suddenly felt pity for the woman in the tomb. "Oh, my. He did love her, didn't he? With all his heart. And she, poor thing, was promised to another."

"That's it exactly." Ravensfield smiled with something that was almost relief. "Their love was doomed from the start. And when they could not be married—"

"She died rather than face the prospect of a life without him." Lynnette touched a hand to her cheek. It was damp. "It is a tragic story."

"Yes. And you see now why this place is here. As a sinner, she could not be buried in the churchyard. But the baron refused to see her treated as others who take their lives are. They are buried at a crossroads to dilute their evil by spreading it to the four corners of the earth. A stake is driven through their hearts—" He demonstrated, pounding an imaginary hammer in one hand into the imaginary stake in the other. The force of the movement made Lynnette jump.

Ravensfield's eyes glittered. "It keeps them from rising, you know. So the baron, he built his lady love this tomb but they say she goes out in search of him still. She haunts this place. Especially at this time of day, when the shadows are growing long and the air is—" He shivered as if against the touch of an unseen hand. "It is better if we leave."

Lynnette swallowed hard. "But surely you do not believe it?"

Ravensfield shrugged. "I have always been a most practical man," he said. "Yet no one can deny the mystery of this place. You see, once the baron buried his lady here, others brought their loved ones. Those who could not be buried in churchyards."

It was no wonder the place held such an emotional charge.

Lynnette glanced around at the names she could see. James Whitcomb and Clarice and all the others whose lives had ended so sadly.

"There are those about here who say they have seen her and the others."

She was so lost in her melancholy thoughts that the duke's voice startled her.

"People say these poor lost souls are nothing now but a mist moving through the deep shadows. But sometimes, they claim, you can see features in that mist. Faces horribly disfigured due to the nature of their deaths. Eyes filled with tortured memories. Bodies broken. And they say you can feel them here, as well. Not just in the tragic atmosphere of this place. I mean really feel them." He skimmed a finger over her cheek and Lynnette shivered, but whether it was from the potency of his story or the touch of his hand, she could not say. "They are the passing chill you sense in the air. The icy feeling against your skin. You can see why I think it better if we don't linger, Miss Overton."

Lynnette's eyes were wide, her voice as small as a whisper. "Yet you were here. And by yourself. Are you not afraid, your grace?"

He raised his chin. "I am the duke. As such, it is my duty to oversee all my land. I walk through now and again. Just to be sure nothing is disturbed. That no one and nothing is . . ." He glanced all around again. "Lurking."

Lynnette ran her tongue over her lips. Her mouth was very dry. Her knees trembled. It was just as well for when she made to take a step back toward the wall and the path that led away from the place, she faltered.

"Please." The duke offered his arm. "Let me assist you. Perhaps you've come too far on your first day out of the house."

"Perhaps. Yes." Lynnette gathered her cloak around her. Her fear was at least good for something, she reminded herself, and with one last look at the dreary graveyard and one last prayer for the sorrowful souls doomed to walk its grounds, she wound her arm through Ravensfield's.

"Beggin' your pardon, miss." Jenny, the maid who had been assigned to help with Lynnette's personal needs, pushed open the door to Lynnette's chamber and toed the threshold. "I do not mean to interrupt, miss."

Lynnette closed *Greystone Castle* and bid the girl closer. "There is no problem in that. I have been here alone these many hours. And it is very quiet."

"Yes, miss. I heard. About you goin' out, that is. His lordship was not happy. He said as how we should keep a better eye on you. To make sure you recover proper like, miss."

"Word travels fast here at Broadworth."

"Yes, miss." Because she obviously did not know what

else to do, Jenny curtsied. "It's not as if we gossip and I hope you don't think it. It's just that . . ." Jenny pleated her white apron in nervous fingers. "Flossie who helps in the kitchen, she saw you return. With the duke. And I was just wonderin' . . . That is to say, I do hope you're all right, miss. I mean, I do hope his lordship, he didn't—"

It was a terribly forward thing of the girl to imply but before Lynnette could even tell her as much, she realized that Jenny was not talking about the same thing Lynnette was thinking about. Lynnette was thinking about the thrill that sizzled through her when Ravensfield offered his arm and she accepted.

"What is it?" Lynnette could not help herself. The worry on Jenny's face was so real, she could not but feel sorry for the girl. "Jenny, why is it that the duke worries you so?"

"Shouldn't say it, miss." Jenny took a step inside the room and looking back over her shoulder, closed the door behind her. She shifted from foot to foot. "It ain't somethin' you talk about, after all. Leastways, Mrs. B and Mr. Worthy, they say if they ever hear one of us speak it out loud . . ."

Her vacillation made Lynnette more curious than ever. "Tell me why it is you're so afraid. I swear . . ." She crossed a finger over her heart. "I won't say a word. Not to anyone. And most especially not to Mrs. B."

"I wouldn't, miss. Except as it's for your own good. You see . . ." Jenny hurried to stand closer and again shifted from foot to foot. "It all started with that there room. The one right across the passageway."

Lynnette had seen the room just that afternoon when she slipped out of the house. The way she remembered it, the door was closed and from what she could tell, there was nothing at all remarkable about it.

"It's strictly forbidden to us, miss. That room there? The door is kept locked. Always. And as if that ain't curious enough . . ." Jenny sidled closer. "There's the blood."

Lynnette wasn't sure she'd heard properly. She shook her head. "Blood? Are you saying—"

"I'm saying, miss, and don't take it wrong because I would not be sayin' anything at all as it ain't proper, especially as how you're a guest of the duke's and all . . ." Jenny hauled in a long breath. "I'm sayin' that the duke spends his nights in that there room. And none of us is ever allowed in except for the duke himself and Mr. Worthy. Not even to clean or air it. But Mary . . . she was the scullery maid once, before the new cook arrived who is such a turk when it comes to keepin' things clean and the like . . . and Mary, who is now helpin' with the dustin' and such especially since Emily who is supposed to do it all sometimes helps herself to the sherry down in the kitchen . . ." Another gulp of air got Jenny back to the subject at hand.

"Mary said as how once when he didn't know she was about, she saw the duke go into that room and the door was open long enough for her to have a peep inside. And what was in there? Books the likes of which no gentleman should be readin', that is what. And a coffin—I know it sounds daft, but Mary swears it is true. And a glass of blood, there upon his lordship's desk."

"That is a great deal for Mary to have seen when the duke was simply walking into the room."

The logic of Lynnette's argument was lost on Jenny. "It's as true as Sunday, and it means you must be careful." The girl leaned closer and lowered her voice. "You see, miss . . ." Just to be sure they were still safely alone, she looked again at the door. "He's what you call . . . leastways it's what the other girls say about him . . . He's one of them there . . ." She swallowed down her misgivings. "Bless me, miss, the Duke of Ravensfield, he's a vampire!"

5

"She saw the names, Worthy. And she is no fool. If we are not rid of her . . ." Ravensfield did not dare to finish the sentence. He knew exactly what would happen if Lynnette stayed at Broadworth much longer.

There was his secret to consider, of course, and she had come dangerously close to discovering it.

Then there was his bachelorhood.

He twitched away the thought. "We must do something," he told his valet. "And soon."

"Well, she's forever readin' Mrs. Mordefi. *Greystone Castle* to be most particular."

Ravensfield looked up from his desk and the blank sheet of paper that was staring at him from atop it as if in challenge.

"What's that you say?"

Worthy was seated in front of the fire, going through the correspondence that had been forwarded from the duke's London home. He was a wiry man and so short, it was difficult to see him above the wing chair. His hair, though, was impossible to miss. It was the color of sand and so thick and curly, it always looked in want of a good mowing. Ravensfield knew when Worthy set down the letter he was reading and turned his attention the duke's way; he saw his hair twitch.

"It's Miss Lynnette you are talkin' about, is it not, sir? Beggin' your pardon for bein' so forward, your grace. But you have been spendin' a good deal of time thinkin' about the young lady."

Ravensfield did not have the stomach to ask how Worthy knew.

Had he been sighing too much of late? Or simply sitting here and staring into space as he had caught himself doing more than once in the days since Lynnette had arrived so dampishly on his doorstep?

He rose from his chair, rubbing a hand to the small of his back. There were things a man could share with his valet. Things he couldn't say to any other man. And never to a woman. It helped that Worthy had been with him since before he'd inherited his father's title and that, unlike the other servants here at Broadworth or his staff in London, Worthy had his trust and was in his confidence.

None of which made it any easier for Ravensfield to face the truth.

He had been thinking about Lynnette. He had been wondering what might have happened that first morning had he kissed her. He had been speculating about how she might taste. And how it might feel to have her body moving beneath his. He had been pondering what would happen if she put two and two together and discovered why he'd been in the graveyard.

"Damnation!" The duke tossed his quill pen onto the desk where it landed with a splash that sent dots of India ink all around. "It is an infernal problem," he told Worthy. "She is an infernal problem. Every day I rise from my bed hoping that she will once and for all find herself recovered, imagining my joy as I watch her hop into her carriage and I see the last of her. And every day—"

"She is still hobbled and not nearly well enough to leave." Finished with the letter, Worthy filed it along with the others he had handled that morning in the coffin that took up a goodly portion of the other side of the room. "Not that it is any of my business, sir, but I have noticed that with her here, you are getting even less done than usual." He looked forlornly at the sheet of paper on Ravensfield's desk. It was covered with nothing other than inky dots. "If you never finish, sir, we will never be back in London for the Season."

"And that means you will miss out on the company of that lady's maid who has caught your eye. That pretty little thing who travels with the Duchess of Falstars. Yes, yes, I know, Worthy. It's not as if I'm trying to keep you from your lady love."

"Only with Miss Lynnette here—"

"Ah, that's it. That's it exactly!" It wasn't, of course and even as he said the words, Ravensfield supposed that in some corner of his mind, he knew the truth of the matter. He could not—at least not in good conscience—blame Lynnette for a problem that had started long before she came to Berkshire. Still, it was easier to blame her than it was to take responsbility himself. Desperate to find some solace, he latched on to the lie like a limpet to a rock.

"That is where the problem springs," he told Worthy with all the conviction he could muster. "It's all Lynnette's fault."

"Exactly what I have been thinkin', your grace. And it's not as if she ain't as pleasant as the day is long. And good to us what is belowstairs. Even slips a sovereign or two to them what helps her out in a special sort of way."

"I have no doubt of the lady's generosity." That much was true. What Ravensfield was beginning to doubt was his own sanity. For no matter how many times he reminded himself that Lynnette was far and away the wrong kind of woman with whom to indulge his desires, he found himself as many times wondering just what it might be like. "It's her lack of regenerative powers that make me come over uneasy. Will we never see the last of her?"

Worthy nodded in understanding. Even when he was done, his hair continued to sway, emphasizing his point. "Can't blame you for wantin' her gone for she's not at all the kind of woman you allow yourself. That, of course, would be on account of what happened with Lady Moore-Chastain."

As soon as the words were past his lips, Worthy knew he'd made a mistake. Under its thick coating of freckles, his face blanched. His eyes widened and he swallowed a gulp of sheer panic.

Worthy was a very wise man to be wary.

Before he even knew it, the duke's hands were curled into fists. "Christina Moore-Chastain has nothing to do with this."

"Of course not, your grace," Worthy stammered.

"And don't think she does."

"Of course not, your grace."

"And don't think that I think that she does."

"Of course not, your grace."

"If I am not mistaken, Lady Christina was a good friend to Lynnette's mother. But other than that, I think we both agree . . ." He pinned Worthy with a look, the better to send the message that they *did* both agree, whether Worthy knew it or not. "Other than that, her name should not be spoken in the same breath as Miss Lynnette's."

"Of course not, your grace. What I meant, of course, is—"

"Miss Lynnette is, after all, a gentlewoman, even if she is a goosecap now and again. But I must admit that for the most part, she is pleasant enough. Unfortunately," he added below his breath.

"Lady Christina, on the other hand . . ." Ravensfield knew he did not need to finish the sentence. Worthy had been with him at the time of the debacle. An older, sophisticated woman. A younger, far less experienced man, newly come into his title. It was the stuff that dreams were made of. At least a young man's dreams. It might have remained so—at least for as long as they satisfied each other—had not Ravensfield discovered that just because a woman was beautiful and sophisticated did not mean she had a heart.

Though he was long past the emotional wreckage that resulted from the affair, it was one lesson he never let himself forget. And one reason he refused to allow himself to get emotionally involved with any woman. Doxies could be used and discarded. Just as they used him. Gentlewomen, on the other hand . . .

Ravensfield dismissed the thought with a twitch of his shoulders. For teaching him the lesson early on, he supposed he owed Lady Christina a debt of gratitude.

Holding tight to the thought, he allowed his muscles to relax. He uncurled his fingers, let go a long breath. "Have no fear, Worthy. I will not lop off your head for mentioning the harridan's name."

"Thank you, your grace."

"Of course, if I was in a less pleasant mood . . ."

Realizing just how lucky he was to have escaped his master's wrath, Worthy hurried to change the subject. "I have been thinkin', sir. About how much of a . . ." He carefully searched for the right way to say it. "How much of a distraction Miss Lynnette might be to a gentleman such as yourself. I can understand why you think it would be a blessing to see the last of her."

It was what Ravensfield had told himself a dozen times.

Now all he had to do was convince himself that he believed it.

He went to the sideboard and poured himself a brandy. "I say, Worthy, something tells me you have a plan."

"Indeed I do, your grace. It was like I was sayin'. She reads Mrs. Mordefi. If she is so taken with stories such as that and if, as you told me when it happened, sir, she was truly frightened by the things you told her at that there graveyard—"

"If she is as taken as all that, she is a poor honey, indeed, and more of a cawker than I ever imagined."

"She is a female, after all, your grace." As if it was as sad as it was true, Worthy nodded solemnly. "Even the best of them come over all preturbed like when it comes to the supernatural."

"Indeed!" Ravensfield took a sip of his drink and waited while it burned down the back of his throat. "She carries that infernal book with her everywhere. And she proclaims the woman her bosom-bow. Can you believe it? Says she thinks of them as friends because of the hours of pleasure she's had from the silly stories."

Worthy grinned. "Which tells me, your grace, that Miss Lynnette is . . . How shall I put it? Beggin' your pardon if I'm not gettin' it right, but I do believe the word is 'susceptible.' "

"It is, indeed!" Seeing a glimmer of hope on the horizon, Ravensfield grinned. "What do you have in mind?"

"I must admit, I have been thinkin', since she is so

taken by them rum books and stories what is filled with ghosts and ghoulies—"

"That if we cannot wait for her to recover and be gone, we might, perhaps, hurry her on her way."

"Exactly, sir."

"Yes!" Ravensfield rubbed his hands together, getting rid of some of the tension that had been building inside him like an electrical charge ever since the day Lynnette appeared. "She is surely the type who frightens easily. We might yet use that to our advantage."

"Just so."

"That's it." Ravensfield did a turn around the room, suddenly flush with satisfaction. It was a brilliant plan and it might just kill two proverbial birds with one very large stone.

"If we can frighten her . . ." He lifted his own glass in a toast to himself. "I will be rid of the distracting Miss Overton. And if I am able to frighten Lynnette, that means the idea I concoct to do it is frightening enough to frighten anyone." It was a remarkably muddled sentence for a man who prided himself on his phraseology but Worthy got the message.

"And if you can frighten her, sir, it just might help you get the juices flowin', so to speak, and give you back that bit of confidence you need to finish what you're doin'."

"It just might. It just might, indeed." Ravensfield drained his glass and thumped his valet on the back.

It was a capital scheme. He would use it to rid himelf of Lynnette and the hold she had on his mind and body. It would also help him find the words that had been eluding him in the months since he'd retired to Berkshire.

For what no one but Worthy knew was that the Duke of Ravensfield was having a devil of a time finding the inspiration for his latest project, the gothic romance that would see publication under his *nom de plume.*

Mrs. Mordefi.

"I will be polite," Ravensfield reminded himself. "And not so overeager as to make the lady suspicious. Polite. Yes." He paused outside the door of the room where Lynnette had taken up residence and drew a long, calming breath. He was a man who valued his solitude, and for good reason. If word went around the *ton* about how the Duke of Ravensfield really made his fortune, the scandal would destroy his family name. Not to mention the fact that it would take the shine off the delicious anonymity that made Mrs. Mordefi so popular, sold so many books, and made him so very much money.

Keeping his secret was only one of the reasons he was eager to see Lynnette on her way, of course. He didn't need to remind himself of everything that happened the last time they were alone together in her chamber. The memory burned through him like fire and, instantly, his body tightened with awareness. He banished the thought—and his response to it—with a curse that rumbled through the passageway and caused a passing maid—he never could remember their names—to scurry off like a frightened mouse.

"Polite," Ravensfield reminded himself. "Well-mannered. No use giving her something else to prattle about once she is frightened out of her wits and runs home."

Cheered by the very thought of her leaving, he rapped on the door. When he heard a muffled, "Come in," from the other side, he snapped the door open, more than ready to play the consummate gentleman.

It would have been considerably easier if he had not found Lynnette looking like a paragon in green silk. Her gown had the sort of short, puffed sleeves that showed off the tender flesh of her arms. The kind of high bodice that made the most of her figure. A deep neckline that revealed the sweeping column of her neck and was cut low enough over her bosom that if he just happened to—

It wasn't until he was already leaning over to get a better look that Ravensfield realized it and pulled himself back from the brink and his own errant urges. He forced his gaze upward. Tonight, Lynnette's hair was high on her head and tousled at the top. One long curl kissed her cheek. She said nothing when he came into the room. She didn't have to. She had been told that there were festivities planned for the night and the excitement of expectation sparkled in her eyes. They were as bright as the diamonds she wore on her ears and at her throat.

"You're angry at me." Ravensfield regretted the words as soon as he spoke them. She didn't look angry, damn it, she looked like a dream, and it was want-witted for him to even bring up what had happened the day he was so bold as to examine her ankle. He was not looking for absolution. Nor was he here to appease his conscience. He didn't have one, and besides, he never made excuses. Not for his behavior. And never for the way he treated women.

"I am afraid that when last we spoke together here in your chamber, I was too forward. You think that I—"

"Oh, no, your grace." A delightful wash of dusky pink stained her cheeks. "You were merely concerned about my injury. As any good host might be. And I was merely—"

"Embarrassed? Then I do beg your forgiveness, Miss Overton." He was not a man who offered apologies, either, but somehow, the words slipped out, as smooth and as natural as the bow he gave her along with them. "If there's anything I can do to make up for my indiscretion—"

"I should at least be gracious enough to accept your expression of regret and have an end to it. Yet if I did that, I would be less than honest. Your kind attentions . . ." She was seated on the couch where said attentions had been administered and she looked up at him with a flutter of lashes.

"I did appreciate your ministrations," she said, her voice huskier than he remembered it and all the more enticing because of it. "It was very kind of you to care so much and really quite . . ." She darted her tongue along her lips. "Quite comforting."

"Excellent!" Ravensfield breathed a sigh of relief. The awkward part of the evening was over and they could get on with it. And, with any luck, with Lynnette's upcoming departure. "I am glad you hold no grudge and that we are of one mind on the matter. If that is that—"

"You did ask if there was anything you could do for penance."

Ravensfield could hardly believe his ears. A man offered polite words and a woman—at least any woman who knew her manners and her place—should have had the sense to accept them at face value. Not to take him up on his offer. "Are you telling me you want—"

"Just a conversation, your grace." Lynnette had been reclining with her left ankle propped on the couch and she swung around and settled both feet on the floor. She folded her hands neatly in her lap and sat very straight, the better to emphasize the graceful curve of her figure.

"I have not had a chance to speak with you privately since the day we met in the graveyard. You have been busy and I have been recovering. Ever so slowly, of course." She touched a finger briefly to her ankle. "But I think you should know that I have been talking to the servants."

The comment snapped Ravensfield out of the fantasy that threatened to upend his better judgment. The one that reared its head when she bent to lay her hand upon her ankle and the bodice of her gown dipped just enough for—

He shook his head, bringing himself back to the matter at hand. There was nothing Lynnette could have in common with his servants. There was nothing they could tell her. Unless—

If he was wise—and he had always thought himself to be—he would have celebrated this turn of events. Local gossip might yet bolster all he was hoping to accomplish this evening. He should feel giddy. Instead, all he felt was annoyance.

"You don't actually believe that twaddle, do you?" he asked.

She didn't answer, and from the look on her face, half eager anticipation, half trepidation, he couldn't tell what her answer might be.

Ravensfield let go a long breath and did a turn around the room. "What is the current gossip belowstairs? Am I some sort of monster? Or a wraith risen from that dusty tomb you discovered? A specter full-fashioned of nightmares and mist?"

Lynnette cleared her throat. When she hazarded another look in his direction, her brows were low over eyes that sparkled with an awareness of the awkward situation she found herself in. It was a credit to her character—not to mention to the force of her will—that she chose to confront him with the facts.

"A vampire," she said, and followed the comment with a smile that threatened to annihilate the solemnity of the announcement. "I know in my head that such things as vampires are impossible," she added quickly and quite obviously because she knew it was what he expected her to say. "Such things are against the laws of both God and nature and I would not even bring it up with you, your grace, if I had not been so recently reading Mrs. Mordefi." Her hand strayed to the book on her lap and she closed it.

"When I read these books, the impossible seems so real that my stomach jumps and my breaths come hard and my heart feels as if it might sometimes leap from my chest. At times, I have to remind myself that they are only figments of that lady's wondrous imagination."

He stalked across the room to stand closer to her. His voice was a growl. "Are they?"

Was she frightened at the very thought? Gad, but he hoped so! Of course, that didn't explain why she looked more delighted than frightened or why her reaction made him feel as if he must exonerate himself.

Ravensfield crossed the room and stood directly in the pool of late evening sunlight near the door. "Shall I prove it, then? See here? What is it your Mrs. Mordefi says? That a vampire cannot abide the sunlight? This proves it, eh? I am as real as any other mortal man."

Was it disappointment that clouded her expression? Or did she need more proof still?

Ravensfield raked a hand through his hair. "What else does that woman say about the subject? That a vampire is averse to garlic? Remind me to eat some at table tonight. That he cannot sleep but in a coffin? Then when you are healed and up and around, I promise you a tour of the house and a peek into my own bedchamber. If you are brave enough." He wiggled his eyebrows, the better to emphasize his point and underscore his own reputation. "And Mrs. Mordefi, does she say that a vampire has no heart?"

As swiftly as Ravensfield had crossed the room, he headed back in the other direction. He sat down next to Lynnette and grabbed for one of her hands. He held it to his chest.

"There. You feel it?" Ravensfield certainly did. There was something about the touch of Lynnette's small, well-shaped hand against his linen shirt that made his heartbeat quicken to a wild, boisterous rhythm. When he realized it, he dropped her hand as if it were on fire. It wasn't until he found himself breathing hard that he realized Lynnette was, too.

"Do forgive me, your grace." Her voice bumped over the words in much the same way Ravensfield's heart was knocking against his ribs. "It was wrong of me to listen to such gossip. You've been nothing but kind and I—"

"Am all alone in the home of a man you hardly know except by reputation which, I admit, is not the best. You must forgive me for teasing you."

"Only if you'll forgive me for considering, even for a moment, that you could be anything less than a gentleman."

"Or more!" Now that the impasse between them was broken, Ravensfield laughed. "I do believe that is what your Mrs. Mordefi says in that book of yours." He tapped a finger against the cover of *Greystone Castle*. "That vampires are more than mortal men. Stronger. Swifter." He looked into her eyes. "Far more intense in their appetites."

He was surprised that he'd so quickly forgotten the promises he made to himself only a short while before. But he certainly did not expect a response from Lynnette that included uncontrolled laughter.

"You, sir, are a humbug!" Though the criticism was real enough, Lynnette's eyes danced. "You've read the book, surely."

"I have not." Appalled by the thought that she could so easily come so close to the truth, Ravensfield pulled back his shoulders. "I would not know such nonsense at all except for the fact that people talk. This Mrs. Mordefi, she's a popular writer and no doubt. I cannot go anywhere without hearing someone discuss her latest tome. I find it remarkable."

"And I find it curious." She tipped her head, studying him. "You say it is fustian yet you listen when people talk about Mrs. Mordefi's work."

"A fellow can hardly help himself! Go to a soiree, and they talk about Mrs. Mordefi. Attend a musicale, and they speak of the woman no end. Whether I want to hear it or not, there's no escape from the gabble."

"Her readers love her."

"Do they?" Ravensfield was honestly surprised. Certainly, he knew they bought enough copies of the books to keep him living in the lap of luxury. But love? "They might enjoy her stories but—"

"Readers are nothing if not loyal. Especially when they find an author whose words are as engaging as Mrs. Mordefi's. I think she is truly wonderful."

The compliment settled deep inside Ravensfield, in a

place he was not used to acknowledging. He did his best to cast aside the warmth that tangled around his heart but even before he tried, he knew it was a losing cause. He was used to women whose veneer of sophistication kept their emotions—and whatever character they might actually have—suppressed. Even ladies of accommodating morals, traditionally more direct than their well-bred sisters, were never entirely honest. They were paid to tell a man what he wanted to hear. As good as it was for his self-esteem, it did little to reveal the lady's true temperament.

Yet Lynnette . . .

He found her still smiling and the warmth of her expression intertwined with the feelings that were already as convoluted as the hedge maze in the garden.

Lynnette had the temerity to tell him to his face what others only whispered behind his back.

"I will make note of it," he told her, forcing himself to keep to the subject. It was, at least, a better alternative to kissing her. And kissing her was what he really wanted to do. "I will read your Mrs. Mordefi someday. If I find her books half as enjoyable as you do, I know I will be richly rewarded." Ravensfield studied Lynnette closely. She was a fetching thing and, if what he heard about her was true, more intelligent than any woman needed to be. It had not occurred to him until this moment that she might not be fooled by all he'd planned for the night.

"Do you think that such things as vampires are possible?" he asked her. "I know you enjoy the stories, but do you really believe in shrouded figures and hidden treasures and mysterious intruders?"

Her eyes widened and her breath caught. Her hand strayed to the cover of her book and she pressed it there protectively. "It can all seem, sometimes, to be very real," she said. "At those times, it can be difficult to separate fact from fiction. There are times when a woman feels . . ." She leaned nearer. Just a bit. Just enough for Ravensfield to catch the heady scent of roses.

"Vulnerable," she said, and Ravensfield cursed himself for a fool. She might be talking about being vulnerable but there wasn't a feather's chance in hell that she was feeling as vulnerable as he was right now.

Rather than consider it, he rose to his feet. "I hope you will never feel like that inside the walls of Broadworth. Now, we must head downstairs. It is time for my guests to be arriving." He offered her his arm.

She made a game attempt at complying. But no sooner was Lynnette on her feet than she staggered. She leaned against the duke to support herself.

Damnation!

The curse echoed in Ravensfield's head yet even he wasn't sure if it was aimed at Lynnette and her still-weak ankle. Or at himself and his instinctive reaction.

Before she could move and be subject to any more pain, Ravensfield swept her into his arms.

"Good heavens, your grace!" Her protest was breathy and not very convincing. "You have guests. You certainly cannot carry me into dinner."

"Dinner?" Ravensfield chuckled. "There will be refreshments, certainly, but we have more than dinner planned for this night. I know you will not admit it but I must confess, Miss Overton, I could tell when we visited the graveyard that you were fascinated with the stories about it. Just as you are fascinated with those books you read. I have planned something appropriate, I think. We are on our way, my dear, to a séance!"

Lynnette's eyes went wide and round. Her breath caught, then escaped on the end of a sigh that was part exhilaration and part frisson of fear.

The duke tried his best not to think about it. At least not the fear part. For when he did, he also must acknowledge the thread of guilt that chilled his insides. He had nothing to feel guilty about, he reminded himself. All he was trying to do was hurry her on her way. All he hoped to accomplish was to frighten Lynnette.

And that was only fair. Because Lynnette Overton scared him to death.

6

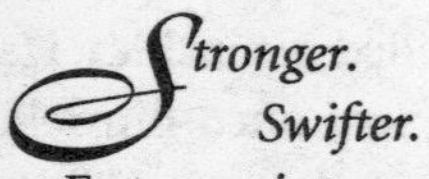

Stronger.

Swifter.

Far more intense in their appetites.

The words floated through Lynnette's head along with the haze of enchantment created as the dozens of sparkling candles that had been lit around the duke's impressive library were snuffed, one by one. Caught in the bewitchment and the hush that suddenly fell over the small crowd of Broadworth neighbors gathered there, she glanced to where Ravensfield was instructing the servants on the last of the preparations for the séance.

When they were finished, the duke invited his guests to be seated. Careful to remember that she was supposed to be incapacitated and disappointed that Ravensfield was too occupied to assist, Lynnette accepted the arm of Howard Wayne-Smith, a member of the local gentry. She hitch-stepped her way to the table that had been placed in the center of the room, careful not to lean too heavily on Wayne-Smith's arm. He talked incessantly of dogs and he smelled a bit like one, too, and as soon as she was able, Lynnette disentangled herself from the man. She stepped past Vanessa Grant, a woman with large blue eyes and a head of frizzly yellow hair. She excused herself around a local belle by the name of Emily Carminster and a young fellow named Theodore Bearingbone, who were deep in conversation.

And she found herself . . .

Lynnette smiled and sat in the seat next to the one reserved for Ravensfield.

Stronger.

Swifter.

Far more intense in their appetites.

Just thinking of the words he'd spoken in her chamber made her feel as if, head to toe, her bloodstream was abuzz, her skin was on fire, and her imagination was being tickled to go in places it would not have dared to venture only a short time before. Places that made her think that—vampire or not—Ravensfield was stronger and swifter than ordinary men. That he had appetites that were more intense. And that she would very much like to explore those appetites with him.

The very thought caused a rush of heat and she was

glad there was only one candle left burning. When Ravensfield sat next to her, he could not possibly see that her cheeks were just as hot. It might be easier to control her errant urges if not for the memory of her trip downstairs to greet his guests.

Though she had played upon the notion of her injured ankle in the hopes of nothing more than the chance to lean on the duke's arm, he had surprised her with his gallantry. He had picked her up and carried her as if she were no more trouble to haul along than a child might be. There was something appealing about such strength, just as there was something comforting about his promise to keep her safe here in the confines of Broadworth.

There was something even more fascinating about the feel of his body moving against hers.

Another rush of heat assailed her. This time, it snaked deep inside, warming her within. She shifted in her seat, both uncomfortable with the sensation and intrigued by it, and while the duke introduced a woman by the name of Madame Sophia who would serve as medium, Lynnette relived the delicious sensations that tingled through her when his superfine coat rubbed against the skin exposed by the short sleeves of her gown. The memory made her shiver with delight, as did the thought of the scent that rose off Ravensfield's skin. Bay rum and limes, clean and delicious. As intoxicating as the warmth that spread from his hands, burning through her green silk.

"So now we will extinguish the last of the candles . . ."

Ravensfield's words snapped Lynnette out of her thoughts. Bad enough she was being a poor guest and allowing her fancies to get in the way of her manners. Worse, she thought, if her host were to learn that the very reason she wasn't listening was that she was too absorbed in thoughts no proper lady should have about any proper gentleman.

Except that if half of what she heard about Ravensfield was true, he was no proper gentleman at all.

The very thought started up a tattoo of anticipation in Lynnette's chest. She watched him lean forward to snuff the candle in the center of the table. The room was plunged into darkness. The next second, he sat down again. And Lynnette was keenly aware of the warmth of his body next to hers in the dark.

How could she possibly concentrate? She was too occupied with the sensations that erupted through her.

Heat, like summer lightning. Chills, like the invigorating splash of an ocean wave. His presence soothed her at the same time it made her feel as if she were soaring.

"Hands, Miss Overton."

Ravensfield leaned nearer, his voice in her ear. Now that her eyes were adjusting to the darkness, she saw that his hands were on the table in front of him. It was, apparently, exactly what they had been instructed to do. Exactly what she had missed hearing because she was so busy thinking of other things.

Lynnette put her hands on the table and forced her mind to the entertainment. It was, after all, the least she could do. She knew the duke was not in the habit of welcoming guests to Broadworth. When he came to his country home, he came to enjoy his solitude. The idea that he had planned this night for her entertainment and opened his doors to his neighbors on her account was enough to warm Lynnette anew.

Now that she had their attention, Madame Sophia touched a hand to her turban and ran her fingers through the multitude of chains and amulets she wore around her neck. She cleared her throat, and little by little, the warmth inside Lynnette evaporated beneath the cold mix of fright and anticipation that crept into her bones.

"So . . ." Madame Sophia's voice was low and heavily accented. "We begin."

Her words subsided in a whisper. Her breathing quickened. Though Lynnette could not see her clearly, she knew her eyes were closed and, lulled by the dark and the gratifying knowledge that Ravensfield was but a few inches from her, Lynnette closed her eyes, too.

They flew open again when Madame Sophia began mumbling in a language that sounded both ancient and mysterious.

Shivers raced up Lynnette's spine. A tiny hiccup of excitement escaped her lips. She did her best to suppress it, one hand to her mouth, but Ravensfield caught sight of the movement. Before anyone else could notice, he took her hand in his and placed it back on the table. Just to make sure she wouldn't make the same mistake again, he held his hand over hers.

How could a woman focus on the supernatural when the physical was so potent?

Lynnette did not even try and work through the problem. Whether the fluttering she felt from her head to her toes was the result of Madame Sophia's communion with the spirits or her own fierce reaction to Ravensfield, she couldn't tell. She didn't care. She gave herself over to the suspense and the eager expectation that sizzled in the air all around.

Perhaps it was her receptivity that caused Madame Sophia to call her name.

"Lynnette! Lynnette!" It was the medium's voice, surely, but it sounded like it came from a very long way off. "We have a message. For you."

The tingling in Lynnette settled to a steady thrum, and before she realized she was doing it, she wound her fingers through Ravensfield's, the better to control her excitement.

"Lynnette!"

"I am . . ." The words barely made their way past the knot of delectable terror in Lynnette's throat. She tried again. "I am here," she said.

"The spirits . . ." Madame Sophia moaned and swayed. Her chains and amulets rattled. "The spirits say . . ." She made a sound that was half gurgle, half growl. "They send a warning!"

Lynnette trembled. Perhaps the spirits knew about the paper tucked into her copy of *Greystone Castle?* Perhaps they were aware of the burglar and of Lynnette's own attempts to keep her mother's message safe? Perhaps there was even a chance they could tell her what had become of Madelaine's diary?

Fascinated and eager to know more, she scooted forward in her chair. "What sort of warning?" she asked.

"You—" Madame Sophia made a gurgling sound. She hauled in a breath. She moaned. "You . . . must . . . return. To London. You must—"

The draperies that had been pulled closed over the French windows on the other side of the room parted as if by the urging of some unseen hand. The doors that led to the veranda burst open. A rush of night air poured into the room. And there, right outside the door, was a ghost.

The phantom was cloaked, its head covered with a cowl that hid all but the gleaming twin fires of its eyes. There was little in the way of moonlight yet the figure glowed, the light as white as bleached bones and as cold as hell.

Miss Carminster clutched her throat and screamed and Mr. Bearingbone chivalrously put an arm around her shoulders. Vanessa Grant pressed a hand to her heaving bosom. Mr. Wayne-Smith mumbled something that sounded like "the bloody blighter!" and Ravensfield . . .

She was so fascinated by the spectral figure, Lynnette could barely tear her gaze away. When she did and turned to Ravensfield, she found that he was not even looking at the ghost. He was watching her.

It took only that for the truth of the matter to hit her as clearly as the sounds of Madame Sophia's continued moans.

Quickly, so that he would not think that she noticed, Lynnette turned away from Ravensfield, hiding the smile that threatened to blossom across her expression. So, there was a tender side to the man! She would not have guessed it. But now that she knew, she would not for the world disappoint him.

He knew how much she admired the intrepid women in Mrs. Mordefi's books. He knew she ached for just such adventure in her own life. He saw as much for himself when they visited the graveyard and she was taken by the stories of its sad residents. To amuse her, he was giving her the opportunity to be a heroine for the night.

Unless the ghost was indeed, real.

A tremor of fear assailed her and Lynnette did her best to hold it at bay. She took another long look at the specter outside on the veranda.

She was just in time to see the cowl droop a bit.

The specter's hair twitched.

Hiding a smile, Lynnette leaped out of her seat. "That is no ghost," she cried, raising one fist in righteous indignation. "I do believe we have been hoaxed and I shall prove it!"

Before anyone could stop her and ruin the delightful scenario Ravensfield had constructed for her benefit, she raced out to the veranda.

It wasn't until after she was there that she remembered her ankle was supposed to pain her and by that time it was too late. It hardly mattered at any rate. Chaos reigned in the library and she doubted anyone noticed her suddenly healed limb. She heard the noise of chairs falling over, the sounds of running feet. The phantom was doing his best to disappear over the balustrade and into the protective darkness of the garden but his cloak caught on a branch and he could not extricate himself. She caught him up, snatching at his hood.

"Mr. Worthy, I presume?" She plucked the hood from the specter's head and Mr. Worthy's hair sprang free. His face looked pale against the luminescent paint that had been applied to his clothing and all around his eyes to make them look like pools of fire.

"I say! I say, indeed." Behind her, Lynnette heard the sounds of Mr. Wayne-Smith's admiration. "How ever did you know we had been humbugged?"

"And imagine a woman who is valiant enough to go charging after a ghost!" Mr. Bearingbone joined in the chorus of praise, his voice brimming with laughter.

Seeing that it was all a lark and all in great fun, everyone joined in. They congratulated Lynnette for being so clever and so brave. They peppered Worthy with questions about how he had arranged the escapade and how it felt to be a ghost. They drank the health of Madame Sophia who, as it turned out, was really one Mrs. Betty Binks who lived in a nearby village; she was known to bake the finest bread in all of Berkshire and was a skilled actress besides.

And if Ravensfield did not join in the merriment?

In between accepting the compliments that were showered over her like flower petals on the head of a conquering hero, Lynnette chanced a look over at him. Ravensfield was standing just inside the library, drinking a glass of brandy. She watched him down the liquor in one swallow and pour another. He looked nothing if not morose, but Lynnette was sure she must be mistaken about his mood.

He was simply standing back and letting her take full credit. Just as he'd expected her to.

Affection bubbled through Lynnette and she found herself smiling.

So, there was an endearing side to Ravensfield, after all. It seemed all it took to bring it to the fore was the right opportunity.

And the right woman.

It wasn't until after his guests were thanked for their participation and sent home that Lynnette had the chance to have Ravensfield to herself.

"I think you will admit that it has been quite an evening." The duke's words were breezy but his shoulders were rigid. He nodded in Lynnette's direction without looking at her. "Good night, Miss Overton."

His attempts at formality were not nearly enough to dissuade her from what she knew she must do. The duke was not a man who accepted compliments easily. He knew she would be grateful for letting her play the heroine just as she knew that he would be embarrassed by her gratitude.

But that did not mean she didn't have to try.

"It is early yet. And I was thinking . . ." Knowing the

perceived need for assistance might serve her yet, she was not inclined to relinquish the pretense of a wounded limb. As soon as they returned to the library, she pretended that her injury flared again. Now, Lynnette sat in a chair near the fire, her left leg propped on a footstool. "It is a beautiful night. We might, perhaps, take some air."

"Together?" It did not seem such an odd request, yet Ravensfield, who had been busy staring into his brandy glass, looked at Lynnette as if she'd suddenly started spouting Chinese. "I think we have had quite enough excitement for one night."

"It isn't excitement I'm looking for," she told him, at the same time she knew that looking for it or not, she would find it any time she was in Ravensfield's presence. "It is a turn around the veranda."

"The door is open." He swept an arm toward the French doors that had so dramatically flown open during the séance. "You are free to come and go."

"Yes. But . . ." She glanced down at her ankle.

He set his brandy snifter down, and it must certainly have been a trick of her imagination, but she could have sworn he grumbled something below his breath as he stalked across the room. "If I might assist." He gave her a smile that glittered in the candlelight and offered his arm.

Lynnette gladly accepted. She snatched up the walking stick but didn't use it. Leaning far more heavily on Ravensfield than she ever had on Mr. Wayne-Smith and being careful to take small steps, she allowed him to lead her out to the veranda.

It was long past dark and there was little to see. Still,

Lynnette was overwhelmed by a riot of sensations she had not had time to notice when she took off, hurly-burly, after the ghostly Mr. Worthy. There were roses and lilacs growing somewhere nearby; she could smell their sweet scent. Above her, the sky was filled with stars and a half-moon whose light created soft shadows. A bat swooped overhead. Her head whirled when Ravensfield fitted his hands around her waist and lifted her. He settled her on the wide marble balustrade that encircled the veranda.

Lynnette waited for him to speak, and when he did not, she gave him a probing look. "So?"

"So . . ." The duke was far more modest than she expected him to be.

"You are a scapegrace, sir, and no mistake."

"It isn't the first time I've been called such."

"But it is the first time, I think, that you dressed your valet in glowing rags and sent him to surprise your company. I can't thank you enough."

"Thank me?" He was close enough for Lynnette to touch and she saw the flash of surprise on his face. "Are you sure that's what you want to say?"

She laughed. "Of course I'm sure. It isn't often a woman has a chance to live out her fantasies."

"And I've given you that chance."

He didn't sound sure of it himself.

"You are entirely too modest."

"I am."

This comment too hovered somewhere between commentary and question.

"You know how much I love Mrs. Mordefi's stories. You know how much I admire the women in them who, against all odds and all reason, head out to confront their worst fears. It was just like in the books! There is something supernatural happening and the heroine is certain it cannot be for real. She investigates, and reveals the fraudulence. Then the next time there is a similar occurrence, she is certain that too is a hoax."

"Only the next time, it really is some ghostly happening."

"Just so!" Lynnette laughed. "You know how dull the country can be and you know that with my injured limb I have not been able to enjoy your hospitality as much as I would like. You designed the séance expressly for me. You have given me the opportunity to play the heroine and I cannot tell you how much fun I had! Or how much I appreciate your kindness. Thank you, your grace."

For a moment, he didn't know what to say. But whatever uncertainties tangled his tongue, he cast them away with a twitch of his shoulders. "I would very much appreciate it if you would dispense with the foolish habit of calling me 'your grace.' "

"Of course, your grace, but—" She caught herself. "What shall I call you, then?"

"I have other titles. Earl This and Baron That." He did not seem as pleased by the distinction as most men surely would. "My father preferred to go by one of the older titles, but I like to think of myself as my own man."

"Which is why you prefer Ravensfield."

"Exactly." He smiled and acknowledged her discernment with a tip of his head. "Ravensfield will do fine," he said. "If, of course, I may call you Lynnette."

All her friends did. It was far less cumbersome than "Miss Overton," far more amiable, and more in keeping with the less-than-formal relationships she liked to establish with those she knew.

But somehow, when Ravensfield said the name—

"I've offended you."

"Oh, no!" It wasn't true, even if her hesitation did send the message, and she wouldn't allow him to believe it. "It's just that hearing you say my name . . ." She considered the wisdom of telling him the truth even though she knew she would in the end. "When you say it, it sounds less like a name and more like poetry."

Ravensfield laughed, and though she did not see him move, she sensed that he stepped closer. The air grew warmer. The shadows thickened. It was a trick of the light, surely, but she could have sworn that the stars flared and brightened. "Then perhaps I should become a writer! What do you think? I might give your Mrs. Mordefi some competition."

"Mrs. Mordefi writes of fabulous things. Flights of the imagination. Figments of nightmares. I think, perhaps, that your talents lie in things that are more corporeal."

The moment the words were out of her mouth, Lynnette pressed a finger to her lips. As if she could somehow call them back. "I do beg your pardon. It is the excitement of the evening that causes me to talk so foolishly. Forgive me!"

"Do I need to?" He was near enough for her to feel the warmth that rose off his body and Lynnette breathed in the scent of soap and bay rum.

"Have you ever played commerce, Lynnette?"

It was not something she expected him to ask, and for a moment, she could not find the words to answer.

Ravensfield was not a man to wait. "Commerce? The card game. Have you never played?"

"A bit," she answered, not sure where the conversation was headed and not sure she liked not knowing. "My cousin Nick has tried to teach me. And his friends, the Duke of Latimer and Mr. Palliston and Mr. Hexam—"

"Ah, the Dashers! They are fine gamesters, all, though none as brass-necked as your own cousin. He has nerves of steel and an eye for a man who is less than honest. You, madam, would be a terrible commerce player. Part of the game involves making your opponents believe that you are holding better cards than you actually have."

"Lying, you mean?"

"Indeed!" Ravensfield chuckled. "And I think you are not very good at lying."

"You make it sound as if it is a bad thing."

"Not at all." He rested his hands on the balustrade on either side of Lynnette and leaned forward. "As we've all been taught, honesty is a virtue. It's just that women of Society . . . well, it isn't often I find one about whom I can speak and use the word 'honesty.' "

"Nonsense." She shook away the compliment along with the guilt that rushed through her. If he knew about the wager the Blades had proposed and how easily she was willing to be a part of it, if he knew about her ankle . . .

She managed a laugh. "Surely, I am not the only one—"

"The only one I have ever met."

"Then perhaps you are not meeting the right women!"

It was another faux pas but while Lynnette cringed, Ravensfield took it in stride. His laughter rumbled through the darkness, so close it vibrated against her skin along with the warmth of his breath. "My dear Lynnette, you are extraordinary. Let's see, you've told me my female friends do not come up to snuff—"

"Never, your grace!" She blanched at the very thought, but Ravensfield would not listen. He went right on.

"You've told me my talents lie more in the physical than they do in the mental or the spiritual."

"I certainly never intended that!"

He wasn't listening. He leaned in closer still, his mouth dangerously close. "Is there anything else you'd like to tell me?" he asked, the words a murmur against her lips. "What is it you would like?"

It was insanity, surely, to choose the truth over a lie in a situation such as this. Yet there was no way Lynnette could bring herself to equivocate. What did she want?

The feelings that rioted through her told her as

much. The warm rush of heat. The tingle of anticipation. The words that rushed out on the end of a sigh.

"Oh, your grace, I would very much like it if you would kiss me."

He was tempted. Good Lord, but he was more than tempted.

Ravensfield was spellbound by the sparkle in Lynnette's gray eyes, charmed by her lack of artifice, beguiled by her faith in a man she hardly knew. And so hungry for the touch of her and the feel of her body against his, he could taste it.

What he wasn't, was insane.

If he thought her a distraction before, she was certain to be more of one once he kissed her. If he thought of her as an inconvenience, he knew he did not fully know the meaning of the word. Once he committed himself with a kiss, she would not easily leave. He wouldn't let her. For he knew himself, and he knew he could not stop at a kiss. And he would no sooner compromise her than he would ensnare himself.

The thought spread a chill through him like icy fingers, and acting on instinct and instinct alone, he backed away from Lynnette and from his own errant longings.

It would have been a damned sight easier to come to terms with his decison if Lynnette hadn't taken her lower lip in her teeth. If she hadn't looked away.

If she hadn't looked so terribly hurt.

She lifted her chin. "I could have sworn—"

"Don't." He backed away even farther. From her. From all he was tempted to do—to her and with her. "If your good cousin knew what I had nearly done—"

"No more than he has done, surely. Before he met Willie, that is."

"With a woman such as yourself?" The very idea was as impossible as blood from stones and Ravensfield snorted his disbelief. "I know the viscount well, and though we pretend to a certain animosity, you should know that I admire him. He's a gentleman, and no gentleman would ever take advantage of a woman in his care. You must forgive me." He used the same formal tone of voice he usually reserved for court and for the old tabbies at Almack's who, against the odds and all reason, thought chivalry was still alive.

"It's the night air." He was enough of a realist to know it wasn't true. And enough of a fabulist to try the explanation on for size. Just to ease his conscience. "I suppose the moonlight and the soft breezes, the starshine and the scent of flowers . . . That would explain why I nearly—" It didn't. Night air was hardly a reason for finding himself suddenly susceptible to the kind of woman who usually made him run for the door.

The only thing on the other end of a relationship with a respectable woman was marriage. Long ago, he had promised himself that he would marry only for love, but he had learned at the hands of Christina Moore-Chastain that love was as ephemeral as a spring breeze. There was nothing to be gained from allowing himself tender feelings for a woman.

Nothing but heartache.

Uneasy with the thought, he spun away to do a quick turn around the veranda. Better to pound through the dark than risk another look at the way the moonlight washed Lynnette's dark hair with silver. The way her gown molded to her breasts. Surely she was equally responsible for the awkward place they found themselves in. If it wasn't for her Cupid's-bow lips, he never would have thought of kissing her. If it wasn't for her perfect body, he would not have considered how good it would feel to take her into his bed. If it wasn't for his own good sense, a quality many would have sworn he lacked completely, he might not have found himself in a place he did not know how to get out of.

He grappled for some explanation—any explanation—that would allay his scruples and soothe her pride.

Pity he couldn't find one. Nothing could excuse what he'd nearly done.

Fortunately, Lynnette was not the type who shirked her responsibility. "You must forgive me, your grace—" She caught herself, and even from across the veranda, he saw the quick flash of her apologetic smile. "Ravensfield, you must think me a perfect nodcock. I'm afraid I was still caught up in the romantic excitement of the evening. Otherwise I wouldn't be acting like a Drury Lane Vestal."

The comparison was too much and Ravensfield sucked in a breath, the better to control the fantasies that raced through his mind with all the subtlety of cannonshot. If Lynnette was acting anything like the canary birds who plied their wares in town, she'd already have her clothes off.

And he'd be well on his way to gratifying her. And himself.

Lynnette was never so grateful for the darkness of night. It covered the embarrassment that flushed her face and for that she was thankful. It hid her disappointment, as well.

For one second, she could have sworn Ravensfield was going to ignore propriety and follow the same wild urgings that were coursing through her. She was sure he was going to kiss her.

The thrill of expectation still tingled along her skin. It sizzled deep inside her like a flame.

Now, she found herself rejected.

She swallowed down her disappointment and consoled herself with the fact that it was only natural that he should be hestitant. After all, they hardly knew each other. What was not so natural was that he would take her inexcusable behavior in stride.

The very thought warmed her in a different way.

"It is kind of you to ignore my boorish behavior," she told him.

"Kind?" She did not expect Ravensfield to laugh. "I am fairly certain that is a word that has never been used to describe me."

She owed him her gratitude. She might have found the words to tell him as much if a movement in the shadows hadn't caught her eye. Curious, Lynnette peered into the darkness over the duke's left shoulder. "Your grace?"

He looked over his shoulder to where she pointed toward the wide, shallow steps that led into the garden.

"Your grace, I thought I saw—"

"Not another ghost, I hope!" He chuckled, grateful that the subject had changed and they no longer had to step around the sorry fact that she had acted too brazenly and he had been—if only for a second—eager to accommodate her. When she did not join in his laughter or leap the balustrade and head into the garden to expose the unwanted visitor like the heroine in one of Mrs. Mordefi's books might have done, his brows dropped low over his eyes.

"What is it?" he asked.

"I thought I saw . . ."

But by then, Lynnette already had the thing figured out. She exhaled, getting rid of the momentary misgivings that had her looking toward the house and wondering if her copy of *Greystone Castle* and the precious paper inside it were still safe. "It isn't going to work. Not again." She shook her head, amazed that he would try the trick a second time. "If you think you can frighten me—"

"Not at all! I've learned as much this night, haven't I?"

"Yet you've sent Worthy out into the night again, poor man. What's he supposed to do this time? Pop out of the nearest tree screaming like a banshee?"

Ravensfield tried his best to look solemn. But his smile gave him away. "You're right. And I am terribly sorry. It seemed a pity to waste the costume and all that phosphorescent paint. Come. I think we have had enough ghosts for one night." With a last look toward the garden, he scooped her into his arms and carried her into the house. He didn't say another word, not until a final "good night" when he deposited her in her chamber and rang for Jenny to help her into her nightclothes.

After that, Ravensfield hurried back downstairs and on to the veranda, being sure to close the library doors behind him. He twitched his shoulders against the feeling of unease that sat upon them like a stone. He peered into the darkness, and seeing nothing there, he headed into the garden for a quick look around.

For what he had not confessed was that he had seen someone in the garden, too. A figure outlined as if by India ink in the milky light. A man dressed all in black.

He had not sent Worthy out to try and frighten Lynnette again.

Which made him wonder who was prowling the grounds. And why.

7

Lynnette had been hurt by Ravensfield's easy dismissal of her affections. She could not deny it. But she was not one to let herself wallow in self-pity for long. Really, he should have known her better than that. She was not so quickly put off. Or so easily fooled.

He had, after all, taken enough note of her likes and dislikes to know how much she enjoyed Mrs. Mordefi's stories. Otherwise, he would not have arranged for the wonderful séance and made sure that she was allowed to play the role of the heroine. Afterward, he had been modest about it all and so much the gentleman as to be understanding and even tender in his response to her brazen request for a kiss.

He had been paying close attention. To her. And that could mean one thing only: he was beginning to realize that his affection for her burned as bright as hers for him. Any day now, he was sure to declare the depth of his feelings. All he needed was a little more time.

And perhaps, just a little encouragement.

With that in mind, Lynnette arranged for an amusement of her own and invited those from the neighborhood who took part in the séance to join them. They had eagerly accepted and she kept an eye on the weather and waited for just the right day. In the meantime, Ravensfield was sequestered behind the door to his study so Lynnette kept to herself. It was only natural that the time alone and the memory of the man she could have sworn she saw in the garden would make her think about her mother's diary. It was enough of a reminder that she would need to deal with the problem of the diary when she returned to London. It wasn't too soon to consider her next step. Sure that the diary went missing in the days just after her mother's death, she wracked her brains to remember every person who had paid a sympathy visit to Plumley Terrace.

During the long hours of the three gray and gloomy days following the séance, she made a careful list and went over it again and again. Who on the list might have taken the diary? And what did that person intend to do with it?

Now on this, the fourth day, the sun was shining, the sky was brilliant blue, and Lynnette was convinced that her brain needed a rest, her spirits needed reviving, and the Duke of Ravensfield needed yet another little push in the direction of true love.

She could think of no better way to do it than to put her plan into action, and with that in mind, she breezed into the breakfast room just minutes after she knew he'd sat down to table.

"I have wonderful news!"

Ravensfield looked up from his plate of sausage and eggs to where she stood. "You've recovered."

Lynnette cursed herself for forgetting to limp. Now that she was standing in front of him, as fit as a fiddle and as radiant as the spring day, it was difficult to pretend to her former injury. She leaned against the table, nonetheless, just so he wouldn't forget it.

"I am much better," she said.

He rose from the table, his breakfast untouched, and taking her elbow, he walked her to the door. "I can see why your spirits are sparked. After such a long, dull visit to the country, you must be eager to be going."

"Indeed! For we are going to a picnic."

He did not look convinced. "Picnic? We? Who have we invited?"

"Why, Miss Carminster, of course, and Miss Grant. Mr. Wayne-Smith and the Bearingbone boy. They are the only of your neighbors with whom I am acquainted. They have been waiting for the summons and word that the weather is perfect, and today . . ." She looked toward the windows where the morning sun shone like a newly minted sovereign. "Today is perfect."

"And we're going—"

"To the abbey ruin that I hear is nearby!" Lynnette could barely control her excitement. She was eager to see the ancient abbey that the servants told her was even more haunted than the little graveyard. "I hear there are ghostly monks and there is talk that once there were blood sacrifices by the light of the full moon."

"Really, after what happened here the night of the séance, aren't you afraid?"

Lynnette laughed. "Oh, no, your grace!" She smiled into Ravensfield's dark eyes. "I do believe that with you by my side, I shall be quite safe!"

Broadworth Hall had been built most specifically for one thing and one thing alone: to give Ravensfield a place where he could go to get away from the whirlwind of town life. A man needed solitude, after all, most especially when there was work to be done. He could not accomplish that work with the endless parade of temptations that were part and parcel of London life.

Social obligations. Clubs. The theater. Sport. Gaming. Women.

And he couldn't wait to get back to all of it.

The country might be picturesque, but it was as dull as ditchwater. That was, of course, the whole point of being here. The duller the better, for the more he felt himself in the doldrums, the sooner he would be likely to complete his newest book.

It was a perfect plan, elegant and simple. Brilliant in its own way because, after all, he would tolerate nothing less.

Pity it wasn't working.

As restless as he was dissatisfied, Ravensfield kept to the shadows and skirted the sun-drenched clearing that was once the south transept of St. Swithun's Church.

His solitude was getting him nowhere. His isolation was doing nothing but making him more restless, and less productive, by the day. The peace and quiet were wearing on his nerves, stretching his patience to the limit. He sat in his study all day and night but, except for a scene in which a heroine unmasked a fraud at a séance, he had yet to come up with even a glimmer of an idea for the latest Mrs. Mordefi work. If something didn't change—and soon—he'd never get back to London.

A burst of laughter erupted from the knot of people sharing a picnic lunch in the center of the clearing, and like it or not, Ravensfield's thoughts were drawn in that direction.

Bad enough that he could not write his book and be finished with it.

Worse yet when further distraction was added to the mix.

"Your grace!" Howard Wayne-Smith waved to Ravensfield and pointed toward the overflowing baskets of food Mrs. B had tucked into his carriage before they left Broadworth. "It is time for luncheon, your grace," Wayne-Smith called out. "You will be joining us?"

Luncheon was not what Ravensfield wanted.

What he wanted was to be left to himself. What he wanted was to be rid of the constant, nagging voice in the back of his mind, the one that reminded him that each day he did little and accomplished less meant he was one day further from returning to London.

What he wanted . . .

His gaze wandered over to where Lynnette was chatting easily with Theodore Bearingbone. In white muslin sprigged with tiny pink rosebuds, she looked as fresh as a garden flower, and watching the way the low-cut bodice of her gown caressed her breasts when she moved, Ravensfield sucked in a breath to steady himself.

What he wanted was Lynnette Overton, damn it, and if it wasn't for her and his own mystifying attraction to her, he wouldn't be here right now.

A stiff and rather painful smile hiding his thoughts, he strode over to where the company was setting out the meal.

"So kind of you, your grace." When he came within range, Emily Carminster beamed a smile at Ravensfield. "So kind of you to invite us along on this little excursion."

She could not possibly have known how very wrong she was.

Kindness had nothing to do with it.

"We do not often see you when you are in residence at Broadworth." Though he had not noticed it the night of the séance, in the daylight he saw that Miss Grant had crooked teeth and sallow skin. She also had a penchant for stating the obvious. "You must tell us, your grace, why you chose such a delightful diversion."

Must? Ravensfield was tempted to throw the word back at her. Nearly as tempted as he was to tell her the truth. Why choose a company of sadly flat country bumpkins?

The answer was as plain as the rather large nose on Miss Grant's face.

It was that or disappoint Lynnette.

He cast the thought aside. It was not what he'd meant

to think at all. He'd had to agree to Lynnette's plan for the day. After all, she had already sent word around for his neighbors to meet them here. To do anything else would have been the height of rudeness. Besides, once she had this notion of a haunted monastery out of her system and now that she was feeling better, she was sure to be on her way. This last excursion was the least he could do for Lynnette, and with any luck, the last thing he would do for her. Ergo, it was something of a celebration as well.

Heartened by the thought, Ravensfield accepted the plate of food that Miss Grant handed to him. As usual, Mrs. B had outdone herself. Figs and olives. Cheese and bread. Portuguese ham, Russian caviar, plump roast chicken. For good or ill, the only seat left was one next to where Lynnette sat on an overturned portion of one of the pillars that used to brace the nave of the monk's church. He sat down on what was left of a tree trunk that had fallen years before.

"We were just saying . . ." Finding herself suddenly in the presence of a man whose reputation was scandalous and whose social life was, for the most part, nonexistent when he was at Broadworth, was apparently too much for Emily Carminster. She flushed a rather unbecoming shade and giggled rather loudly. "We were just saying, your grace, that it is a perfect day and that you have chosen a most perfect spot for an outing."

"Do you think so?" Ravensfield was talking to Miss Carminster, but he was looking at Lynnette. He wasn't sure why—aside from the fact that from beneath the brim of a fetching little bonnet, her eyes sparkled like the sunlight itself—but it suddenly seemed very important to know if her impromptu party was all she'd hoped. "Have we come to just the right spot?" he asked her.

Lynnette was too wise to pretend she did not know what was behind his question. She was too prudent to do anything but take it at face value. She shook her head sadly. "I have yet to see one ghostly monk," she said, and there was a thread of devilment in her voice that was all the more appealing because it was meant only for him. "And as for blood sacrifices in the light of the full moon—"

"Surely you of all people don't believe such things, Miss Overton!" Aside from being an expert on dogs and bitches, Wayne-Smith considered himself something of a man of science and a rationalist, as well. His argument—such as it was—would have been more persuasive if his mouth wasn't full of half-chewed ham. "You proved yourself that such things are an impossibility. Just the other night. Ghosts and vampires!" He barked a laugh. "Peasant rumors! That's all there is to it. You must not give such stories credence. It is impossible, after all, for things such as phantoms to exist."

"Impossible, yes. But isn't that why we find it so intriguing?" Lynnette was talking to Wayne-Smith. She was looking at Ravensfield. "The more impossible a thing is, the more likely we are to want it. It is human nature, don't you think?"

"Human nature? Bosh!" Wayne-Smith pointed with a

chicken bone. "That is the excuse people use, Miss Overton, when they refuse to take responsibility for their own actions."

"Do you think so?" Lynnette's voice was low, her question meant only for Ravensfield. "Do you think—"

"Overton." Miss Carminster had clearly not been following the conversation. She tipped her head to one side. Used to being the center of attention as she was so often here in the country where there was so small a crop of women to be toasts of any crowd, she had no qualms about interrupting. Thinking very hard, she tapped one plump finger against the side of her plate. "The name is familiar, yet I cannot place it. I thought as much the other night when we met at the Hall. Overton. Overton. Wasn't there some to-do in town some years ago? Something about a woman named Overton? I say!" Her mouth fell open and her eyes grew large. She stared at Lynnette with nothing short of unabashed wonder. "You aren't related to Madelaine Overton?"

The truth dawned. For Miss Carminster and for the rest of the assemblage. Miss Carminster, awake to her blunder and just as certain that there was no way now to redeem herself, blubbered unintelligible words below her breath. Miss Grant looked down at the ground, suddenly intent on the grass growing at her feet. Wayne-Smith gave the full of his attention to a passing cloud.

Though he may have heard some rumor of the story, Theodore Bearingbone was too young to know the whole of the tale, just as he was too young to pretend, as the others were trying so mightily to do, that Miss

Carminster had not misspoken. Sensing a good story and curious as the young always are, he leaned toward Lynnette, his nose twitching. "Madelaine? Madelaine Overton? I must confess, I do not know the name. Did you say, Miss Carminster"—he turned toward the lady—"that this Madelaine Overton has some connection with our Miss Overton?"

Miss Carminster's face turned a rather unbecoming, waxy color. She ignored Bearingbone, and though she spoke to Lynnette, she did not meet her eyes. "I do beg your pardon. I did not mean to bring up so unpleasant a subject."

Until that moment, Ravensfield would have sworn that Lynnette had not taken a breath since Madelaine's name slipped so carelessly from Miss Carminster's fleshy lips. Now, she set her plate on a portion of the column next to her and turned her gaze on Miss Carminster.

"You are quite wrong to be distressed," she told the woman. "And please don't think that the mention of Madelaine's name has disturbed me in any way. She was my mother and I have nothing but good memories of her. It is always pleasant for me to think of her. Even though she has been dead these seven months now," she added for Bearingbone's sake. "And every one of those days, I have sorely missed her."

"As well you should." The last thing Ravensfield wanted to do—now or ever—was step into the middle of a societal quagmire. It was not in his nature to gossip, just as it was not in his nature to come to anyone's rescue. Still, he could not help himself. Lynnette's quiet mastery of what might have been a social disaster elicited his deepest admiration.

"I knew Madelaine Overton," he said. "She was a diamond of the first water. The most beautiful and charming woman in all of London for some Seasons. I was quite young myself when we first met," he added for Lynnette's benefit, though he wasn't sure why it seemed so important that she know. "And still, I remember the first time I ever laid eyes on her." His mind drifted back. "She wore white. And she smelled like jasmine. She was as beautiful a woman as the *ton* had seen in many years. And as graceful."

Lynnette gave Ravensfield a smile of thanks that warmed him far more thoroughly than the sun. "I am afraid I do not at all live up to her memory," she said, and she did not sound disappointed, only sensible of the fact that she and her mother were very different women. From what Ravensfield knew of them both, he would say it was an understatement.

"Ah, look at that, will you?" Wayne-Smith might be more at home with hounds than he was with humans, but he knew how to change the subject when it needed changing. He pointed toward a quail that had the temerity to peek out from the tall grass to the far side of what was left of the abbey church. "A beautiful specimen," Wayne-Smith said, and for all his youth and apparent scatter-brained appearance, Bearingbone had the good sense to join in.

A spirited discussion of hunting and fowling began.

Through it all, Ravensfield said little. He was too busy keeping an eye on Lynnette. Too absorbed in reminding himself that he had best tamp down the admiration that flared inside him like fire to kindling.

For just as distraction was something he had no time to deal with, admiration was one indulgence which he could not afford.

"Thank you." No sooner were they in the curricle that would carry them back to Broadworth than Lynnette knew she had to speak. Before she missed her opportunity. After luncheon, the rest of the afternoon had been pleasant and boisterous, with Miss Grant and Mr. Bearingbone leading a game of Twenty Questions and the rest, except for Ravensfield who was noticeably quiet throughout, joining in. She had not had a chance to talk to the duke privately.

"I appreciate everything you said."

"About Madelaine?" Ravensfield took her gratitude in stride. He picked up the reins, ready to guide the horses up the overgrown path that led between what was left of the church and the hulking, moss-covered wreckage of the building where the monks once lived and worked.

"There's no need to thank me at all," he said, his words as matter-of-fact now as they had been when Miss Carminster first brought up the subject. "I spoke only the truth."

"You knew my mother well?"

He did not have an opportunity to answer, and though Lynnette could not say why, the delay made her feel as if she'd been stretched taut. Miss Grant called out her thanks and a farewell from the dogcart that she and the others were piled into. Ravensfield grunted. Lynnette waved. It wasn't until they trotted off and the curricle was left, alone, that he turned to her.

"Not in the way you think," he said, and there was something about the tone of his voice and the level look he gave her that told her he thought it vital for her to know. And something else about his words caused a wave of relief to wash over Lynnette. "I was not one of Madelaine's lovers."

Lynnette considered herself sophisticated. But she was not worldly enough to dispassionately discuss her mother's dalliances. From what she knew, they were legion. She turned away. "I never would have dared to think—"

"Spare me the girlish bleatings. Of course you did." Ravensfield snapped the reins and the horses began to pick their way up the narrow, winding path. "You are not so green as to have not heard all there was to hear about your mother, Lynnette. You must admit, the moment I mentioned her name, the thought must have crossed your mind. You wondered, if only for a moment. Lay those thoughts to rest. I was very young, Madelaine was older and much too well-bred to tolerate a rakehell pup such as me. Of course, she was a beautiful woman and forgive me if I am too bold but I think we both know the truth. Her reputation back then nearly equaled mine now."

"It did." Even if she had not heard the rumors, Lynnette would have known it was true. She remembered the men who used to call on her mother. "My parents were not happy together." She sighed, and caught herself, afraid she'd said too much.

Ravensfield's deep-throated laugh told her otherwise. "It is the curse of being among the *haut ton*," he said. "Our lives are fodder for every gossip mill. Your parents were no different. It was no secret that they lived their separate lives. So did mine, though my mother was less inclined to adventure than yours. She was more apt to compensate for her loneliness with the words of Shakespeare than the whisperings of a lover. The good news, I think, is that most people have more sense than does our prattling Miss Carminster and therefore do not mention things they know little about. Still, I think it is probably not surprising to you. There is still a buzz now and then about your mother. And the Wonderlee Diamond."

For the space of a dozen heartbeats, Lynnette found her tongue tied and her breath caught behind a tight knot. Everyone knew about the diamond, of course. The people in her immediate social circle. Her betters. The tradesmen who came to call. Though they never said a thing, she knew that even now, so many years later, they had not forgotten. She could see it in the looks they gave her when they thought she didn't notice. She could hear it in the unspoken words that shouted out from between the lines of everything they said.

Everyone knew about the diamond and about how Madelaine had been accused of stealing it. Everyone knew that though no proof of her crime was every produced, Madelaine's integrity had been compromised. She was a suspect and that simple fact caused tongues to wag. No sooner had the rumor started than she was banished from Society and ostracized by all but her very dearest friends.

Everyone knew.

No one dared speak of it.

No one but Ravensfield.

The realization slapped her like a cold wind and Lynnette hurtled back to reality. "She didn't steal it." Her voice rang with conviction. So much so that she startled a hawk in a nearby tree. It screeched its opinion of the disturbance and wheeled off into the clear blue sky. "Madelaine did not steal the diamond," she said again, quieter this time but with just as much conviction, her look daring Ravensfield to dispute her.

She might have known he would not be put off. His eyes glittered in the late afternoon light, and he cocked his head as if ready to measure and evaluate her response. To measure and evaluate her.

"Do you think so?" he asked. "The robbery occurred some nine years ago. You were very young. How do you know what really happened? How do you know your dear mother didn't—"

"I know. Isn't that enough? For all her faults—and she owned to many—my mother was not a thief. To her dying day, she swore that she had no part in the disappearance of the diamond. She even said she had proof, but . . ." Lynnette's gaze strayed to the copy of *Greystone*

Castle she'd left on the floor of the curricle. When they left Broadworth earlier in the day, she did not think to have time to read while they were out and she was right, but she carried the book with her nonetheless, just to assure its safety.

"Even without proof, I know it is the truth." She lifted her chin and pinned him with a look, telling him what she'd told herself a thousand times on a thousand different nights when the dark closed in and the memory of her mother's final, sad days pricked her like so many knives. "Why would she want the diamond? What would she do with it? The Overtons have never lacked for money."

"Some say the diamond is precisely why you never lacked for money. Wait!" he added quickly when Lynnette's mouth dropped open and she spun in her seat toward him. "I did not say it was true or even that I believed it. But like it or not, it's what the *ton* believes. Or at least some of the *ton*. How can they think anything else when the case the jewel was kept in was found among your mother's things?"

"It was put there, of course. By the thief. To deflect suspicion from himself and onto my mother."

"You're very sure."

"I am." The truth of the matter was as much a part of her being as every breath she took, and Lynnette could no more deny it than she could escape the whiff of scandal that hovered still over the Overton name like a flock of crows around a graveyard. "Someday, I intend to prove her innocence."

Although she might have expected at the worst some word of criticism and at the best a bit of advice from Ravensfield, she did not expect outright laughter. Nor did she expect that when she heard it, her temper would flare as quickly as it did. Or as dangerously.

"You may stop the carriage," she said, her voice icy even though sunshine spilled over the path ahead of them.

"Don't be a ninny!" Ravensfield kept right on going. "I will not stop the carriage. You cannot get out, anyway. Your ankle—"

"As you, yourself, noted this morning, my ankle is much better. And it is none of your concern. Neither is my life. Nor my mother's reputation. Nor where the Overtons get our wherewithal. Stop the carriage. Now! Or I shall leap out while it's still moving."

He looked at her out of the corner of his eye. "You'd do it, too, wouldn't you?" His question was punctuated by laughter and his laughter only made her more angry. And more determined.

When he saw her jaw clench, he pulled the horses to a stop. "Very well. There. You see, I've stopped the carriage. You've proven your point. You've won this battle. No need for you to dive over the side."

Fortunately for Lynnette's resolve, the carriage came to a halt near the ruins of what had once been the gatehouse. There was a tumble of stones on the ground nearly level with the carriage opening. Gingerly, she stood and evaluated her options.

"You're being a gaby and you know it," he told her,

obviously reading her mind as well as the look she gave the mound of rocks.

Lynnette tested her weight against the tumble of rock and finding it stable enough, she stepped out onto the highest of the stones. "I will not listen to you laugh at me, sirrah, not when I am talking about something so important."

"I was not laughing at you." Even without looking at him, she knew he *wasn't* laughing. At least not now. His voice was tight, as if his jaw were clenched and his teeth were gritted. "You can be devilishly annoying."

Lynnette gave his opinion an indignant "harrumph." At the last second, she remembered *Greystone Castle,* and reaching for it, she tucked it under her arm and carefully lowered herself to the ground.

She smoothed the skirt of her gown and clenched her hands against the cover of her book. Her ankle felt fine, just as it had all day, but she limped a bit at any rate, just to pull at the strings of Ravensfield's heart.

She might have known he didn't have any. Or a heart, either, if the way he looked at her with utter disdain meant anything.

Lynnette straightened her shawl and raised her chin.

"And what is it exactly that you intend to do?" The duke's question was as pointed as the look he gave her.

"I don't know." It was true, and just so he knew she wasn't going to let that stop her, she squared her shoulders. "I suppose I will walk back to Broadworth."

He nodded. "Just like you walked *to* Broadworth the night you arrived? May I remind you, Miss Overton, you were not very successful. You would still be lost somewhere in the woods if it wasn't for me."

"If it wasn't for you, I'd be in your curricle right now, riding back to Broadworth in comfort. That is, if you weren't so ill-mannered."

"Ill-mannered?" This time, Ravensfield didn't just chuckle, he threw back his head and laughed, the sound of it echoing against the walls of the ancient abbey and frightening a flock of doves roosting in what was left of the eaves of one of the buildings. It wasn't until they scattered that he bothered to turn his regard to Lynnette again.

"You think me ill-mannered, madam? Then who am I to argue with you?" Ravensfield tipped his tall top hat. "I suppose I have no choice but to prove it."

With that, he snapped the reins and the horses trotted off.

"Ill-mannered and no mistake." Watching him go, Lynnette grumbled the words and when he rounded a bend and was out of sight—and she was therefore out of his sight, too—she plunked down on the nearest stone.

"Annoying, am I?" She tossed the question after the curricle. "Not nearly as annoying as a man who dares to laugh when a woman is speaking of something weighty. Something significant. Something that is more important to her than—"

The sound of a branch snapping nearby caused Lynnette's philippic to end in a breath of surprise. She glanced over her shoulder toward the thicket from which the sound emanated, and seeing nothing there but a curtain of green, a splash of late spring flowers, and shadows that were longer than they had been only a short time before when the rest of her luncheon companions departed, she continued her harangue. This time, it was aimed at herself, and her overactive imagination.

"Quail," she said. "Nothing but quail and certainly not long-dead monks or tortured lost souls or—"

Another sound from that direction and she thought it best to keep quiet.

Just as she thought it best to start moving away from the ruin. Before the shadows were longer and darker than ever.

Her mind made up, she steadied one hand against the nearest stone and pushed herself to her feet. She would be at the front door of Broadworth in no time, she told heself, calling for Mrs. B to see to it that her things were packed and for Garvey to ready the horses. She'd put Ravensfield and his impertinence, his angel's face and his devil's smile and his cold, cold heart behind her once and for all, that's what she'd do.

The very thought fueled her determination and her steps. Before she knew it, she was nearly to the place where the road down which Ravensfield had disappeared in a cloud of dust met the less-used path that led to the ruin.

At the same time Lynnette congratulated herself, she knew it was time to rest. Fifteen feet off the main path was all that remained of an ancient well, its wall waist-high and the stone steady looking.

The ground between herself and the well was dotted with rocks and tumbled-down bricks and she picked her way through them. She was almost to the well when the tall grass to her left ruffled. As if with someone's passing.

Before Lynnette could move another step, a man clothed head to toe in black, his face obscured by a black Barcelona handkerchief, stepped out of the woods and closed in on her.

8

"Annoying' is hardly a strong enough word for it!" His voice unwavering, his back as rigid as his resolve, Ravensfield hurried the horses along, widening the distance between himself and the abbey. Between himself and the annoying, hardheaded, bedeviling Miss Overton.

"All I did was laugh," he told himself, even now defending what was nothing more than a natural reaction to the situation. And an instinctive one at that.

"I laughed because I could not help myself. You'd think the little fool would realize that. She had that steadfast gleam in her eyes. That unwavering note of righteous indignation in her voice. I was quite overcome. The least she could have done is take that into consideration before she got a bee in her bonnet about getting back to the house on her own. Goosecap! And now she wants to—"

He reined in the horses, peering toward the far end of

a broad clearing that on one side ended at the river that flowed across all of the Broadworth property and on the other bordered the dense stand of trees that ringed the abbey ruin.

If his eyes weren't playing tricks on him, there was a carriage stopped in the deep shadows there, tucked between the row of apple trees that was all that was left of the monks' orchard and a line of towering pines.

As if whoever left it there didn't want anyone to see it.

The thought sat uneasy with him. He flicked the reins to get the horses moving again, but he did not let them have their heads. They walked along at a pace far slower than the furious rush of thoughts that sped through Ravensfield's mind.

The carriage was a crane-necked phaeton, a high flyer, and a bang up to the mark one at that. He could tell as much, even from here. It had a fine matched team and equipage the likes of which was seen only at those places that men such as the duke himself frequented. All the right clubs. All the wrong gaming hells. All the good families. All the very, very bad brothels.

If there was someone visiting from town, surely he would have heard. The phaeton was, after all, on his property.

Concealed on his property.

Not far from where he'd last seen Lynnette.

"Annoying Lynnette," he reminded himself. "Hard-headed, bedeviling Lynnette."

He was certain that with every chance he gave her, Miss Overton would continue to prove just how annoying, hardheaded, and bedeviling she could be. He also knew that, annoying or not, there was never any doubt about what he would do. It took some maneuvering in the narrow lane, but Ravensfield was a crack hand and he had the curricle turned around soon enough.

Before another few minutes had passed, he was headed back to the abbey.

There was a line in one of Mrs. Mordefi's books. *The Beast of Carnaby Hall,* Lynnette thought. It spoke of fear. And how it wound its tentacles around the poor, unsuspecting person it attacked. How it eroded confidence. Ate away at intellect. Gnawed at sanity the way a dog picked at a bone.

It seemed, once again, that dear Mrs. Mordefi knew what she was talking about.

As she stared across the glade of knee-high vegetation and stunted trees that were all that separated Lynnette from the man in black, that same fear took hold, immobilizing her. She listened to her blood rush inside her ears. She felt her heart hammer against her ribs. She watched the man close in on her.

And then she remembered another line from the same book.

One that talked about how, often and quite unexpectedly, fear could give a person wings.

The memory was like the sting of an insect, and

just like the sting of an insect, it made Lynnette start. The next second, she whirled around and took off running.

It might have been easier to negotiate the rock-strewn landscape if her skirts were not so long, her copy of *Greystone Castle* was not so heavy, and if she hadn't slipped and twisted her already tender ankle. Pain shot up her leg with every step she took.

She didn't let it stop her. She hobbled around the monk's well and scrambled over what was left of a stone wall. Safely on the other side of it, she turned. The man was busy negotiating his way around the tumble of rocks and debris that ringed the well, and hoping he would not notice, she dropped *Greystone Castle*—and the single sheet of paper hidden inside its cover—between the wall and a wild rosebush. If she could not keep herself from falling into the hands of the man in black, at least she might be able to keep her mother's message safely out of his grasp.

That done, she ducked under the low-hanging branch of a tree and glanced over her shoulder. The man was only steps behind her but that did not keep her from breathing a sigh of relief; he jumped the wall and hurried past the rosebush. He had not seen her hide the book.

"I say! Excuse me, miss!"

He was as polite as if they'd met over tea.

Which did not make Lynnette feel one jot better.

Polite or not polite, he made a grab for her. She dodged out of his reach but she knew she would never be that lucky again. As if to make up for all the times she pretended to hobble when she was actually quite well, her ankle throbbed. Her lungs were starved for breath. If the man in black tried to catch hold of her again, surely she would be trapped.

She was nearly to the lane when he clamped a hand down on her arm. At the same moment, she heard the sounds of hoofbeats. Or perhaps it was simply the frantic pounding of her heart.

The next thing she knew, Ravensfield racketed around a corner, so quickly she could have sworn the carriage tipped. As easily as kiss my hand and as swimmingly as if he'd been born fingering the ribbons, he pulled the horses to a stop and jumped out. Lynnette whirled to point toward the man in black, but he was already gone. The glade was empty except for the sounds of his retreat into the woodland that surrounded them.

Ravensfield rounded the carriage, the fire in his eyes fueling his every footstep. "What are you doing running about? And you look a fright." He shot a look all around and, seeing nothing, turned a glare full on Lynnette. "What the devil is going on?"

"A man." This time, she had no intention of doing it, but as soon as Ravensfield was close enough, Lynnette found herself with her hand on his arm, the better to support herself and take the weight off her reinjured ankle. "He was there." She pointed to the now-empty spot. "He came at me."

Ravensfield slipped an arm around her shoulders.

The better to brace her against him. A muscle jumped at the base of his jaw. His voice was no more than a growl and so grave it shot dread through Lynnette, not for herself but for the man in black if Ravensfield should ever get a hold of him.

"Did he hurt you? Did he harm you?" He turned her just enough to look down into her eyes. "If you're injured—"

"No more injured than I was when I first began." As much as she hated to admit to the weakness, there was only so much she and her ankle could endure. She did a little hop, the better to position herself and keep her weight off her ankle. "If we could just sit for a bit and—"

She might have known he would not wait for her to complete her request. Ravensfield lifted her into his arms and carried her back to the curricle. He settled her gently enough but there was nothing gentle about the expression that settled over his face. Back in London, she had often heard the Duke of Ravensfield's eyes compared to the darkest pit of hell. Like hell, they smoldered with discontent and burned with unspeakable anger.

"If you weren't so obstinate . . ." The duke ground the words from between clenched teeth. "If you weren't so insistent that you could find your way back to Broadworth on your own—"

"If you weren't so rude." She tossed her head, just so he wouldn't forget that for all his harsh words, he was the source of the problem and thus had no choice but to accept full responsibility. "If you had only taken me seriously—"

"Madam, I will take you seriously when pigs fly." Ravensfield jumped into the curricle. He gave the reins a masterful touch and the horses obeyed instantly. They took off at a far more comfortable pace than the one that ushered the duke back to the ruin in a cloud of dust.

All of which made Lynnette wonder if he was not more bluster than he pretended.

She turned to watch his expression. "You took me seriously enough to rush to my aid when you suspected that something was wrong."

"Bah!" They came to the place where the road met the narrow lane that led down to the ruin and he gave the ribbons a tug that quickened the horses' pace.

"You took me seriously enough to believe me when I told you there was a man there at the abbey."

"I saw his carriage."

So much for thinking that he had faith in her.

Lynnette sat back. There was a sharp turn up ahead and, though the carriage was elegant and the ride as smooth as could be expected on country roads, she instinctively grabbed for a handhold.

It was a good thing she did.

No sooner had they negotiated the curve than they heard hoofbeats on the road behind them. Coming fast.

Because of the curve, it was impossible to see who might be behind them, but there was no mistaking the sounds of fine horses running full speed. Ravensfield's brows dropped low over his eyes, his mouth thinned. "Too fast for any normal driver or any normal carriage out for an ordinary run."

Lynnette looked back, too, and listened. Each second, the sounds grew louder. Closer. "You said there was a carriage. Near where I saw the man."

Ravensfield did not bother to answer. He cracked the reins. The horses took off and after that all Lynnette could do was hold on. That, and pray.

The next second, the phaeton rounded the bend and hurtled after them. It was a well-appointed rig driven by a man whose face was obscured by a black Barcelona handkerchief tied just below his nose. There was another man dressed in similar fashion in the carriage with him and it was pulled by a matched team that was every bit as sprightly and as fast as Ravensfield's.

The duke urged his cattle to go faster.

The other carriage closed the gap.

"Have no fear. There is spirit left in this bit of cavalry and no mistake!" He touched the reins to the horses' backs and they picked up speed. "And no one knows Broadworth land better than I do."

There was some comfort in the fact, even if it was difficult to acknowledge with the wind beating Lynnette's cheeks and the air rushing so fast at them that she had to hold her bonnet on her head or risk losing it. The curricle slapped into a furrow in the road and her teeth banged together.

Undaunted, Ravensfield urged the horses on.

He was a skilled driver and he took the next turn smoothly. So did the carriage behind them.

"Hold on!" Ravensfield called, his voice raised so that she could hear him above the sounds of pounding hooves, jangling metal, and the wind that whipped by them.

Lynnette dared a look over her shoulder. The phaeton was closing in, bit by bit, the men inside it whooping and bellowing as if the race were nothing more than a game.

It was that, perhaps, that tipped Ravensfield's mood from simple anger to out-and-out fury. His eyes narrowed, his jaw rigid with the kind of determination Lynnette had seldom seen in any man, he flicked the reins and the horses flew like the wind.

Lynnette remembered this part of the road from earlier in the day when they'd traveled to the abbey. There was a stone bridge up ahead that spanned a river and, just beyond that, the turnoff to the long tree-lined avenue that led to Broadworth Hall. If they could make it that far—

The right wheel of the curricle bumped into a deep track cut into the road and when it bounced out again it hit a rock. The carriage swayed. It shot into the air. It all happened so fast, Lynnette did not have a chance to brace herself. She didn't need to. Ravensfield's hand clamped down on her arm, keeping her in her seat. With his other hand, he expertly plied the ribbons, slowing the horses just enough to regain control.

Unfortunately, the men in the other carriage were

just as skilled. The phaeton avoided the rock completely, swerving onto a grassy embankment, then back onto the road again. The horses took the maneuver in stride. The driver and his passenger whooped louder than ever.

Ravensfield glanced at Lynnette and certain that she was safe he grabbed the reins with both hands, his concentration fully on the road. It took her no more than a moment to see why. There was a hay wagon up ahead, slowly lumbering over the bridge and coming in their direction. The wagon was wide. The bridge, narrow. There was only the most constricted of spaces for them to get through and only if Ravensfield was enough of a dab hand to squeeze the curricle between the wagon and the wall—no more than three feet high—that was all that kept travelers from plummeting into the river below.

Ravensfield gave her another quick look, and Lynnette knew exactly what he wanted. One word from her and he would rein in his team and stop the carriage before they came to the bridge, pursuers be damned.

If he knew her better, he would know he didn't have to ask.

There wasn't a feather's chance in hell of her giving up. Not when they were this close to besting the men who hounded them. Not when all that stood between them and a victory of sorts was the daring to make the impossible move, a low stone wall, and twenty feet of nothingness that ended in a wash of chilly water.

Because she could not get the words out loud enough

to compete with the wind and the sounds of the labored breathing of the horses, she nodded instead. Ravensfield's eyes sparked and he gave her a thin-lipped smile. Right before he guided the horses through the absurdly small space between the wagon and the side of the bridge.

Perhaps their pursuers were less skilled. Or possibly, they simply had more sense.

Lynnette heard the other driver bark out a curse. The phaeton slowed.

Ravensfield didn't. The team still moving at top speed, the curricle still flying over the road, they turned onto the broad avenue that led directly to the front door of the Hall. Only then did the duke let up. He slowed the horses, then stopped them, turning as he did to look back toward the road and growling, "They wouldn't dare follow us onto the very drive of Broadworth."

He was right. The next second, they heard the jangle of equipage. The phaeton raced past and continued down the road.

Lynnette pulled in one deep breath after another, a hand to her bosom, the other automatically checking to see if her bonnet was still atop her head. Amazingly, it was. Ravensfield was not so lucky with his high-crowned beaver. His hat was missing completely, his hair was mussed. A curl of it hung over his brow like an inky question mark.

It gave her fair warning, she supposed, for what she knew was to come.

"Who—" Ravensfield began, but she stopped him, one hand in the air as if to deflect the query.

"What—" He tried again.

Again, she stopped him before the question was fully formed.

"How—"

"I do not have all the answers," she told him. "But I can explain at least some of it, I think."

"Then do it." It was as simple as that. At least to Ravensfield. He waited, his brows knit and his posture as rigid as a soldier's.

"I cannot." Lynnette shrugged and then instantly regretted the gesture. It made her look uncertain, and though she may have been guilty of other things, doubt had never been one of them.

She pulled in a breath to steady herself and started in again. "I cannot. Not until we go back to the abbey."

"Are you completely insane?"

It was not one of the questions she was expecting, which might have explained why Lynnette could not find her tongue to answer. It was just as well. From all indications, the duke was not going to give her a chance to get a word in edgewise.

"May I remind you, madam, that you were just recently at the abbey. And had I not returned there when I did, you might have been hurt. You might have been killed!" He turned to her so quickly, she did not have time to back away. Just as quickly, he had her by the shoulders and he gave her a little shake as if that might stir some reasonable explanation out of her. "If you hadn't been foolish enough to think you could stay there at the abbey all by yourself—"

"You are quite wrong, your grace." The shake knocked Lynnette's bonnet loose and rather than try to right it, she slipped it off her head. She ignored the flare of anger in Ravensfield's eyes. It was not so easy to ignore the feel of his hands where they rested against her shoulders. His touch was hotter than the flame of outrage in his eyes, and like that flame, it burned through every portion of Lynnette. It took more self-control than she knew she had not to melt beneath the heat. Instead, she looked him in the eye.

"As you will remember, I never intended to stay at the abbey. I said I was leaving. Returning to Broadworth."

"Sprouting wings?" With a grunt of disgust, he dropped his hands and backed off. "How in the name of the Good Lord Mike—"

"No need to be profane! You are the one who left me—"

"For no other reason than you wanted to be left. And you are the one who said—"

"For no other reason except that I did not have any choice. May I remind you that I would not have had to say anything at all about finding my own way back to Broadworth if you had not been so rude as to laugh—"

"Not because I was rude! Because you were—"

"Simply stating the facts about my relationship with my dear mother. As I recall, I mentioned that I believed in her innocence. That I was devoted to her memory. Which seems to me more a thing to—"

"It is more a thing to admire, damn it!" Ravensfield's words rang through the twilight air, frightening the horses. He did not even bother to try to settle them but let them dance upon the drive, dispelling their energy.

"If you weren't so damned serious. If you didn't look so damned delicious while you were being so damned serious." As quickly as he'd dropped his hands, he grabbed her again, his fingers pressing into the flesh just below the bouffant sleeves of her gown. "Damn it, Lynnette. I was not laughing at you. And certainly not at your devotion to your mother. I was laughing at the very thought of a woman with so much spirit. I was laughing at myself. At my own foolish—"

"If it is so foolish, your grace, perhaps you'd best keep your hands to yourself."

Her voice was unwavering, her look steady. And something told her Ravensfield had never been so openly challenged. Or so easily taken unawares.

She might have known even that would not be enough to stop him.

"I was right when I said 'annoying.' " His words shivered in the air between them. "You are quite the most irritating, the most exasperating—"

"And you are still holding on to me."

"It's not all I'd like to do! Damn it and damn me, for admitting it." He cupped her chin in his hand and looked so intently into her eyes that she could read the mirror image of her own sudden longing. "Does my impertinence surprise you, Miss Overton?"

"Yes."

"Does it frighten you?"

"No."

He laughed. "It should."

"Do you think so?"

"I think—damn it," he growled. "I'm done thinking." With that, he brought his mouth down on hers.

9

It was not a gentle kiss. Nor was it brief. Ravensfield's lips were firm and insistent, persuading Lynnette ever so skillfully, and not at all subtly, to drop her guard.

It took little urging.

In the first moment of contact, she was too bedazed to do anything more than sit as still as a statue. But after that . . .

After that, Lynnette gave herself over to the mastery of Ravensfield's kiss. When he tunneled his fingers through her hair, she tipped her head back, opening to him so that he could touch his tongue to hers.

The kiss was fire, and as if he'd been burned, the duke ended the contact as abruptly as it began. Without a word, he picked up the reins, flicked them over the horses' backs, and turned the carriage.

They drove back to the abbey nearly as quickly as they left it and before Lynnette had time to consider what had happened, or how she felt about it and what it all meant, they were stopped where a jagged portion of the wall of the church threw a saw-toothed shadow against the ground.

Ravensfield was breathless and Lynnette wondered if it was from the pace of their drive. Or from the kiss. She wished she knew. Then perhaps she would be well on her way to understanding her own reaction. For she was just as breathless.

"Very well. You wanted to return to the abbey, we are back at the abbey." The duke's voice was as devoid of emotion as his expression. He glanced around at the little glade, now empty, before he turned to her. "You owe me an explanation."

"No more than you owe me." Lynnette congratulated herself. Even if her insides were roiling and her blood was so hot she swore she could feel it searing every inch of her, she managed to keep her voice as level as the duke's. "You simply cannot kiss a woman and—"

"Of course I can." The smile he aimed in her direction was half fire, half ice. It did not light his eyes. "Surely you've heard talk of my reputation, Lynnette. You know that I can—and do—kiss any woman I please."

"You're far too bold and no doubt. I suppose you think that any woman who earns your attentions should be grateful."

"Do you think so?" Ravensfield's laughter echoed through the ruin. "I wish you had been with me through my younger years, Miss Overton. There are a dozen women at least who would have benefitted from your wisdom. Grateful? More often, they looked at it the other way around. They thought it only right that I was the one who showed my gratitude. Money. Homes. Gifts. Clothing. If they were nearly as grateful to me as I have always been to them, I would have far more of the blunt still left in my pockets."

"Balderdash!" It wasn't. She had no doubt it was the absolute truth, yet there seemed no other remark fit for the moment. Rather than sit there like a lobcock while she tried to think of one, she decided a change of subject was in order. "We are here because of what we discussed earlier. About my mother. And the proof of her innocence. We had best do what needs to be done before it gets even darker and those ghostly monks of yours start walking about. I will get the book." She slid over in her seat to lower herself to the ground.

"I will get the book." Ravensfield put a hand on her arm. "Better than letting you traipse all over hell's half-acre while you are hobbled like an oldish horse." He leaped out of the carriage and landed lightly on his feet. "Only you must tell me what book. And where I am supposed to look for it."

She pointed toward the shrub now in deep shadow. "There," she said. "Between the wall and the rose. *Greystone Castle.*"

"*Greystone Castle.*" She heard him grumble before he went in search of the book. It wasn't hard to find and he recovered it and brought it back, still mumbling. "Do you never leave this book at home where it belongs?" he asked. He got back into the carriage but he did not give the book to her but, instead, sat with it on his lap. "I hope you are not going to tell me we've come all the way back here because you cannot wait to read what's going to happen to that paperskull Clarice."

"Clarice is not a paperskull, and it's true, I cannot wait to read what's going to happen to her. But that is not why we came after the book. It is also not why those men in black were after us. At least I don't think so. If they are so anxious to find out what happens to Clarice, they can buy a copy of *Greystone Castle* for themselves." She pulled the book out of his hands and flipped it open. The slit inside the cover might have gone unnoticed by anyone who wasn't looking for it. Being careful to make it no bigger and no more obvious, Lynnette slipped her hand inside it and pulled out the single folded sheet of paper written in her mother's hand. She unfolded it and handed it to Ravensfield.

"I cannot say for certain but I am fairly sure that this is what they are after," she said. "It is Madelaine's. Written long before she died."

Ravensfield glanced down at the paper and the series of small drawings on it. His mouth screwed into a disbelieving grimace. "It's gibberish!"

"Is it?" Lynnette retrieved the paper from his hands. She had studied it so many times, she hardly needed to glance at it again. She knew exactly what it contained: drawings of twenty-six small boxes, each with three sides only. Some of the boxes were tipped to the right, some tipped to the left, some were open at the bottom, others at the top. A few had small dots inside them. Others had stars drawn within their boundaries, sometimes one, sometimes two, sometimes more. Still others of the boxes were empty.

She angled the paper so that Ravensfield could see it better in the fading light. "Don't you see? It is a cipher."

"Code?" He sat up and cocked his head but his wonder lasted no longer than the time it took for his skepticism to come rushing back. He waved a dismissive hand over the paper. "You've been reading far too many romantic books and surely your imagination has run away with you. Why would Madelaine—"

"Her diary is written in code."

Lynnette allowed the words to sink in before she continued.

"I should qualify that, I suppose. Not all of her diary. Just portions of it. The portions *after* the disappearance of the Wonderlee Diamond."

A new note of interest brightened Ravensfield's eyes. "Are you saying—"

"I am saying what I said earlier. My mother always maintained her innocence. And I always have and always will believe her. Don't you see? I cannot say for certain but I believe that she knew something about what really happened to the diamond. And whatever information she had, she knew it was important and that there were others who might want to lay their hands on it. Until she was ready to reveal her secret, she knew she had to keep the information safe. That's why she made up this code. See?" She pointed.

"Twenty-six little boxes. Each surely stands for one letter of the alphabet. It may be simple. For instance, this box . . ." She touched a finger to the drawing in the topmost left-hand corner. "It may stand for *A*. This one . . ." She pointed to the next box drawn on the paper. "This one may be *B*, and so on. That would be the simplest way of keeping the code in order, but of course, it could be more complicated than that, written end to beginning, for instance. Or vowels first."

"Do you think so?" He did not look convinced, and as if it would somehow prove the theory, he took the paper out of her hands and looked at it closely. "It is a singular idea, surely. But how do you know—"

"That the diary is written in code? Really! You make me sound as if I have no more wit than a sawney. I've seen the diary, of course. I've read a good portion of it because a good portion of it is *not* written in code. But when I came to the end, I marveled at the little drawings that covered the last pages. Unfortunately, by the time I found the diary, Madelaine was too ill to explain what the cipher meant."

Lynnette looked away, the better to hide the fact that she could not speak of her mother's last, sad days without her eyes filling with tears. She cleared away the sudden knot in her throat with a cough. "She was—"

"Abandoned by most of Society. Though the robbery happened some nine years ago, I remember it well enough. It was the talk of the town." Ravensfield nodded solemnly. "They say there were a few—"

"Who stood by her side. Yes. And those few kind people have made sure that my place in the *ton* has not been sullied by the lies that surrounded my mother. But even those few friends . . ." This time, it was not so easy to control the mixture of anger and heartache that thickened her voice. She might not have found the words at all if Ravensfield had not closed a hand over hers and given it a squeeze.

With a small smile, she thanked him for the show of support. "Even Madelaine's friends could not help her keep her spirit or her mind," Lynnette said. "One year slipped into another and with each passing season she grew more despondent. She lived in almost complete isolation and it was that more than anything that ate away at her. After all, her whole life revolved around the beau monde. She was born to it."

"And she was marvelous at it!" Ravensfield's voice warmed with admiration. "I remember her. As I told you earlier this afternoon. I remember her as the most beautiful of women. The most gracious of hostesses. The most charming of conversationalists. She was a paragon and the whirl of London life revolved around her, like the unlighted planets spin around the sun. Other women dressed the way Madelaine dressed and served what she served at soirees. They danced the way Madelaine danced, laughed the way Madelaine laughed. And the men . . ." He gave her a sidelong look, and seeing that none of this was news to her, he continued. "Well, you know that the men adored her."

"And when all that was taken from her . . ." Lynnette swallowed the sour taste in her mouth. "Some people like nothing better than seeing those who are at the top go tumbling to the bottom. When the rumors started about Madelaine and the Wonderlee Diamond, there were many who were only too anxious to seize the news like a terrier does the neck of its prey. Even though there was never any more proof than that jewel case found in Madelaine's rooms, they didn't let go."

"They were envious and found some perverse pleasure in her disgrace."

"And she knew it. Just as she knew she was innocent. But that didn't change a thing. When the *ton* turned away from her, Madelaine felt alone and heartsick and there was nothing any of us could say or do to console her. Not even me." She coughed away the lump that blocked her breathing, the one that always formed when she thought of how hard she'd tried and how little she'd been able to do to help her mother through those painful times.

"Her health deteriorated along with her mind," she told Ravensfield. "It wasn't until some years after the jewel went missing that I found her diary. And read it." She looked away, mostly because she could not bear to look into the duke's eyes while she thought of the details of her mother's life: the lovers, the trysts, the betrayals.

"But when I came to the end, to the coded portion . . . when I asked what it all meant . . . by then, she was too ill to explain."

Ravensfield's eyes narrowed to slits and he looked at the paper in her hand. "But you have the key!"

"Now I have the key," Lynnette explained. "I found it among Madelaine's papers just recently. After her death. I cannot tell you how happy I was! Finally, I thought, I was close to solving the mystery. But when I went to look for the diary—"

"Let me venture a guess. It was gone."

She nodded. "And it was no accident. I think we both know that. Someone took it."

"And you have no idea who."

"After Madelaine died . . ." Lynnette closed her eyes, thinking about the list she had completed in the last days. "There were people in and out of the house for weeks. Her friends, certainly, those who never lost faith in her. But some of the others of the *ton*, as well. The gossipers and scandalmongers, come to express their sympathy even though they were never there for her when she needed them. I suppose any one of them might have somehow come across the diary and taken it, sensing I suppose that there might be something sensational in it. Something scandalous. Or something damning. That same someone has the diary still and I am certain that he suspects I may have found the key. Only three months ago, I received a letter, offering me money in return for a way to decode the diary."

"You refused." It was not a question; Ravensfield nodded as if he expected nothing less of her. "And then?"

It was easier to tell him the truth than it was to try and find some fabrication to fit the facts.

The prospect was both frightening and freeing. She sighed, releasing some of the tension that had been building ever since she realized someone was interested in the diary. And willing to do anything to take possession of the code.

"There was a burglary," she said. "At Brighton when I was in residence there. Someone waited until I was out, then went through my things. Fortunately, after the letter arrived offering me money in exchange for the code, I thought it wiser to carry the paper with me everywhere. He did not find the code but that did not stop him. When I returned to London . . ." At the thought of the face on the other side of the door that led to her balcony, she shivered. "There was an attempted burglary. Very recently."

His hands clenched into fists. "Were you—"

"I was home. But my doors were locked." She couldn't resist the temptation to add, "Thanks to Mrs. Mordefi."

He eyed her skeptically. "I thought you said—"

"That the woman is a recluse? It is certainly true. But it is also true that her words send shivers up my spine. I am embarrassed to admit . . ." She glanced away. "I was so frightened by what I was reading, I locked my doors."

"Then it seems your Mrs. Mordefi serves some useful purpose after all!" He grinned but the expression lasted only a moment. The next second, he was as sober as a judge. "Tell me what you think. These fellows who are after the code, how did they know you were here?"

Lynnette may have been upset by the appearance of

the man in black. She may have been upended by Ravensfield's kiss. But she was not so upset or upended to forget the story she'd concocted to explain her presence in Berkshire.

"I suppose it would not be so difficult," she said. "Though I left for Bath as quietly as possible, I did not sneak away in the middle of the night. My staff in London, they knew where I was headed, and because I did not want to arouse suspicions or worry anyone, I swore no one there to secrecy. And we did have to stop along the way," she added, reminding Ravensfield of what she'd told him when she first arrived at Broadworth.

"You'll remember that my abigail fell ill. If anyone asked, I am sure the people at the inn where we left her to recuperate might have mentioned which road I had taken when I left and in which direction I was headed."

"Which brings us to another question and though I am reluctant to ask it—"

"You mustn't fear upsetting me." She smoothed a wrinkle from the skirt of her gown, refusing to admit that she did not need his warnings to worry her. Ever since the first burglary attempt, she had been worried enough.

"Then you must ask yourself why these men want the code so badly."

She glanced at him and saw the truth there in his dark eyes. He knew just as surely as she did why they wanted the code and what it all meant. He was simply trying to ascertain if she understood the fundamentals of the problem.

"It is kind of you to be concerned," she said.

"Please!" He cast the very thought away with a shrug of his broad shoulders. "I am simply trying to see if you understand exactly what you've gotten yourself into."

"Gotten into?" She sat up straight. "You make it sound like some pickle that I have brought on myself."

"And I certainly did not intend to. I merely wonder if you know—"

"How very serious it is?" She nodded and wondered if, now that the light was fading fast and the shadows were deeper than ever, he even saw the gesture. "Yes," she said, in the event that he didn't. "The men who are searching for the key must have some reason they desperately want to keep the information in my mother's diary a secret. Madelaine's life was an open book. Except for the affair of the Wonderlee Diamond. It is no stretch of the imagination at all to suppose that they realize what I myself know must be true: the coded entry in the diary reveals the truth of what happened that weekend the diamond disappeared. If I am not mistaken, I believe it also reveals the identity of the true thief. I don't know how Madelaine found out, but I am very sure she did. She had a network of connections and, scandal or no scandal, many people owed her favors. Now, someone will go to any length to keep that information from becoming public knowledge."

"And what does your cousin, the Viscount Somerton,

say to all this? I know him, and I cannot believe he hasn't gone from one end of London to the other, bashing heads and asking questions later." A new thought occurred to him and his eyebrows rose. "I say! You haven't told him, have you? About the diary or the code. About the burglary in Brighton or the attempted burglary at your London home. If you had, he wouldn't have let you out of his sight."

"I haven't told him," she admitted. "I haven't told anyone. I've only told you because you've been so very kind."

"Devil take it, woman! Promise me you will never go crying the news about town. If anyone knew—"

"It would ruin you completely. Yes, I'm sure." Feeling as if a weight had been lifted from her shoulders, she smiled at him through the gathering gloom. "I did not mean to hand over my troubles to you but I do appreciate that you listened. I think what I must do—"

"What *we* must do is make sure this paper never falls into the wrong hands." Carefully, Ravensfield folded the cipher and handed it back to her. "You have my word, Broadworth will be made safer than houses. You need have no fear of further trouble while you are here. There will be a footman stationed on the drive and outside the front door itself. Once that is taken care of, we will begin to make our inquiries."

When she did not immediately respond, he peered at her. "You have made inquiries, have you not? About the diary? About who—"

"I have tried to work through the thing. I've made a

list. Of all the people who may have had a chance to pinch the diary. I've asked, as discreetly as possible, if anyone of my acquaintance may have picked up something—by accident, of course—that did not belong to them." She sighed. "I've gotten nowhere. There's only so much a woman alone can accomplish."

"Do you think so?" Though she saw nothing amusing about the subject or the situation, Ravensfield laughed. "I have seen you in action, Miss Overton. Something tells me you could move mountains if you had a mind to."

"Mountains, perhaps. But a woman asking questions of people she hardly knows about subjects about which she is not supposed to be cognizant . . ."

She didn't need to elaborate. He understood perfectly. Just as she knew he would.

Without another word, he tugged the reins and they headed back to Broadworth.

He had not meant to kiss her.

Ravensfield stalked into his study, swinging the door closed behind him. He dropped into the chair behind his desk, and though he stared at the empty piece of paper that he'd left on the desktop the night before, he hardly saw it. He saw instead those clear gray eyes, steadfast and unshakable. That mane of chestnut hair, as rich and as soft as silk. He felt the thrill that tingled through Lynnette's body when he kissed her, the one that was echoed in his own along with a rush of exhilaration that told him—

"Oh, hell!"

Too edgy to keep still, he got up and paced to the other side of the room. Although he had a costly and quite complete library in a room two floors below, he kept his favorite—and more personal—books here in the private room his staff was not allowed to enter. Now, to give himself something to do that might keep his mind off all that had happened with Lynnette, he ran a finger over the bindings and read each title over to himself. Some of the books were so old, the words were barely legible, the covers cracked. On others, the leather was so mellowed with age that it was as smooth as butter and as soft as—

"Damnation!" Ravensfield grumbled to himself, whirling away from the books. "As soft as the touch of Lynnette's lips against mine."

Disgusted with himself, he paced back the other way. He had not meant to kiss her, he reminded himself. Even though he'd wanted to. Even though he'd been wanting to practically since the moment she landed on the tips of his boots in the middle of a rainstorm.

He thought he knew better than that.

He should have known better than that.

After all, a man of his experience was not easily unhinged. Especially by some sprout of a female, half temptress, half innocent.

Used to working on his books late at night and away from the prying eyes of servants, he kept a sideboard in the study so that he might have the promise of a bit of claret now and again. He went over to it and filled a crystal glass, glancing at the door as he did. It was late, dinner had been served hours ago, and just across the passageway, he had no doubt that Lynnette lay sound asleep.

And here he was, his mind so filled with all the things she'd told him about her mother and the Wonderlee Diamond, he could not get it to settle down so that he might concentrate and get to work on his next book. His body so tight from wanting her, he could barely make himself keep still.

"Damned woman," he grumbled, and he wasn't sure if he was talking about Lynnette or about Madelaine. After all, both Overton women had somehow gotten themselves involved in something they did not know how to get out of.

Just as Ravensfield had.

There might be consolation in claret, but there was none at all in the thought.

He tossed back the liquid, and when it failed to wash away the dry-as-dust taste in his mouth, he filled his cup anew.

Involved was something he didn't have the time for, he reminded himself. *Involved* was something for which he had little patience. *Involved* was the one thing he'd promised himself he'd never be.

And the one place he found himself now, so utterly and completely, so unexpectedly and so amazingly, that he knew there was no way out for him, either.

There was only one thing for him to do.

He had always meant to help Lynnette. From the

moment she told him the story of the cipher and her mother's diary, he had thought there might be something he could do to discover who the man in black was and rid her of him. He had thought of lying in wait for the man himself and of the real satisfaction he'd get from pounding him into the ground. It was, after all, exactly what the blighter deserved for frightening Lynnette.

But he decided a more rational approach might work best. For Lynnette's problem and for his own.

He had friends, after all. Powerful men who might have heard a word or two here and a rumor there. Dishonorable, some of them, which made them all the more likely to have heard some news about an infamous diamond and the even more infamous woman who was said to have purloined it.

Rubbing his hands together with satisfaction, Ravensfield sat in his desk chair and pulled a sheet of paper in front of him, determined to open the lines of communication and help Lynnette solve the mystery. He had to if he ever hoped to put an end to the swirl of mystery and temptation she'd brought to Broadworth with her.

If he ever hoped to expel her from his home.

And his heart.

10

Heat.

It enveloped me. It filled me. It coursed through my body, liquid fire, burning through my mind, annihilating my senses, incinerating all that was left of my will and my reason until I could feel nothing. Not the bed beneath me or the air around me. Not the soft woolen blanket I knew covered me or the pillow where I laid my head. My world shriveled, closed in, and collapsed.

All that was left was the heat.

As I write this, so far removed from that night and all that happened there in my bedchamber at Greystone Castle, I am sorely tempted to understate the incident, to bury the memories that are, after so many years, still so raw and so powerful. Yet I know I cannot. I must dare to confront them. Just as that night, I confronted the very Thing that had, these last weeks, haunted my nights and thrown a shadow across my days.

I will not say that this was heat of the kind that leaps

from a fire, for to do that would be to give the wrong impression, dear reader. This heat was not spawned by something so earthbound as flame. To say so—to try to convince myself that it is true—would be to do an injustice to a sensation that blistered through every inch of me.

This was, rather, the heat of an inferno. The kind of heat that could only be engendered by the deepest conflagration of Hell.

Trembling from the intensity of it, I fought my way out of the arms of sleep and the dream that held me in its thrall. I had been dreaming; I knew that as surely as I knew my own name. Yet I could not say what the dream was about no more than I could say where it ended and where reality began. I only know that when I finally forced my eyes to open, I was breathing as hard as if I had run up the stone stairs that led from our tiny chapel to the bell tower beside it.

I was smothered, spent, and I discarded my blankets and struggled to sit up, looking across the room as I did, sure that the small fire laid earlier in the evening to warm my chamber had somehow leapt from the grate and caught the draperies on the window across the room. But the fire in the hearth had long gone out. The air all around me was inky and cold.

Yet I burned.

Lynnette fanned her face with one hand, trying—just as poor Clarice was doing—to dispel the heat that built within her. In the hours since they left the abbey, a storm had started up. But though rain beat against her window, her room was as comfortable as any she'd ever been in. Still, Mrs. Mordefi's well-chosen words painted pictures of a world that was very real. She knew it was fiction. Yet she swore that like Clarice, she could feel the fire.

All was quiet yet I knew that, in and of itself, did not guarantee that I was safely out of harm's way. It had been quiet all those other nights, as well. All those other nights when I sensed His presence. This time, though, it was more than a sense. It was a certainty, and when I peered across my room and into the shadows and saw a deeper shadow there, I was not surprised. I heard a whisper on the night air, though what words it said, or even what language it spoke, I could not say. I felt a touch, like the brush of candle flame against my skin.

And then He was with me.

A boom of thunder shook the air. Between the startling noise and the fact that the appearance of the mysterious phantom who had been plaguing Clarice for the first two hundred pages of the book took her unawares, Lynnette gasped.

She was still waiting for her heartbeat to settle when she swore she heard a sound out in the passageway, like the sound of someone passing her door.

And just as quickly, she knew that her mind was playing tricks on her.

It was the suspense of the book that caused her to hear noises where there were none. Reminding herself that it was that and nothing more that accounted for her imaginings, she went back to her book.

Oftentimes I had felt His presence. Even more frequently, His face appeared in my dreams. But I had never really seen Him before. I sat like a person transfixed, too frightened to scream, too spellbound to do anything but wait as He slowly approached my bed, his movements so smooth and so silent, it was as if his feet did not touch the floor.

He was tall and broad shouldered. His face was just as I have described it to you before, so handsome I could not help but think that were I at a ball, I would be the envy of all the other women if a man of such looks and such bearing had but glanced my way or asked me to partner him in a dance. His jaw was as firm as if it had been chipped from stone. His lips were full, as a man's often are when he is pleasure-loving. He did not smile but looked at me steadily, his eyes flaring with a twin flame of the fire that burned within me.

Was it merely a physical reaction? I cannot say, dear reader, no more than I can venture to guess if it was some aberration of my brain that made me feel this way, as if our minds were already one. As if the next measure of this fierce symbiosis must be something more tangible. More physical.

He put a hand on my shoulder.

Even through the layer of my nightdress, his skin burned mine, branding me as his. He increased the pressure, bit by bit, and before I could stop it, I felt myself falling. The next thing I knew, I was lying once again with my head on my pillow.

I knew I should scream. In my head and in my heart, I knew that I should struggle with all my might. I cannot explain why I did not. I only knew that I could not. My strength had disappeared and I could do nothing more than watch as He came ever closer.

I could not speak. I could not move.

Not when He put a finger beneath my chin and tipped my head back, the better to look into my eyes.

Not when He moved closer still, so that I could feel the touch of His lips against my cheek.

Not even when He glided his mouth down from there, and nuzzled it against my neck.

The shiver that raced up Lynnette's back and across her shoulders was half terror, half delight. She burrowed further into the blankets, anxious to keep reading.

A task that might have been easier to accomplish if, again, she hadn't heard a noise from out in the passage-way.

"Not the man in black," she assured herself. Though she had known Ravensfield for but a short while, she was sure of one thing: he was a man of his word. He might kiss a woman and then laugh about it—every bit as shameless as his reputation led her to believe—but he was not dishonorable. She was as certain of Ravens-field's promise to keep her safe as she ever had been of anything.

At the same time she told herself that the wisest thing

she could do was keep to her bed, her ankle throbbing afresh and propped on a pile of pillows, she knew it was a losing cause. She had never been strong enough to withstand the pull of a mystery. She slipped out from beneath the covers, wincing just a bit at the pain when she landed on her feet.

Grabbing hold of the walking stick, she put her weight against it and limped to the door.

The passageway was dark but for a flash of lightning that shone from a window far to her right and another light, either candle flame or firelight, that gleamed from the perimeter of the door of the room across the way. It was the room the servants were never allowed to enter. The door was shut but the scrap of light that escaped from around its edges told her that it was not closed completely.

As much as Lynnette knew that whatever was on the other side of the door was none of her business . . .

As much as she knew the walk across the passageway was not good for her ankle . . .

She could not resist.

When another rumble of thunder shook the house, she crept across the passageway.

Whatever the noise that had disturbed her reading, it was gone now; the house was quiet but for the pounding of the rain. Aside from the steady ticking of the tall-case clock at the far end of the passageway, the only other sound she heard was a faint scratching, like pen against paper. Curious to see if she was right she leaned the walking stick against the wall and peered into the slit of an opening between the jamb and the nearly closed door.

From this angle, it was difficult to see much of anything.

Lynnette leaned nearer. She saw a wall of shelves overflowing with books, an overstuffed chair in front of a fireplace, and—

Convinced her eyes were deceiving her, she scrubbed them with her fists, then moved closer to get a better look.

In a flash of lightning, she saw a long mahogany box in one corner of the room. It was studded with brass fittings, wide enough to repose in, long enough to hold a man.

"Coffin?" She whispered the word, then just as quickly told herself she was being a cods-head. Still prickling from the excitement of all the goings-on at Greystone Castle, she was giving the servants' rumors about Ravensfield too much credence. And letting her imagination run away with her.

The sound of the duke's pen on paper kept up, and sure that he had not heard her, she angled herself so that she could see into the room from the other direction.

She caught a glimpse of his dark head bent over the desk as he continued to write. Next to him sat a glass of liquid, the color as deep and as crimson as—

Blood?

A shiver ran through Lynnette. A warning sounded in her brain. But like a spectator at the scene of some particularly gruesome accident, she could not look away. It was foolish. It was madness. But she had to know more.

In a quest to do just that, she slid to her right. From there, she spotted even more of the room's curious furnishings: an ancient, moldering book opened to a page adorned with a gilded star, an unsheathed, wicked-looking knife, its razor-sharp blade edged with red by the firelight. And Ravensfield.

Some time while she was busy trying to see what she could see, he had finished what he was writing. He stood and, even as she watched, rounded the desk and walked toward the door.

Fear streaked through Lynnette along with a healthy dose of embarrassment. She made a grab for the walking stick, missed the ivory head and slapped the shaft. The walking stick clattered to the floor, the sound as loud as musketshot. She scrambled to turn and lost her footing. Her reaction was instinctive, she put a hand out to brace herself.

Unfortunately, what she chose to brace herself against was the door. It flew open and Lynnette flew into the room with it. She tried to right herself but the movement only caused her to spin. In a flash of lightning and a boom of thunder, she landed—hard—on her backside.

The Duke of Ravensfield was standing directly over her.

"Do let me guess." He let go an exasperated sigh at the same time he caught hold of both her arms and lifted her to her feet. "You heard a mysterious bump in the night."

"Something like that." Lynnette's hair was in her eyes and she pushed it back with one hand. Ravensfield did not look as angry as she expected him to look. He looked angrier. She swallowed down whatever excuse she might have given him, and while she tried to think of some explanation that might account for her presence, she glanced around the room.

There *was* a coffin in one corner of the room. There *was* a glass of liquid that sparkled, bloodred, in the flash of the next lightning bolt. Upon the desk was a bone of some sort used as a paperweight and, next to it, the knife that she'd seen gleaming even from the door.

"It's no wonder you don't want the servants coming in here." It was a bird-witted statement to say the least yet Lynnette could not help herself. As overawed as she was suddenly terrified, she gulped in a breath for courage.

It didn't help.

Yet somehow, she found the strength to look into Ravensfield's eyes. Earlier in the day, she'd seen a reflection there of her own longing. Now, she saw another emotion, one she could not read. He was angry, surely, but he was wary, as well.

She wondered why.

"Done looking?" He was standing close, holding her still, and the question ruffled a single strand of hair that lay across her cheek. It was a strangely pleasurable sensation, and rather than be distracted by it, Lynnette brushed the curl away.

"I wasn't looking at all. I was—"

"Looking."

"I heard a noise."

"You violated the one rule we have here at Broadworth. This room is off limits to all but myself and Worthy."

"I did not mean to—"

Still holding on to her, he backstepped her over to the chair in front of the fire. It took little more than a nudge from him to make her sit. "Of course you did! You thought you could spy on me."

"I didn't think it. I did it." Lynnette grimaced at the honesty of her own statement. "I mean, I did not mean to spy, only to see what might be causing the noise that disturbed my reading."

He glanced over his shoulder toward the window. "The storm?"

"Not that, surely. Something else. Something inside the house."

"The perfect excuse to nose about. So . . ." His arms out at his sides, Ravensfield turned all around, as if proudly displaying the room and its contents. He was still dressed in the clothes he'd worn at dinner—black trousers and tailcoat, a waistcoat of the same color, and a shirt, collar, and cravat that were luminous in the next flash of lightning.

"Now you know! You've breached the doorway. You've crossed the threshold. You've seen the sanctum sanctorum. Now you will tell the world my secrets."

"No!" She dismissed the very notion with a shake of her head. "I do not know your secrets, and even if I did, I would never reveal them. Not to anyone. Not after you've been so kind and—"

"Spare me, Miss Overton!" Ravensfield whirled around and walked away. When he got to the other side of the room, he turned to her again, and leaned back against the desk, his head cocked to one side. "What will you tell them?" he asked.

"Tell?" She ran her tongue over her lips. "I would never—" But she realized she would. At least that was her intention before she arrived in Berkshire. She remembered the Dashers and the Blades and how they'd wanted nothing more than to know what kept the duke so occupied here in the country. She remembered that at the time, and in an attempt to make the duke's acquaintance and spark his interest in her, she'd been more than willing to go along with the lark, more than willing to spy on Ravensfield and reveal his secrets.

Just as he accused her of doing now.

The very thought caused mortification to streak through her. She looked away and, too late, realized that the gesture exclaimed her guilt.

"Was this part of your plan? Damn me for an idiot but I thought you different than that. Better."

She did not know what he was talking about until she looked his way. He was studying her closely, his gaze gliding from the hair that hung around her shoulders and down farther still. For the first time, she realized that having thought no one would see her, she'd come out of her room wearing nothing but her nightdress.

Instinctively, her hand went to the high collar of the gown. As if that might make the slightest bit of difference.

It didn't. Even through the fabric, she could feel the heat of Ravensfield's gaze every place it touched.

Her neck burned, and then her cheeks. His gaze slipped and though she was tempted to cross her arms over her chest to keep the look from touching her breasts, she knew it was no use. Like flame, the sensation cascaded over her body, enveloping her. Filling her with liquid fire.

"I did not plan to intrude upon your privacy in the manner that I did," she said, her voice skipping over the words. "If you think I often drop in on men wearing nothing more than my—"

"The thought had occurred to me. But then, you must forgive me, I'm afraid I am rather suspicious by nature. At least suspicious of women who visit in the night in little more than the skin God gave them."

Appalled at the very thought that she would try blatantly to trap him, she sat up straight and realized, too late, that when she did, her breasts were outlined more clearly than ever by the firelight against the fabric of her gown. "Seduction? I would never—"

"Never?" He closed in on her, step by careful step. "You would never lie? You would never use your womanly charms to get your way?"

It was, after all, exactly what she'd been trying to do

since first she came to Broadworth. It was not a pretty thought and, ashamed, she let whatever protest she might have made die on her lips.

Another bolt of lightning ripped the night sky and the searing light outlined Ravensfield with fire. She had studied him enough in these last days to know him well, but she never realized how very tall he was or how broad his shoulders were. At the same time she was fascinated, she was frightened, as well. By the anger that simmered in him. By the strange furnishings of the room. By the coffin and the blood and the storm that increased in fury with every passing second so that this one quiet place was her only refuge. And here, there was more danger than even out in the storm.

She was too spellbound to do anything but wait and watch as Ravensfield slowly approached, his movements so smooth, it looked as if his feet did not touch the floor.

"You cannot think me so crafty." Lynnette scrambled to redeem her reputation lest he think less of her. "You cannot think I would try to deceive you so completely as to—"

"Would it deceive me, do you think?" He was nearly to the chair now, and at this close range, the question washed over her like a wave and left her breathless. "Would it surprise me, do you think, if a woman used her feminine wiles to get what she wanted from me?"

"Perhaps not. Not some other woman. Some other women, perhaps I should say. But I would never do so. I hoped that you thought more of me than that."

"Did you?" He chuckled. In any other situation with

any other man, it would have been enough to dispel the energy that built in the air between them. Now, it simply added to the heat.

When Ravensfield put a hand on her shoulder, a frisson coursed through her and the heat of his skin branded her. He knelt beside her chair and looked into her eyes. "What do you think of me now? Now that you've seen this room and everything in it?"

"I think . . ." It was hard to think anything. Especially when her head was whirling and her breaths were coming so fast it felt as if she'd run from the front door to the attic of her London home and back again. Captivated by the reflection of the firelight, she stared into Ravensfield's eyes. Her words sounded disembodied, even to her own ears. "I think, your grace, that there is a very good chance that you have been lying to me."

"That I am a vampire?" He leaned in close and his deep, soft laugh whispered against her skin. "I thought that I had proved to you that I am not."

"But the coffin . . ." Though it was nearly impossible, she managed to pull her gaze away from his. She slid it to the mahogany casket along the far wall then back the other way toward the crystal goblet that sat upon his desk. "The blood . . ."

"Blood? Is that what you think?" He chuckled again, louder this time. Longer. His gaze flickered from her eyes and down to her mouth. It stayed there but a brief moment before it slid to her breasts. He reached for her and cupped one breast in his hand, his thumb and forefinger kneading her nipple until he elicited a moan from her.

Lynnette knew she should offer a protest. But she could not speak or even move.

Not when he put a finger beneath her chin and tipped her head back, the better to look into her eyes.

She pulled in a breath, as afraid of what might happen next as she was eager for it, and when he loosened the bow that was tied at the neckline of her nightdress and inched the fabric open, she could do nothing at all except wait.

Thunder rolled through the night air. Lightning flashed. Its fiery light glinted against the coffin and the blood and Lynnette's mind spun out of control along with the passion that swelled inside her.

She thought of Clarice and the phantom.

She thought of the mysterious book open upon Ravensfield's desk and the heat of his mouth where it pressed a kiss against her cheek.

She thought of the blood when he glided his mouth down and nuzzled it against her neck.

It was the last thing she remembered before everything went black.

11

"I had the most remarkable dream last night."

Lynnette set her fork next to her plate and looked across the table at the Duke of Ravensfield, wondering what his reaction to her comment might be.

His reaction was no reaction at all. Just as it had been through all of dinner. He was glowering and morose, quiet and preoccupied, and while she thought of what she might do to bring him out of this fit of the blue devils and herself out of the confusion of memory and sensation that had assailed her all through the day, she took another bite of Cook's excellent turbot and chewed thoughtfully. She made sure to swallow before she continued.

"My dream was . . ." She chose her word carefully. "Turbulent. Perhaps it was caused by the storm."

"Storms frighten people with malleable minds."

"Indeed." Grateful for at least this much of a response, she leaned forward. "Yet I have heard tell that storms can also awaken a sort of primitive energy within those who are sensitive."

He quirked an eyebrow but did not comment.

She cleared her throat.

"I dreamed of a secret room here within the walls of Broadworth. And of the mysterious things in it."

"Really?" Ravensfield finished his dinner and pushed the plate away. "What sort of things?"

She had hoped the mention of all the things she'd seen—or thought she'd seen—the night before would draw the truth from him. Was it a dream? It seemed very real at the time. But when she woke . . .

She shook her head, hoping to order the thoughts that had, throughout the day, been bounding through it with all the unrestrained energy of a terrier pup.

When she woke that morning, she was safely in her own bed, tucked under the blankets as neatly as if she'd never left. Yet she swore she could recount every detail of Ravensfield's study. Just as she swore she could still feel the touch of his hand every place he caressed her. And the heat of his mouth against her throat.

"You for one thing," she said. "You are one of the things I remember. You were in the room. And if I'm not very much mistaken, it was the room across from the one in which I'm staying."

"Then it must have been a dream. I haven't used that room in years."

"Broadworth is newly built. It hasn't been here for years."

His forehead creased and his brows knotted. "I don't use the room," he said.

"Then the coffin? The blood?" She congratulated herself. She was brave enough to confront him with the facts. Even if she was not bold enough to mention them all. It was one thing to discuss the fantastical with her host. It was another altogether to look him in the eye and mention the fire that erupted inside her when he untied the ribbon on her nightdress and—

"I stand by my original theory."

The sound of Ravensfield's voice interrupted the tumble of memories and Lynnette jumped. He had the good grace to ignore the reaction and continued on as if nothing had happened.

"People with malleable minds are often frightened by storms."

"Yet mine is a mind that has never been malleable."

He scraped his chair back from the table, signaling that dinner was over.

Lynnette was not about to let the matter pass so easily or so quickly. If all she remembered was nothing more than a dream, she needed to know. So that she might stop deceiving herself.

And if it wasn't?

She sucked in a sharp breath, overwhelmed by the thought and the possibility of all it meant.

If everything she remembered actually happened, then there were depths to Ravensfield that she had never imagined. And new and exciting sensations she wanted to explore. With him.

She rose from her chair. "I have been fancying a walk on the veranda."

He looked surprised but he surrendered to her whim with as much good grace as she suspected he ever surrendered to anything. He held out his arm to her. "Not afraid of those mysterious men in black, eh? Why am I not surprised that it would take more than that to frighten you?"

She laughed in spite of herself. "You give me more credit than is my due," she said, winding her arm through his and walking slowly at his side. "I was frightened enough at the abbey when that fellow came at me."

"And still able to remain enough in control to have the good sense to hide that book of yours and the paper inside." He glanced at her out of the corner of his eye. "Are you never terrified?"

"Frequently, your grace." When they came to the library and he opened the French doors that led to the veranda, she smiled and led the way outside, her steps surer now that she'd had an entire day of inactivity in which to rest her leg. Putting her weight on the stick he had given her, she carefully made her way to the balustrade. She turned to face him, leaning back, the better to give her ankle a rest. "I am always terrified when I read Mrs. Mordefi's books."

Was it her imagination, or did the mere mention of the woman make Ravensfield start?

Lynnette watched him carefully. "You think little of such nonsense."

"I think it . . ." He paused, searching for the right word. "I think many people find it entertaining," he said finally, adding a curt nod to the word as if to emphasize its rightness. "And I know it is lucrative," he said, and added quickly, "at least I imagine so. You claim you are but one of many who purchase and read the books."

"Indeed!" Lynnette grinned and wondered if he could see her expression through the darkness. Just as she wondered if he realized he had given her the perfect opening to begin her inquiry again. "Do you suppose my reading preferences account for why I dreamed of coffins and blood last night?"

He hesitated. As if weighing the wisdom of answering. "Do you suppose it was a dream, then?"

"Do you?"

He laughed and it must have been a trick of the darkness. He did not sound at all like the rake whose reputation was so scorching, it was the talk of the *ton*. He sounded unsure of himself. As unsure as Lynnette felt.

His voice dipped and he took a step forward. "Do you wish to believe it was nothing more than a dream?" he asked.

"I wish . . ." It was Lynnette's turn to hesitate. She weighed the benefits of the truth against the propriety of the situation. As always, the truth won. "I wish I knew if it was a dream, because if it was, I would gladly excuse myself and go up to bed so that I might dream again."

He pulled in a sharp breath, but whether he was intrigued by her admission or simply scandalized by it, she never had a chance to find out.

Behind her, Lynnette heard a sound, like the snapping of a twig. She spun around and saw a slither of dark shadow just beyond the veranda.

"Damnation!" Ravensfield saw it, too, and the oath rumbled through him like cannonshot. "I'll not tolerate this one more minute," he grumbled, and before she could say a word or make a move to stop him, he leapt onto the balustrade. In another second, he was over the side. He was not a small man and though she suspected he was as graceful as a man was meant to be if he was dancing or on a horse, he landed in the garden with little fanfare and less decorum. She heard a bush of some sort crush under his weight. Ravensfield grumbled a curse.

The sky was overcast and there was not even a spot of moonlight to assist her; still, Lynnette leaned over the balustrade and peered into the shadows. She was just in time to see Ravensfield haul himself to his feet. The next moment, he caught sight of a deeper shadow in the darkness. A man dressed all in black. Ravensfield was after him in an instant.

She heard a thump and a mumbled word she had never before heard used in mixed company. She saw the garden vegetation shudder. Someone threw a punch and it must certainly have connected. She heard the slap of flesh against flesh and a muffled groan.

Her only thought was for Ravensfield's safety.

Lynnette spun toward the broad, shallow steps that led into the garden, not sure what she could do to help but sure that she must try. She grabbed the walking stick and took it along with her. When she was done using it as a brace, she might yet use it as a cudgel.

She hurried as much as she was able across the veranda, all the while listening to the sounds of the fight in the garden below and imagining the worst. It was dark, and she was all the way to the steps before she realized there was another figure there, blocking her path.

The second man in black.

Lynnette sucked in a breath of surprise and clutched the walking stick tighter. When the man made a move in her direction, she was ready for him. She clutched the stick in both hands and raised it. Her aim was steady, her eye was clear. She thumped him on the head.

"Ow! Miss Lynnette!" The man's voice was muted behind the Barcelona handkerchief he had tied over his nose and mouth. "That is a dashed beastly thing to do to an old chum!"

"Chum?" Ready to strike again, Lynnette stopped, her hand—and her stick—in the air. She was just in time to see Ravensfield come out of the garden with the other man in black caught by the scruff of the neck.

"If I am not very much mistaken, I think we have solved your mystery, Miss Overton." Ravensfield did not pause. His shoulders firm and his jaw set, he marched to the French doors, and when he got there, he dropped the mysterious intruder unceremoniously on the library carpet. The second man followed though he gave the duke wide berth and stayed close to the open windows. Just in case he needed to make a quick exit.

Ravensfield was none the worse for wear after the rough-and-tumble. His neckcloth was askew and he smoothed it down with one hand. His hair was mussed but he did not bother to run a hand through it. He propped his fists on his hips and looked from one intruder to another.

Lynnette looked, too. She was just in time to see the man whom she'd walloped pull the handkerchief away from his face.

"Mr. Hexam!" Lynnette's voice came out an octave too high. It lost none of its amazement when the man closest to Ravensfield removed his face-covering, as well. "And Mr. Palliston!"

His jaw as steady as if it had been carved from granite, the duke strolled closer to Roger Palliston. Palliston was a tall thin man with a fair complexion that was his bane. It betrayed his emotions too easily. He flushed from chin to forehead. His pale eyes were wide and when Ravensfield stopped but an arm's length from him he gulped.

"I say! Good evening, your grace." Palliston smiled, though how he managed when his knees were shaking and his voice was breathy, Lynnette was not sure. "And Miss Overton." He bowed in her direction. "As always, it is a pleasure to see you, ma'am. You light the night."

"Like the fair moon itself," Arthur Hexam added. He was the heavier of the two men and his pudgy face split with a wide grin. "It looks as if we've been found out."

"Indeed." Ravensfield's voice was ice. His look was fire. When he turned it on Hexam, his smile melted and Arthur took a step back, away from the duke and closer to the door. "It was you in the phaeton."

Neither Hexam nor Palliston denied the assertion.

"It was you who frightened Miss Overton there at the abbey and again the night she thought she saw someone out in the garden."

"Oh, no!" Palliston held both his hands in the air, distancing himself from the accusation. "I swear, sir, this is the first time we have ventured as close as your garden. That was not us at all. As a matter of fact, I have it on good authority that it was none other than your own good friend James Varclay along with some others of the Blades."

The news hit Ravensfield like a stone and he pulled himself up to his full height and looked down his nose at Palliston. It was all poor Roger needed to complete his total intimidation. It was a good thing there was a chair nearby for his knees gave way and he dropped into it.

The truth of the matter dawned on Lynnette and she understood all. She let go a breath of relief. "Good heavens! I've been so worried. And all this time, it had to do with the—"

"Yes, of course." Glad to be exonerated, Hexam cast

a longing look at the sideboard and the bottle of claret on it. When his obvious thirst was ignored by his host, he got back to the matter at hand. "You see, your grace, though the Viscount Somerton strongly recommended against it, you know yourself that there is little that can dissuade the Blades and the Dashers from engaging in devilment. We are embroiled in another wager."

"Are you? Are you, indeed?" Ravensfield rolled back on his heels. It was a deceptively casual posture, but unlike Hexam and Palliston who took it at its hale-and-hearty face value, Lynnette knew better than to be fooled.

Insensible to the danger, Hexam started in on the telling of the story. "You see, there has been speculation, about what keeps you here in the country."

"So the Blades challenged the Dashers . . ." Palliston chuckled. After all, he thought it all in good fun. "To try and find out what it is you're up to. And the winners will receive one thousand pounds. Alas, it doesn't look to be us. All we've seen is the picnic at the abbey."

"And tonight's dinner," Hexam added. "It isn't nearly enough to satisfy the Blades. We were, however, surprised to see you here, Lynnette." He turned her way. "Last we heard, you'd given up on your plan to spy on the duke."

Embarrassment streaked through Lynnette. But before she could offer an excuse, Ravensfield spoke in her defense. "Miss Overton is my guest and thus is under my protection. And you . . . You, sirs, are leaving."

"Well . . ." Palliston stood and tugged his coat into place. He had a streak of dirt smeared across one cheek and it looked as if by morning the skin around his left eye would be the color of August plums. He sniffed. "Yes," he said. "I suppose we should be going." He glanced toward the sideboard. "I don't suppose that just for old time's sake—"

"No." Ravensfield stepped toward the door, the better to let the men know that the interview was over. "Wherever you're staying, you'd best return there. And if you're wise, you'll be gone from Berkshire in the morning."

Perhaps it was the memory of the duke's healthy right upper cut that helped Palliston make up his mind. Before another moment passed, he was out the door. Mr. Hexam followed behind.

Ravensfield closed it behind them. He stood for a moment, his hand on the knob, his back to Lynnette, who scrambled for some way to explain her part in the bumble broth. Before she could, Ravensfield's voice cut the silence. It was calm, too calm, and nearly as chilling as the pall that assailed her when she thought the men in the garden were there to harm her.

"A thousand pounds is the sort of wager a man makes on a horse. Or a boxing match." Ravensfield turned to face her. "It is hardly a worthy price on the head of a duke. Do you think it worth the trip all the way here to Berkshire?"

For the space of a dozen heartbeats, Lynnette could

not fathom what he meant. The truth dawned and her mouth dropped open. "You cannot think that I—"

"Which of the Blades sent you?" he asked. "Or was it your own cousin who had you playing the spy?"

"No one sent me. You have it all wrong. I—" She forced herself to return his gaze. For all his faults—and to hear the gossip of the *ton,* they were many—Ravensfield had been good to her. The least she owed him was the truth.

She signaled her surrender with a sigh. "Your friends were quite worried about you."

"Friends?" He grumbled below his breath. "Do you suppose a bounder such as I has any?"

"You know you do. There are those fellows who call themselves the Blades, and—"

"And those fellows who call themselves the Blades visited those fellows who call themselves the Dashers and—" He harrumphed his opinion of the whole thing. "They sent you to find out what goes on here at Broadworth."

Was it Lynnette's imagination, or did he tense, waiting for her answer?

She could not bear to keep him in suspense for long. "I offered," she admitted. "I told the Dashers I would come, and that while I was here, I would somehow find out what you were about. But Nick, he said—"

"Your cousin is a wise man." Ravensfield stalked to the far side of the room. His shoulders were rock steady. His jaw was tight. A muscle bulged at the base of it, revealing a fury he was barely able to keep in check.

As if to prove the point, he turned and came toward her just as quickly, his movements as efficient and as deadly as a panther's. "If your cousin convinced you otherwise, then why are you here?"

Lynnette panicked. She might be bold enough to admit to the wager and how she had tried to have some part in it. But she was not so gooselike as to tell him the real reason for her visit to Broadworth. She could not tell him that she had had her heart set upon him for what seemed like forever. No more than she could explain to herself how and when a girl's foolish fancies had turned into a woman's aching need.

"I wanted to help Nick and his friends win the wager. But they would hear nothing of it. So I planned a visit to Bath. So that I might leave London and keep my mother's message safe. I told you."

"I would not have taken you for a liar." Ravensfield's voice was low, a growl that crawled along her skin. "Nor would I have supposed that you could be so deceitful."

"I didn't mean—" She gulped down the rest of her protest. Her reasons did not matter. Making her way to Broadworth was what she'd intended all along, just as he supposed, and now that Ravensfield had discovered at least part of the truth, she felt nothing if not a traitor.

Lynnette pulled in a breath for strength. There was really only one thing she could do, one way she could save what was left of her pride and, hopefully, redeem what she could of their friendship.

"Garvey tells me one of the wheels on my carriage is being repaired," she told him. "Some minor mishap when he took the horses for their exercise this morning. I cannot leave here tomorrow. But the next day . . ."

He did not try to dissuade her.

She did not expect him to.

It was that more than anything that left her feeling cold and empty. Cold and empty, Lynnette returned to her chamber to prepare for her departure from Broadworth and from the Duke of Ravensfield.

"Damned woman." Even after Lynnette was long gone, Ravensfield continued to watch the door, half hoping that she'd return, half afraid she would come back. "I might have known there was more to her than the chirpy spirits and the lighthearted laugh. Damn!" He pounded his fist against a nearby table and the bric-a-brac on it shivered.

So she would have gladly spied on him. And had she learned that he and Mrs. Mordefi were one and the same?

He pictured his reputation and his fortune going up in flames. It was nearly as painful as the disappointment that filled him head to toe.

It was hell realizing Lynnette was just like other women.

A sour taste filled his throat and he drowned it with a

glass of claret, the better to wash away the truth of all she'd told him.

"Wagers and lies. Deception." He hurled his glass against the far wall where it shattered and what was left of the wine in it splattered like blood.

It was his own fault, he supposed, and he should be as angry with himself as much as he was with her. He had learned long ago that there was nothing to be gained from tender feelings for any woman. And somehow while he wasn't paying attention, and though he certainly wasn't trying, tender feelings toward Lynnette were exactly what he'd developed.

He shook his head, as amazed as he was disgusted. "Did you not listen to yourself all those years ago?" he asked himself. "Did you learn nothing from the fiasco with Lady Christina? Isn't it why you've always kept yourself apart and made sure that the ladies you bedded were of the sort who could not lay claim upon your heart?"

He had no answers and it was that more than anything else that annoyed him. All this time, he had kept his distance from Lynnette, thinking her respectable and fighting his passions because of it. He imagined that she was different from other women. Better.

All this time, he'd been wrong.

Another thought struck, and though his initial reaction was to beat it back as both wicked and insane, it would not be so easily set aside.

Lynnette was just like every other woman he'd ever met?

Then there was no reason for him to handle her as if she were porcelain.

And that meant . . .

A slow smile lifted Ravensfield's mouth.

It meant that there was no reason he couldn't seduce her.

12

The summons came at nearly midnight. Odd, indeed, yet since Lynnette was awake and finishing the last of her packing, she thought little of it. Ever since the night before when Mr. Hexam and Mr. Palliston had arrived and her own small part in their scheme discovered, she had seen little of Ravensfield. She did not try to impose herself on him. She'd already acted enough of a fool imagining that he might have feelings for her. She did not need to take the chance of it happening again. Dreaming about the man was one thing. Expecting the waking world to match those dreams was another.

She spent the day making preparations for her departure the next morning, doing her best not to think how much it would please the duke to see the last of her. She was not ready to grapple with that reality.

She was already in her nightclothes when Mrs. B appeared at her door and told her that Ravensfield requested her company, and at the very thought, Lynnette's spirits soared. Perhaps he would yet forgive her for her lies.

She dressed in a hurry and now she wondered if the carmine muslin she'd chosen on a whim was appropriate for evening wear. She dismissed her misgivings with a toss of her head. The bright red of the fabric brought out the mahogany highlights in her hair and, if the light was just so, reflected a certain fetching blush onto her cheeks.

She might yet make one last impression and give Ravensfield something to remember after she was gone.

Satisfied that she was as ready as she would ever be, Lynnette made her way downstairs, pleased to be able to walk without the aid of Ravensfield's stick. The house was quiet, there was no sign of servants or of the duke himself. She peeked into the dining room but it was dark. She looked into the morning room but that room too was empty. Finally, she saw the flicker of a candle from the direction of the library and she followed its shimmery light, convinced that this was where the duke wanted to see her and, as Mrs. B put it at the behest of her master, "have a bit of a talk."

Instead of Ravensfield, all she found in the library was a single candle lit upon the desk. Next to it was a note written in Ravensfield's broad, distinctive hand.

It is a beautiful evening, and if I am not mistaken, you do like a turn about the veranda.

She did, indeed.

Smiling at the opportunity to make amends with her host, she opened the French doors and went outside.

But he wasn't there, either.

Lynnette paused, letting her eyes adjust to the night and the faint glow of silver light that came from a thin slice of moon. She searched the darkness for any sign of the duke and instead saw another candle and another note, these left upon the shallow steps where only the night before, she had—quite literally—bumped into Mr. Hexam.

You have said that you fancied a look at the garden. It's the perfect night for a stroll.

She would not have guessed that Ravensfield could be playful.

Smiling, Lynnette tapped the note against her chin, quite taken by the little game. At the same time she wondered what the duke was up to and what he might have planned, she stepped into the garden.

There was a stone path at her feet and she followed it, sure that she would see another candle soon. She was not disappointed. There was a fountain not far away; in the stillness she heard the pleasant cascade of water. On the low wall that surrounded it, another candle flickered.

She unfolded the single sheet of paper left next to it, realizing as she did that her hands were trembling.

You've gotten this far. I knew you would. You are as good at following clues as those heroines you so admire.

Just like those heroines she so admired, Lynnette's heart beat a rapid pace. Though she suspected Ravensfield had a tender side, he hid it well. She was surprised at the merry treasure hunt as well as at his ingenuity. She was grateful that all was forgiven and that she might yet have a chance to explain.

She followed the little trail of candles past a folly covered with rambling roses and through a knot of herbs that smelled heavenly on the night air. The trail ended at what looked like a wall.

When she saw the next candle, far to her right, she realized that the wall was actually a living thing.

"The hedge maze," she told herself, and went to retrieve the next message.

You are as bright as Clarice and the rest of them, but are you as brave? I will warn you, I designed this maze myself and it is byzantine and (if I do say so myself) quite clever. Can you find your way to the center?

"Of course I can!" She glided her hands along the hedge. It was thick and tall and since Broadworth had been built only the year before, she imagined the shrubbery must have been transplanted from some older place. When she found an opening big enough for only one person to enter, she stepped inside. Almost immediately, she was confronted by another wall of vegetation. She turned to her right but there was no passage there. To her left . . .

Lynnette moved that way, carefully feeling along the hedge for any sign of an opening. She found one, and caught up in the excitement of the hunt and the challenge the duke had laid before her, she continued on, searching for the center of the maze and for Ravensfield himself.

Ravensfield was as nervous as a bridegroom. And he didn't like the feeling. He didn't like it at all.

Though it was a fair night and there was hardly a chill in the air, he rubbed his hands together. He paced as far as the mahogany table he'd had brought out from the house and set in the center of the hedge maze, wondering how long it would take for Lynnette to arrive.

He quashed his misgivings with a sip of claret but the liquor did little to relieve the dryness in his mouth and he set it aside with a grumbled curse.

"Ridiculous to be nervous," he told himself. "She is a woman like any other woman, remember. Like every other woman."

The memory renewed his anger and his anger renewed his determination.

Now if only he could get his beastly conscience to be quiet!

He grumbled another curse. Precisely why he needed

to get this over and done, he told himself. Precisely why he needed to have his fill of her, then put her out of his life.

"Lynnette?"

The sound of a footfall somewhere nearby brought Ravensfield spinning around. But though he could have sworn he heard something, there was no sign of his guest. "Lynnette?"

"You are cheating, surely, your grace." The voice was disembodied, coming from somewhere on the other side of the hedge that surrounded the central portion of the maze on all sides. "If you keep talking, it will be too easy for me to find you."

"Too easy? Do you think so? I have never had anyone tell me yet that this maze was too easy. Are you close by, do you think?"

"Close enough." The voice came nearly from beside him and he spun in that direction, convinced that she had somehow sneaked up on him unawares.

"Where?" he asked. "I do not see you."

"But I see you." The voice moved away and he pictured her winding through the maze, coming sometimes closer and sometimes moving farther away. "You have candles lit," she said, her voice a will-o'-the-wisp in the night. "I can see them."

"But seeing and finding are two different things. And who knows what you might find if you should find your way all the way here."

"A place to sit and rest I sincerely hope."

She was at the far end of the maze now. He could tell

because her voice was soft. Still, when she laughed, the sound stirred the air like the whisper of angel wings.

He hardened his heart to it. She had no angel's spirit inside.

"I have heard that you are much healed," he said, just so she wouldn't think him so inconsiderate as to make her travel so far with an injured ankle. "Mrs. B tells me you walked as far as the stables this afternoon."

"And rode your blue roan mare while I was there. Mrs. B didn't mention that, I will wager, because she made me promise not to even think about riding. And I, of course, swore I would not."

"Of course." As soon as Ravensfield found himself smiling, he wiped the expression away. He moved toward the single opening that led into the heart of the maze. When Lynnette arrived, this was where she'd enter and he wanted to be there to greet her. Properly. Passionately. As any lover would.

"She's a fine jumper," he said, raising his voice so that she was sure to hear.

"Mrs. B? Or the blue roan?"

"Both, I expect. But I was thinking of the horse. You didn't—"

"Jump her? No." As if she'd been born of the night itself, Lynnette materialized just inside the hedge opening. Ravensfield had been out in the dark for nearly an hour; his eyes were well adjusted to the light of the candles he'd lit all around. The flickering illumination washed Lynnette's face with soft color and made her lips look moist.

"Oh!" She took one look around the center of the maze and her eyes widened. "It's beautiful."

Ravensfield had made sure of that. Certain of the lady's taste and just as certain that her head could be turned as any woman's could by candlelight, champagne, and the soft touch of moonlit air, he had set the stage well. In the center of the clearing was a table and on it two crystal flutes that reflected the light of the surrounding candles. There were flowers there as well, freshly picked from the garden and the hothouse on the grounds, along with a bowl of fruit, a plate of figs. He moved back and made a sweeping motion toward it all.

"Welcome," he said. "This is my private place. Few people ever find their way here."

"And no wonder!" Lynnette's cheeks were flushed. Or perhaps it was a trick of the candlelight that made them look so. She hurried into the opening and looked all around. "Yet it seems the servants must visit once in a while. Do they dust and polish in here every day?"

"There isn't furniture here every day." She knew it, of course, the laughter in her voice told him she was teasing. Ravensfield turned his back on her, the better not to think how much he'd come to not only expect to hear her laughter about the house, but look forward to it.

He cast the thought aside as inconsequential. "This is special," he told her, reminding himself to keep his voice low, the better to begin the intimacies. "It is for a special night. A special guest."

"Then you must be expecting someone else." She walked the perimeter of the table, peering at the glassware, sniffing the flowers, fingering the lace cloth. When she'd completed the circle, she paused, one hand on the back of the nearest chair and her eyes on Ravensfield. "I have not been treated as a special guest these last twenty-four hours."

"And I am fully to blame." He bowed from the waist. Though it seemed frightfully old-fashioned, it was the kind of thing women always found appealing. "I have been occupied with a matter of some urgency," he told her. "Business."

"Business?" Her laugh was as gentle as the breeze that swept over them and brought with it the scent of the moonflowers that shone, as pale as ghosts, from one corner of the clearing. "What kind of business occupies a duke? Surely not trade, for that would be far below your station, your title, and your fortune. If I might venture a guess . . ." She stepped nearer and her hips swayed beneath the dainty fabric of a gown that, in this light, looked to be the same earthy color of full-bodied port. "I think you must be preparing for the Season."

"I am," he answered instantly. It was, after all, what he would be doing as soon as his book was finished. As soon as Lynnette was out of his life. "There is much to be done before I return to London."

"Ah . . ." She moved toward the stone bench that was usually the only thing here at the center of the maze. "Exactly what I've been thinking."

When she sat down, Ravensfield sat next to her. It was not difficult to keep to his plan of seduction when Lynnette looked so fetching. Sitting where she was, facing the table and the candles that sparkled upon it, her eyes twinkled brighter than the starlight. Her hair was pulled up, though not so neatly as usual. A few strands escaped their pins and brushed her shoulders. A dark curl caressed her left cheek. She looked like a woman who'd just come from her bed. She *was* a woman who'd just come from her bed, and Ravensfield swore he could still feel the warmth of the blankets rise from her skin and see the last remnants of sleepiness in her eyes, as if they'd just woke—pillow to pillow—after a night of making love.

Just the thought made him tighten like a watch spring.

He did his best to tamp down the rush of desire, reminding himself that a woman as inexperienced as Lynnette could not be hurried. Not without being frightened away. He must remember to take his time.

If only he could remember it when the scent of lavender filled his head.

Unable to resist, he moved closer to her on the bench, and smiled when she made no move to scoot the other way.

"You've been thinking about the Season, too, eh?" Ravensfield smiled and leaned nearer. He laid a hand upon her arm. "I have no doubt a woman such as yourself is busy from first to last. Balls, dinners, musicales."

"As I am sure you know, it all sounds wonderful but

it can be deadly dull!" When his hand slid down to hers, she allowed him to close it over her fingers. The feeling washed him over with warmth. "Yet I am grateful, of course. If it wasn't for the steadfast friendship of a few good people, my mother's reputation would have excluded me from polite society completely. On the whole, people are kind. But there are still some who look the other way when I pass."

"Is that why you're so eager to clear her name, then?"

Lynnette's brows dropped. "To make my own life easier?" She slanted him a look that was nothing less than outraged and he felt, more than saw, her demeanor change from silk to steel. At the same time he cursed himself for destroying the mood, he scrambled to redeem himself.

"I didn't mean—"

"Of course you did!" She controlled her anger, but just barely. She slid her hand from under his. "You think the reason I want Madelaine's diary is so that I might prove she's innocent and thus smooth my own way. To what, do you suppose? A profitable marriage?"

"Of course not!" The idea was ridiculous and Ravensfield dismissed it with a snort. He reminded himself that he was in the center of a seduction, not a boxing ring. He brushed a hand up her arm. "You are not the type of woman who—"

Lynnette moved out of reach. "Then do you think I want to salvage my mother's reputation because I am concerned about the Society folk who do naught but creep into favor with themselves? So that they might know that I'm as good as the rest of them?" Trying to hold her temper cost her. Her voice trembled. "I *am* as good as the rest of them."

"Better." When he made another move closer, Lynnette's back went as rigid as a pikestaff.

"Do you think I am as brainless as so many other women? That I would seek to clear my mother's name so that I might be welcomed by those who treated her so poorly? Invited to their homes so that I can spend my weekends in endless, vapid conversation with vapid people at country house party after country house party? Really, I thought you knew me better than that."

"Not what I meant at all! I—"

"Think little of me, that is as sure as eggs is eggs."

"It most certainly is not! And you are turning—"

"Everything I say on end and—"

"Not listening at all."

Lynnette stood, the action as explicit as a thrown gauntlet. Ravensfield had no choice but to stand, too. That, or look as if he hadn't the backbone to take up the challenge.

"It is clear to me that once again, we are talking at cross-purposes," she said. "And here I thought you might want to smooth the rough edges of our friendship before I went on my way in the morning. I have long overstayed my welcome. I can tell I am an unwanted guest."

"Unwanted" was not exactly the right word. For though Ravensfield had every intention of taking Lynnette's maidenhood before the night was over, he had promised himself he would feel nothing at their coupling. And at that very moment, he felt so much more than nothing, it nearly overwhelmed him. He wanted her more than he'd ever wanted anyone or anything.

The smooth swell of her bosom showed above the dark fabric of her gown, pale in the moonlight when she turned away from the table, sweet and inviting in the candlelight when she spun the other way. There was a soft shadow between her breasts and he wondered what it might be like to taste it. He reached for her arm.

Her gaze skipped to where his hand rested just above her elbow. "If this is your way of saying that you are sorry for your accusations . . ." Her voice was breathy with vexation. Or some other emotion. "If this is your way of telling me that you were too harsh and took my admission of knowledge of the wager too much to heart . . ." She raised her eyes to his, her lashes dark, her eyes inviting pools of starlight.

"If this is your way of saying you are sorry . . ." She yanked her arm from his grasp. "It isn't going to work. As much as I value your friendship, as much as I wished—" She caught herself on the brink of an admission and ran her tongue over her lips. "As much as I at one time wished there could be more between us, I do not need your pity."

So this was how it would end?

Ravensfield might have laughed if he had the heart.

If the Blades could see him now! If the gossips of the *ton* could have but a glimpse of his undoing!

The Duke of Ravensfield, a man whose reputation

was despoiled by years of debauchery, a man who broke hearts with no more compunction than he broke bread . . .

The Duke of Ravensfield at a loss for words? Undone by this slip of a woman?

He backed up a step to allow Lynnette to get by.

The look she gave him was as cool as the note of formality in her voice. "Thank you for letting me stay at Broadworth, and for making sure that I was well cared for. I think that without Jenny and Mrs. B, I would not be recovered enough to return home. Since that is precisely what we both wish . . ." She did not finish the sentence but swept toward the darker place that betrayed the opening that led back into the maze. "Good night. Goodbye."

Ravensfield watched her disappear into the night.

It was what he wanted, wasn't it? He wanted her to leave and finally she was gone. It was perfect!

Which made him wonder why the sight of her walking out of his life left him feeling like hell.

13

"*Lynnette!*"

She told herself not to turn around. She warned herself that it was not in her own best interest to give in so easily to the emotion that reverberated through Ravensfield's voice and caused an answering vibration through to her very core. It did not surprise her to find that she was as powerless to resist as the ocean is against the moon's pull.

No farther than a foot from the wall of the hedge and the narrow passage that would guide her back into the garden, she stopped and spun to face him.

"If you have more to say to me, perhaps you might say it in a letter," she told him, surprised at the coolness in her own voice. "Words on paper seldom sting as much as those spoken with malice."

"Malice? Is that what this damnable feeling is called? I thought it was rather something more like regret."

Pretty words. They may once have been able to turn

her head. No more. If she'd learned nothing else in her time at Broadworth, she'd learned that words and the pictures they painted were often deceiving. And that she was too often too eager to be deceived.

"Perhaps the only thing you regret," she told Ravensfield, "is that I overstayed my welcome."

"The way I remember it, I never exactly welcomed you." His sharp bark of laughter echoed on the night air, taking the bite from the truth. "I say, Miss Overton, it seems we have been at cross-purposes since the moment you arrived here in Berkshire. First my heroic rescue of you in the storm. The one you thought more of a chase. Then the servants' rumors. Since I have yet to suck your blood, I assume you've put those to rest, at least in your own head." He took a step nearer, and as tempted as she was to move away and widen the gap between them, Lynnette held her ground. "We have faced mysterious men in black together, and together, we have conquered. Or at least, we conquered Misters Hexam and Palliston. We were not in opposition then. And you must admit, though there have been stormy words between us, we have laughed together a time or two." He spoke the words softly, almost as a question, as if to measure her reaction. When she did nothing, he took another step closer.

"Will you run away into the night if I come too near?" he asked.

"I should have no reason to do that, your grace, unless you give it to me."

"And am I 'your grace' again? Have we gone all the way back to when we were nearly strangers?" Another step nearer and he was close enough to touch. Lynnette clutched her hands behind her back.

"I do not often apologize. I do not often have anything to apologize for." Before she could point out that it was toplofty of him even to think it, he went right on. "I am not saying that because I am never wrong. I am saying it because I am a duke. Damn it, Lynnette, dukes aren't meant to apologize!"

She tapped the toe of one silk slipper against the stone path.

"You will make me, though, won't you? Very well. I apologize!" Ravensfield scraped a hand across his chin. "I misspoke, surely, for otherwise you would have known that I meant no disrespect to either your mother or to you. You are eager to find your mother's diary. Of course I know it. And of course I know that the reason you seek to do so isn't so you can play the proper miss with those Society cats at Almack's. You are not the type who buckles under such pressure."

"I'm glad you noticed."

His voice dropped, as soft as the touch of the night breeze. "I've noticed your spirit, for surely it is mettle and mettle alone that makes you brave enough to search for the truth. I have noticed that you don't give up. Not even when it's the wisest course of action. I've noticed that you are quick-witted and intelligent and though I admit that quick-witted and intelligent women usually make me run for the door, I have noticed—much to my own surprise—that it is not the way I feel when I'm with you."

One more step closer and she could read the emotion

that shimmered in his eyes. That is, before his gaze slipped to her mouth and from there to her bosom and back up again. "I've noticed that your breath catches when I come too near. Just as it is doing now. It makes me think that your heart is racing. Just as mine is. And that you're thinking not so much of leaving as you are of what might happen if you stay."

"Perhaps what might happen if I stay is exactly the reason I should be leaving." She cringed at her own inability to express herself in a more uncluttered fashion, but Ravensfield merely laughed.

"Your thoughts are clear even if your sentence structure is muzzy," he said. "As for your intentions . . ." He studied her carefully and for long enough that Lynnette felt as if she might burst from anticipation. Finally, he nodded as if confirming something to himself. Or coming to some understanding, though of what, she could not say. "If there's anything I can do to make your journey home more comfortable . . ." He backed away. It was only one step yet Lynnette felt suddenly as if she could breathe more easily.

"Thank you. Your Mrs. B is a most excellent woman. I do believe she has all of my things packed." She forced herself to relax and took a step away from him.

"Once you are gone, things here will be damnably dull."

Lynnette couldn't help but smile. "Dull? Do you think so? I think, rather, that you will be happy to be rid of me. Then you can get back to . . . to whatever it was you were doing here before I intruded."

"Oh, you are brazen-faced!" His look of horror did not disguise the amusement in his voice. "Even now, you'd like to get my secret from me."

"So that I might win a thousand pounds?"

"No." He shook his head and the laughter drained from his voice. "I know that much about you. You would very much like to know the truth for you are not the type who is content with bits and pieces. It takes the whole of a story to satisfy you."

"Knowing the whole of this story might." She could not help herself. Perhaps it was the moonlight. Or the blanket of stars overhead. Perhaps it was the candle-light. She felt as if they were sharing confidences. "Of course if that was to work, you'd need to tell me what your secret is!"

Ravensfield threw back his head and laughed. "You're a vixen and no mistake. But you will not get around me so easily."

She peered over his shoulder toward the table, the candles, the flowers. "As you so clearly thought you could get around me."

"I—" As if he'd forgotten it was all there, he glanced over his shoulder, too. When he turned back to her, she swore she saw a shimmer of hesitation in his eyes. "I thought to make your last evening here pleasant. I thought—" He caught himself on the verge of another fabrication and decided it would get him nowhere. Again, his gaze strayed to the table and back to her. "What if I told you that I brought you here for some other reason?"

"What? So that you might seduce me?" Lynnette laughed. When she realized Ravensfield didn't join in, she pulled in a sharp breath. It was the wrong response and she knew it instantly. It made her look ingenuous and very inexperienced, and although she was ingenuous and very inexperienced, she knew that acting like either or admitting to both was the worst sort of show of weakness. Especially with a man like Ravensfield.

Apparently, he'd forgotten his reputation as a rake. "I'm sorry." He stepped forward and reached for her arm but it was dark and in the dark he somehow took hold of her hand instead. He pressed it between both of his.

Lynnette felt as if she might shatter from the contact. She turned away, the better to not have to look in his eyes. "Dukes don't apologize," she said.

"This one is apologizing. I'm sorry. Really. I never should have—"

"Never should have thought you could seduce me? Or never should have wanted to even try in the first place?"

"Damn it!" As if it were on fire, he dropped her hand. "You take every word I say—"

"Because every word you say is—"

"—twisted and turned and before I even know it, I—"

"—find that everything I knew or thought I knew is—"

"—not what I said in the first place." He pushed a hand through his hair. "There are times I think it would be better if we could simply pretend we'd never met.

Then we could be introduced at some soiree or another and start all over again."

"I doubt it would make the least bit of difference."

"I don't doubt that you are right."

It was the first thing they had both agreed on, and realizing it, they exchanged fitful smiles. Lynnette shifted from foot to foot, wondering what he expected her to say and thinking that if she were not so inexperienced she might know.

"You couldn't possibly have wanted to seduce me." It wasn't what she'd been planning to say for it was, after all, exactly what she had been hoping would happen. "I mean, really, it is the most ridiculous thing."

He neither confirmed nor denied the charge but stood looking at her, his dark eyes as soft as the night air all around them. "Not so ridiculous when you look the way you do."

"That is only because it is dark and it is easy to hide flaws in candlelight." She plucked at the skirt of the dress she'd donned in such a hurry. "I look like a woman who's just risen from her bed."

"Or one who should be taken back to it as soon as possible and with very little fanfare."

"Really! It is too cruel of you to say so. You don't even like me."

"Don't I?" This time when he grabbed for her arm, he met his mark. Hanging on tight, he reeled her in and pulled her close and his arms went around her, keeping her in place. "You're absolutely right. You're not the kind of woman who is usually seen on my arm, and never in my bed."

"And that disturbs you. Why?"

"Why?" As quickly as he grabbed her, he let her go. Standing too close to Ravensfield made Lynnette feel as if she couldn't fill her lungs with air. Standing too far, she suddenly felt chilled.

"You disturb me."

"Which is why you won't try to stop me from leaving."

"Precisely. But it doesn't mean I can't kiss you goodbye."

He didn't wait for her to respond and it was just as well. Lynnette was not sure if she would have allowed him the kiss or not.

But he was not a man who asked for permission. He bent his head and brought his mouth down on hers.

This kiss was nothing like the one he'd given her in the carriage on the day of the abbey picnic. That day, Ravensfield was annoyed and his kiss was as rough-and-tumble as their race with the phaeton had been. Now, there was no doubt that he was fully in control. The pressure of his mouth against hers was deliberate and firm, teasing and tempting until he coaxed a moan from her.

He pulled away long enough to look into her eyes and smiled when she was bold enough to meet the gaze. "What was that sound, Miss Overton? Did I hear you say goodbye?"

"We all say goodbye in our own way," she told him,

and before he could get the idea into his head that she was some shy young peagoose and so easily upended by a man's kiss that she did not know how to respond, she kissed him most thoroughly.

Ravensfield's arms went around her waist. Lynnette linked hers around his neck, her fingers playing through his hair. When he deepened the kiss, she tipped her head back, and when his tongue touched her lips, she opened to him.

It was an astonishing sensation and Lynnette gave herself to the feeling. She memorized the taste of him, the scent of bay rum that rose from his skin, the heat that made her feel as if lightning shot through each and every place he touched. She did not feel him turn her and backstep her toward the bench on the other side of the path, but suddenly she felt the stone press against the backs of her legs. She sat and tugged him down beside her.

"Good God!" When he looked at her, she was certain the fire in his eyes was the reflection of the candle flame. It took her only a moment to see how wrong she was. This was a hotter fire, a brighter flame, and when he tunneled his fingers through her hair and looked into her eyes, she was spellbound. "I am not in the habit of deflowering sweet young things," he told her, and she wondered if he was trying to convince her. Or himself.

"Then I think you'll agree it's a very good thing that I am six and twenty and not so young any longer." His gaze was fixed upon the tops of her breasts where they showed at the low-cut neckline of her gown. The very thought that he might find pleasure in her body sent a shiver through her. "And as you yourself are so fond of telling me, I am anything but sweet."

"Sweet to the touch." He slid his hand down the column of her neck to her shoulder. His fingers spread fire each place they played across her collarbone. He inched closer and skimmed a finger along the swell of one breast. She did not shrink away and he ventured another, firmer touch and dipped his head so that he might press a kiss against the hollow at the base of her throat.

"Sweet to the taste," he said, gliding his lips back to hers. "Perhaps I was wrong all those times I spoke otherwise of you."

"Perhaps you were right, and are even now deceiving yourself."

"Perhaps." He nuzzled a kiss against her neck and Lynnette felt herself tense. Real or imagined, the last time he'd kissed her so, she had swooned. But real or imagined then, this kiss was real enough. And fainting was the last thing on her mind. She tipped her head and arched her back. Was it also her imagination? She thought she heard a satisfied murmur from Ravensfield. He slipped his mouth again to the hollow at the base of her throat, then down farther still and dipped a kiss into the shadowy place between her breasts.

Her eyes drifted closed and she caught her lower lip in her teeth. If she was not very much mistaken, the purr of contentment she heard was coming from her own throat.

Ravensfield took the sound as a good sign. He stroked her breast, his fingers gliding over the muslin of her gown, and when she did not pull away, he slipped his hand inside.

"Oh!" It was the most incredible sensation and Lynnette did not even try to hide her amazement. She nibbled the tip of his ear. She skimmed her hands over the front of his coat, thinking as she did that for all their appetites, men were bundled damnably tight into their clothing. Coat and neckcloth and jacket and trousers . . .

Lynnette's hands wandered along with her mind, cataloguing as she went. Just as Ravensfield's did. He reached behind her and unlaced her gown, and when he pushed it down over her shoulders, the night air brushed her bare skin like a lover's touch.

"You really are lovely." His fingers skimmed across the top of her corset. "Perfect and beautiful and—"

"And I really do think the time for talking is over."

Her frankness was Ravensfield's undoing. It tugged at heartstrings that he had not, until that very minute, known existed.

It tugged at other places, as well.

Desire burst through him like a Vauxhall rocket. It scorched his reason and ignited his passions. Moonlight washed Lynnette's bare shoulders and touched the mounds of her breasts where they showed above the lace edging of her corset. It tipped her lips and he drank deep, congratulating himself at the same time he untied the ribbon that held her corset closed. Lynnette was snugged damnably tightly into her clothing. If not for the fact that he was a man of the world, he might have fumbled his way through this thing.

Fortunately for both Lynnette's pleasure and the need that spread through him like a spark in a tinderbox, he knew his way around her unmentionables. Just as he did every other woman's.

Her corset was loosened in a matter of moments and he spread it apart. Her sweetness was impossible to resist. His fingers followed where the candlelight caressed, across one breast and then the other. With one finger, he outlined each nipple, then dipped his head to take her into his mouth. He listened to her sharp intake of breath and the tiny noise of surprise that escaped her.

He slipped her out of her bloomers as effortlessly as he plied the reins on his carriage, and himself out of his trousers just as easily. His mouth still on hers, his fingers kneading her breasts, he pulled her onto his lap, her gown above her knees. At the same time he claimed another kiss, he slipped into her.

She held her breath for a space of a dozen rollicking heartbeats, her eyes wide with wonder, her body tensed. Right before she threw back her head and moaned.

Ravensfield rocked her to the rhythm that coursed through his body, willing himself to take his time, wanting to pleasure her as much as she pleased him. It was not easy to make himself wait, especially when Lynnette leaned close. When she raked her hands in his hair.

She tightened around him and tensed, and no more able to control the need for release than he was to keep himself from claiming her mouth in one more fierce kiss, he pushed into her, harder and faster than before. She trembled against him in waves of pleasure, again and again, and he gave himself to the same sensations. When the blood stopped rushing in his ears, the only sound he heard was that of his own rough breathing and her voice, soft and sweet where it whispered in his ear.

"Oh, Thomas!"

The sound of the name, spoken so seldom and never so tenderly, startled him. He nudged her far enough away to look into her eyes.

What he saw reflected back at him was enough to annihilate the satisfaction of their lovemaking.

"I—" Ravensfield considered the consequences of saying what he was tempted to say and, just as quickly, threw caution to the wind. This wasn't a time for second-guessing his instincts. Not when those instincts advised self-preservation. A hand on either side of her, he slipped Lynnette off his lap and rose to fasten his trousers. "I do believe I was carried away."

Laughter bubbled from her, the sound as crystalline as church bells on a frosty morning. Though he refused to look her way, he knew she was looking at him. He could feel the touch of her smile, the warm aftermath of her pleasure, the heat that could only by shared by a man and a woman who had been lovers. "I do believe I was carried away, too. And I am more than willing to be carried away again, anytime you wish."

Ravensfield moved a step away from the bench and the passion that simmered in Lynnette's voice. He turned to find her staring at him, her moonlight eyes glazed with the remnants of their intimacy, her cheeks flushed, her lips moist and swollen from his kisses. He fisted his hands at his sides. "You aren't listening."

She was listening enough to recognize that the heat of his passion had turned to ice. A second's disbelief turned quickly to understanding. Lynnette's smile faded and blindly she scrambled to find her corset. It had landed on the ground and she set it down on the bench beside her and pushed her gown up, slipping the sleeves over her arms. It was as much an act of self-defense as was Ravensfield's retreat from the bench. But he could no more tell her that than he could go to her. For if he did, it would be tantamount to admitting that he'd been overcome by her innocence. And upended by her trust. She was supposed to be just like any other woman, and he wasn't supposed to feel any different than he'd ever felt before.

It took more willpower than he knew he had to keep to his place.

"I said I was carried away. What I intended was that I never thought—" He cleared his throat, the better to give her time to digest the meaning behind his words. "I'm sorry."

"Sorry? Are you?" Though Lynnette's eyes were as bright as the candleflame, her voice was softer than the night shadows. She stood, dragging her corset up with her, holding it close to her chest like a shield. She raised her chin and looked him in the eye. "As I am sure you noticed, your grace, I am not a woman of great experience. I am not apologizing for my greenness. Nor am I excusing it. But I am also not a blockhead. I learn very quickly. If you are sorry then I know it means that I must be sorry, too."

And before he could even begin a protest he knew would sound as ineffectual as it felt, she hurried out of the clearing and disappeared into the maze.

"Damn!" Ravensfield stared at the stone bench, cursing Lynnette. Cursing himself.

He might have believed that she was just like any other woman when he planned this madman's scheme. He might have believed it still when she fell easy prey to his charm and he stripped away her clothing and her inhibitions.

He might have gone right on believing it.

Until she broke down the wall he'd built around his heart and the barriers that made him a part of life and yet held back his emotions. Until she called him Thomas.

Lynnette like any other woman, eh?

He had deluded himself into thinking so.

Until he realized what he had never realized about any other woman.

That he was in love with her.

14

"You cannot spend the whole of the Season snug in your little nest like a dormouse."

With no more ceremony than a quick rap on the door, Willie sailed into Lynnette's bedchamber, her voice as breezy as a spring morning but her shoulders set in a way that told Lynnette this was not a social call. As if she knew what she would find and had no need to confirm the sorry fact to herself, she spared barely a look at Lynnette, still in her nightdress and huddled under the blankets. Instead, Willie swept across the room and toward the French doors that led onto the balcony that looked over the gardens of Plumley Terrace. Although it was already early in the afternoon, the draperies were drawn. Willie tugged them open, allowing a stream of May sunshine into the room along with more of a look at the outside world than Lynnette was ready to endure. Lynnette squeezed her eyes shut, reached for her pillow, and dragged it over her head.

"It won't help." Though Lynnette didn't hear Willie come toward the bed, she felt the pressure when Willie sat down. "You can hide in here yet another fortnight. Just like you've been hiding here for the last two weeks. But you might as well know right now, it won't help."

"It won't hurt." Even to her own ears, Lynnette's voice sounded petulant. She didn't care. "It's quiet here."

"If it's quiet you're looking for, perhaps you might have stayed in Berkshire."

"What?" Lynnette was already sitting upright, looking at her cousin in wonder, when she realized she'd been humbugged. "You are too shameful," she told Willie. "You did your best to catch me off my guard, simply to provoke a reaction."

Willie's smile was as bright as the fiery color of her hair. "If nothing else, it got you to remove the pillow from your head."

Lynnette glanced down at the pillow lying beside her, considering the benefits of hiding beneath it again. Unfortunately, if the last two weeks had taught her nothing else, they had taught her that hiding under a pillow, or in her room, or even behind the sturdy door of Plumley Terrace, was not enough to make her forget.

The familiar ache started up inside her. Right at the place where her heart used to be. It was another reminder she didn't need. Of all that had happened. And all she was trying to forget.

"I am far more content beneath my pillow," she told Willie. "More content and—" She remembered Willie's earlier comment and her mouth dropped open. "You said Berkshire! However did you know about—"

"I am not reading your mind, if that's what you're afraid of." Willie's smile faded and she put a hand on Lynnette's shoulder, the better to comfort her. "I have talked to Mr. Hexam and Mr. Palliston, of course. At first, they were reluctant to discuss their whereabouts or the details of their journey. I think they were embarrassed to admit that they had failed in their rattle-brained mission. But they did, finally, confess that they had gone against Nick's wishes and made the trip to Broadworth Hall to spy on the Duke of Ravensfield in order to win the one thousand pounds from the Blades. They reported what they'd seen there. *Who* they'd seen there."

"Good heavens!" Lynnette felt the blood drain from her face. "Nick hasn't—"

"Headed to Berkshire to challenge Ravensfield? Pistols for two, breakfast for one?" She gave Lynnette a steady look. "Should he?"

The very thought made her uneasy and because she refused to let Willie see how uneasy she was, Lynnette got out of bed. Her wrapper was nearby and she slipped it on, then reached for the violet Norwich shawl she kept near the bed and draped it over her shoulders. By the time she was done, she hoped that Willie would be ready to change the subject.

Willie being Willie, she should have known better.

As casually as if they were discussing nothing more pressing than the weather, Willie rose and fluffed the pillows. "You haven't answered me," she said, glancing up to gauge Lynnette's reaction. "Is that because you don't wish to? Or because you, yourself, do not know the answer to the question?"

"Both, I suppose." Lynnette's shoulders slumped under the familiar weight of the green melancholy that had been her constant companion since the night in the garden at Broadworth Hall when what had been the most glorious moment in her life turned—thanks to Ravensfield's cold indifference—into the most bitter. Before she even realized it and long before she could control it or the riot of memories that had haunted her day and night since, a sigh slipped from her along with the comment, "He was so tender."

Much to her surprise, Willie looked neither startled nor scandalized. "I daresay, you are not the first woman to think that about Ravensfield."

"As well I realize. That makes me look all the more the fool." Lynnette plumped down on the bed. "You might have warned me that love is not the simple, happy state portrayed in books."

"Yet it can be. At the right time. With the right man." Willie's smile was gentle. She propped her hands on the smooth swell of her belly. "When a woman's love is returned as freely as it is given."

"Now you are talking about you and Nick!" Too restless to keep still, too miserable with her own plight to think of the happy endings reserved for the privileged few, Lynnette rose and paced to the other side of the room. "I am sorry to put this to you so coldly, Willie darling, but if you are talking reality, you cannot possibly bring up the subject of you and Nick. Your love is the stuff that storybooks are made from. That makes the two of you an abnormality of sorts, a distortion of the kinds of marriages I see all around me."

"And do you think things were always so easy between us?" Willie laughed. "Or that we are forever casting sheep's eyes upon each other? If that's the kind of love you are looking for, you are doomed to disappointment, for you will not find it anywhere in this world. Then again, you cannot be talking about love at all. Not when we are discussing a certain duke." She tipped her head and considered Lynnette very closely and it took her no more than a moment to see that Lynnette was very serious, indeed. Willie's cheeks paled. "You cannot possibly think—"

"Oh, yes! I did think it." Lynnette threw her hands in the air and hurried back across the room, too fretful to control the energy that jumped through her like a cricket on hot pavement. "Now you know the awful truth. I did think it for a while. But you must give me some credit, at least. There isn't a woman alive who could look at him and not think—"

"Yes, that is certain." The fact that Willie didn't look pleased about admitting to the weakness made Lynnette feel better. But only a little.

"I learned soon enough that I was very much mistaken in bestowing my regard before I knew full well what kind of man he was. He is—"

"Quite charming if all the stories about him are true."

The sparkle in Willie's eyes and the honey in her voice caught Lynnette by surprise. "Charming. Yes, he is that." She nodded and pushed the thought aside, no more pleased with admitting it than she was with remembering how Ravensfield's charm had made her feel.

"And he is intelligent," Lynnette told her, cataloguing Ravensfield's attributes in spite of the fact that she'd spent the past two weeks telling herself not to. "And so brave! When he thought there was a threat to me from Mr. Hexam and Mr. Palliston—before he knew they were Mr. Hexam and Mr. Palliston, of course—he raced to my rescue."

"A heroic act that was, no doubt, enough to turn your head."

"I hardly needed it turned." Because she could not stand to look at Willie and see a woman whose life was as well ordered as Lynnette's had not been since the night she'd set her heart on the fateful trip to Berkshire, Lynnette turned away from her dear cousin. She walked to the windows and looked outside. Beyond the garden and the wall that surrounded it, the street was filled with folk rushing back and forth, heading off to lives that must certainly be less nettlesome and far more bucksome than Lynnette's felt to be at the moment.

"He weaves a certain fantasy with the very force of his personality. It would take a stronger woman than I am to resist."

"You didn't?"

Had the question come from anyone else, Lynnette would have refused to answer. But this was Willie and she and Willie had no secrets. For the first time, Lynnette found herself wishing they did. She turned from the window. "Resist?" She laughed at the irony. "I didn't even try."

"I see," Willie said, but Lynnette wondered how she could. "And now you're telling me that you're in love with the man."

"Love?" It sounded odd, like a foreign phrase spoken suddenly in a sentence filled with serviceable English words. "I thought I might be," she admitted, both to Willie and, for the first time in two weeks, to herself. "In spite of his secretive nature. And the fact that he was so often preoccupied I sometimes wondered if he knew I was there." Another thought tickled her memory and, before she could stop it, she found herself smiling. "I do believe my very presence sometimes rankled."

"Yet he didn't send you away."

"No." There was no great comfort in admitting that, either, or the fact that at least part of the reason he did not was because she had been deceitful enough to pretend an injury. Lynnette's smile faded. "I thought we might forge a friendship. Or more. Until . . ."

Lynnette weighed the wisdom of saying too little against the folly of keeping too much to herself. Ever since the night she ran out of the hedge maze and went to the stable to rouse Garvey from his bed . . .

Ever since she'd given herself to Ravensfield most freely and with more joy than she had ever given herself over to anything . . .

Ever since he had looked at her as if she were a

stranger and acted so coldly in spite of the fact that all between them had been heat, Lynnette had felt as if a hand had tangled her insides into a painful snarl. Keeping the secret had done nothing to diminish the pain. Perhaps sharing it would loosen the knots.

"Just when I thought all was right between us, he acted as if he didn't know me."

"It is often the way with men." As if it were a sad reality, Willie shook her head. "They go about their lives, in a world of their own, I think. And though they sometimes succumb to great emotion, especially where women are concerned, they would no more admit it than they would ride Rotten Row in the buff. I stand corrected, I think they might be more inclined to ride Rotten Row in the buff than to admit to feelings and emotions they are not taught to handle. If Ravensfield is all you say he is—charming and kind and accepting of you in spite of the fact that you are such a great annoyance . . ." Willie grinned to show that she could not think of anyone who would believe such of Lynnette.

"If this is what has you so much in the doldrums, you must cheer up, dear cousin. For all his reputation, I think there is great character beneath Ravensfield's surface. And I do believe he is a man of wisdom. Surely he may come around yet to see what he's missing."

"I don't think so." The certainty weighed Lynnette down like a physical thing. She dropped into the nearest chair. "I do believe he had as good a chance as any man ever gets and yet it changed nothing. Except that it made everything worse."

"As good a chance?" The truth sank in and Willie's face grew pale. She plunked onto the bed. "You mean—"

"Oh, Willie! I was such a fool!" Lynnette dropped her head into her hands. "He turned my head and it took but little turning. I was so eager to fall in love and to have him love me in return. I was ready to believe anything. Even though I knew full well that I was nothing but another in a long line of women who'd had their hearts broken and their feelings hurt."

"He didn't . . ." Willie's shoulders went back. Her jaw went rigid. "He didn't force—"

"Good heavens, no!" Lynnette could not help but defend Ravensfield. And impeach herself. "He didn't need to," she told Willie. "I was putty in his hands, if you will forgive the very bad pun."

"And when it was over?"

"When it was over . . ." Lynnette looked all around. Her copy of *Greystone Castle* sat on the table next to her bed, untouched since she'd left Berkshire even though she was so near the end of the story. Even Clarice's fate was not enough to draw her away from the blue devils, no more than was thinking of the coded page tucked into the book.

"I have been hiding here in the house for close on two weeks now," she reminded Willie. "I think that will tell you something about how he reacted when it was all over. He was silent. Distant. Finished with me as soon as we were finished—"

"Nonsense!" Willie got to her feet, her voice vibrating with outrage. "He cannot think that he can simply—"

"He can. He did. I let him." Grateful that Willie was incensed on her account, Lynnette stood and hurried to give her a quick hug. "There's nothing I can do to change any of it," she said.

"You can stop acting as if you have something to be ashamed of and get on with your life."

"I can." There was only so long that Lynnette could sound as brave as she wished she was. Her shoulders drooped. "I could. If I felt like getting on with my life."

"That is nonsense, as well." Willie wound an arm through hers. "What matters is that you are safe and as well as can be expected and not . . ." She hesitated, obviously trying to spare Lynnette's feelings. "Not compromised in any tangible way." Her eyebrows rose as if it were more a question than an observation and she put a hand on her own growing stomach.

It was sweet of her to even think it. And unnecessary. "No, there's no worry there," Lynnette assured her.

Willie breathed a sigh of relief. "Then that is that, as they say. And we won't speak of it again. Unless, of course, you feel the need."

"I—" Lynnette hesitated, but only for a moment. She surrendered herself to Willie's uncommon common sense. "As always, Willie, you are absolutely right. Hiding here in my bedchamber, feeling sorry for myself, it won't change a thing."

"That's the spirit." Willie smiled. "And you will come for a carriage ride with me this afternoon?"

"I—"

"You told me that you realized that hiding wasn't going to help."

"I know." Lynnette looked toward the door, weighing the benefits of venturing again into the world against those of staying where she could swaddle her heart against the bumps and bruises that were sure to come to it from outside. "It's simply that—"

"I will be around to collect you at four and we will go for a drive. Wear something colorful and bring out your best bonnet. It won't make everything better, but it is a good first move and I know that will cheer you." She walked across the room and did not pause until her hand was on the doorknob. "And I will brook no argument. You are coming with Nick and me to the masquerade ball next week. It is being given by Lady Christina Moore-Chastain, your mother's dear friend, and I know she would be pleased to see you."

"No. Really." Lynnette shook her head, instantly dismissing the very idea. "I have received an invitation to the masquerade, too, and have declined it most politely."

"Lady Christina will be disappointed."

"Lady Christina will understand, just as she understood when she came to call recently and I sent down a note to say I wasn't feeling well and would see her another time. It was good of her, just as it was good of her to stand by Madelaine in her hour of need. I owe her a debt of gratitude. But that doesn't mean it has to be anytime soon." She scrambled for some reason to excuse herself. "I am not ready to be seen in public. My cheeks are pale, I think, and—"

"Nonsense!" Willie laughed. "You are the picture of health. And I have spoken to Lady Christina only this morning. She's thrilled to hear that you are up and about again."

"Which I am not."

"Which you must certainly be by next week."

"But a masquerade? I have nothing to wear and—"

"It has all been arranged." Willie waved away the objection as an airy nothing. "I've seen the modiste for my costume and have asked her to tailor one for you, as well."

"But Lady Christina's balls are the most fabulous and the most renowned. Mr. Hexam and Mr. Palliston are sure to be there. And if they are—"

Willie's shoulders shot back. "Really! Do you think so little of me? Mr. Hexam and Mr. Palliston have been sworn to secrecy about everything they did—and saw—in Berkshire. I know them well enough to know they will not break their promise."

Lynnette laughed. It was the first time she'd allowed herself the luxury in the two weeks since she'd been back in London. The merriment seemed odd here in her bedchamber where she'd surrounded herself with nothing but the deafening sounds of silence. "I have no doubt that Mr. Hexam and Mr. Palliston will keep their vow of silence. They are too intimidated by you not to!"

"And they care too deeply about you." Willie paused

long enough for Lynnette to realize it was true. "They won't say a word. Not even to Nick."

"You mean, he doesn't—"

The enigmatic smile Willie gave her was all the answer Lynnette needed. "If you are looking for advice about love, remember this. There are things men need to know. And things they are better off never hearing about. This falls into the latter category, I think."

"But you and Nick are—"

"Madly in love. Sharing our lives. Creating a future. Yes, indeed, all that is true. But you see, dear, that's something else you need to learn. Love can be as real as the world outside. It can be as deep as the ocean and as long-lasting as the stars in the heavens." A smile broke over her expression. "But that doesn't mean a woman can't have her secrets. Even from her husband. Especially from her husband. This is our secret and will be unless you decide it's wise for Nick to know. Until then"—she opened the door and swept into the passageway—"I will see you at four, and while we are out, we will stop at Somerton House. The modiste will be there to fit your costume."

"But I haven't agreed to go. Not on the carriage ride and certainly not to the masquerade."

"Of course you'll go. A carriage ride is the perfect distraction and distraction is exactly what you need. As for the masquerade . . ." Willie smiled. "You have nothing to worry about. I have it on very good authority that the Duke of Ravensfield has not returned to London and that he was no plans to return any time soon. He will most definitely not be in attendance."

* * *

Willie's very good authority was apparently neither good nor authority enough.

When Lynnette walked into Lady Christina Moore-Chastain's elegant London town house for the masquerade ball, one of the first people she saw was the Duke of Ravensfield.

He was standing against the far wall, deep in conversation with a man who, because of his monk's robe and cowl, was impossible for Lynnette to recognize. The duke himself was wearing neither a costume nor the kind of half-mask that hid the identities of so many of the other revelers. He was dressed as always, splendidly, head to toe in black. The darkness of his clothing was a counterpoint to the bright colors of so many of the costumes and a sharp contrast to the sudden, fiery color that flooded Lynnette's face. Fortunately, Ravensfield was so preoccupied, he did not turn to look her way.

"Oh!" She had no intention of betraying herself to those around her but the sight of the duke when and where she did not expect to see him made the breath catch in Lynnette's throat. Her heart thumped against her ribs so furiously that she was sure every person gathered there—shepherds, pirates, harlequins—heard the noise and knew instantly not only that something was wrong but what, and certainly who, was the cause of her distress.

To her credit, she had enough presence of mind to pretend to trip on the cloak of her Turkish sultana costume. It gave her the opportunity to delay her entrance into the ballroom. She turned her back so that she might busy herself smoothing her gown into place and took the opportunity to run a fitful hand over her golden turban, pinned with a paste ruby at the front and bedecked with a dramatic array of feathers.

Her mind was made up instantly. If she was quick, she could be back in her carriage before anyone noticed. If she was quiet, she could make her getaway without causing too much of a commotion. If she was lucky, she might yet make it back to Plumley Terrace and be safely locked in her bedchamber before anyone even knew she was missing and long before Ravensfield caught sight of her.

She was none of those things.

Christina Moore-Chastain appeared as if out of nowhere and, smiling, headed directly for her. Lynnette knew all hope of escape was dashed.

"Darling!" Lady Christina was dressed as the goddess Diana. The symbolism, Lynnette suspected, was lost on no one. Like the huntress of legend, Lady Christina was golden-haired, beautiful, and graceful. She had the kind of irresistible charm and dash that made her a sought-after guest as well as a hostess whose gatherings were destined to be the highlight of any Season and the talk of the *ton* for months to come.

As any of the lovers whom she'd left strewn in her considerable wake would no doubt attest, she also had a way of awakening a primitive hunger in men, one which many a man had found himself powerless to control.

Lynnette herself had never seen Lady Christina do an unkind thing or heard her speak an unkind or untrue word, though her wit could be biting. Lady Christina had been some ten years younger than Madelaine, but she and Lynnette's mother had been the best of friends and Christina was Lynnette's entrée into Society when the rest of the *ton* would have turned their collective back on her. For that, certainly, she owed Lady Christina her gratitude and her devotion.

"That is you, Lynnette, behind that mask, isn't it?" Lady Christina asked, and when Lynnette lifted her mask just enough to give her a peek at her face, Lady Christina kissed her on the cheek and stood back to take in the full of Lynnette's costume. "You look splendid! I can see the hand of a Parisian seamstress in that gown. Come, come." She tugged her toward the ballroom, and if she noticed that Lynnette was reluctant, she didn't let it stop her. "The dancing is about to begin and you simply must see all the costumes. I've had a number of men ask if you were going to be here tonight."

"A number? Really?" It seemed as unlikely as the fact that a real Turkish sultana might wear a golden silk gown with Spanish sleeves puffed at the shoulders, a high waistline, and a bodice cut low enough to reveal a hint of bosom.

Once in the ballroom, Lynnette found her gaze traveling automatically to where she'd last seen Ravensfield. At the same time she cursed herself for not being able to control her curiosity and her attraction to a man who was like a flame to a moth, she thanked her lucky stars. He was nowhere in sight.

Lady Christina looked that way, too, and for just a moment, her sapphire eyes darkened behind the ivory-colored silk mask that covered the top of her face and sat upon the bridge of her aristocratic nose. The expression came and went, and when it was gone, Lady Christina had a sly smile on her face. "Worried about someone in particular?" she asked, but before Lynnette could answer with a lie, Christina caught sight of the Duchess of Cranley across the room. She excused herself and, like the goddess who was said to slip in and out of the forest as effortlessly as a ray of sunshine, she was gone.

Lynnette was left to fend for herself.

Careful of where she was headed and who might be lying in wait for her there, she made her way to the fringes of the crowd, grateful as she had never been before for the anonymity afforded by her mask. She nodded politely to the people she passed, and though they did the same in return, there were few she could identify for certain. With any luck, it meant that there were few who might be able to identify her, as well.

She was already near the door of the refreshment room when she saw Nick and Willie. They were dressed as shepherd and shepherdess and, of course, Nick refused to wear a mask.

"Can't stand the folderol." Nick twitched his broad shoulders uneasily inside a costume the likes of which would have cost a real shepherd a year or more of his hard-earned income. "Don't understand why people simply can't get together in their regular clothes."

"Don't listen to him." Willie gave him a playful poke in the ribs. "I've heard tell that a man can grow irritated as his wife's confinement nears."

"Ridiculous." Nick caught sight of someone he knew across the room and Willie hurried him on his way with a little push.

Once he was out of earshot, she turned her attention to Lynnette. "Are you well? You look pallid."

"That may have something to do with a certain someone you mentioned when first we spoke of tonight's amusement. You remember, the one who wasn't supposed to be here."

"Oh." Willie's face paled, too, and she glanced around quickly and seemed relieved when the certain someone in question was nowhere in sight. "Will you stay?"

Lynnette chanced a quick look around, too. "Lady Christina has already seen me so I cannot slip away without being impolite. I will stand with my back to the wall all night, the better to know that at least one side of me is safe."

"Poor darling!" Willie patted her arm. "It's my fault, I'm afraid, and I accept full responsibility. If you need to withdraw, I can pretend to be feeling fatigued."

"You are too dear but please don't worry. I will be fine." Lynnette squared her shoulders. "I will simply have to be. I refuse to spend the rest of my life acting like a Bath miss, peeking around corners and jumping at shadows. I must start back into living my life sometime and this seems as good a time and place as any. I will simply put the past behind me, as you have so wisely advised. I am a new woman, Willie. And that new woman starts her life here. Right now."

"That's the spirit," Willie told her.

Awash with the satisfaction of her new outlook on life and flush with determination, Lynnette headed into the refreshment room for a glass of ratafia.

She might have made it if, just inside the door, a hand hadn't clamped down upon her arm. Startled, she turned to find herself face-to-face with Ravensfield. His grip was unyielding. His expression was as pleasant as a thundercloud.

"We need to talk," he said.

15

Her eyes were starlight, lit from within with a silvery glow that beckoned, brighter even than the candles that sparked all around.

It was hardly the time for purple prose but Ravensfield, so much at a loss for words of late, simply could not help himself. One moment of looking into Lynnette's eyes and even the heap of good intentions he'd piled on his designs for this evening were not enough to muffle the drumbeat that started up in his chest. One touch of her—skin to skin—and his head filled with bits and pieces of Mrs. Mordefi's impassioned composition.

Her lips were satin. Pink, and as pure as a morning sunrise. Moist like the dew, calling to him to drink deep.

* * *

That was from *The Beast of Carnaby Hall* and did not apply, for the lady in the book was also the beast and Lynnette . . .

Ravensfield pulled in a long breath and let it out slowly, refusing as he did to allow his hand to tremble where he rested it upon her arm.

His gaze raked her. From the silly turban with its even more silly regalia of feathers. To the tiny golden coins sewn all about the rim of the turban so that they joggled when she walked. To her eyes.

Because he could not bear to look in them and think of all they'd done together and all it meant to him, he allowed his gaze to drift even farther. From her eyes to her mouth. From her mouth to her chin, as stubborn as ever. From her chin down her neck and from there to her bosom, discreetly accented by the high waist of her dress and just as discreetly displayed at the low neckline.

It was impossible to reconcile Lynnette with the beast in Mrs. Mordefi's book. For the beast was a monster. And Lynnette was a vision.

Her body was lithe and supple, ripe and delicious. Her breath caught and her bosom strained against the gossamer fabric of her gown. My body responded instantly and I—

That wasn't from a book at all but straight from Ravensfield's imagination, unrehearsed and needing no rewriting. He grumbled a curse that rumbled beneath the hum of laughter that filled the refreshment room. As quickly as he reached for Lynnette, he let go her again. He stepped back, away from the words that filled his head, and the images that followed and the temptation that shivered in the air anytime Lynnette was near. "You look well," he said.

Her chin came up. "I look as well as ever I looked," she answered him, and her voice was as icy as the emotion that changed the silvery starlight in her eyes to a color that looked more like moonlight on snow. "Now that we've established that, you'll excuse me."

She turned away, and though he had no patience for melodrama and certainly no intention of being operatic, Ravensfield's reaction was instant and instinctual. Like taking his next breath. Again he reached for her and again, the moment his hand closed around her wrist, he felt a frisson of awareness course through his body. Fire against her ice.

"I said that we need to talk."

She glanced down to his hand, then back up into his eyes. "You did. You said it. And I heard it most clearly. I simply have no wish to do it."

"And I can hardly blame you."

"Really?" There was a hint of laughter in her voice that did not make him feel like joining in. "You have an odd way of showing how very understanding you are."

"I—" He hesitated, mostly because he had no wish to try to explain himself. Not here. Not now. Perhaps not ever. He was not a man who was easily upended by a woman. Any woman. And now he found himself tongue-tied and nervous.

He did not like the feeling.

"I didn't come here to debate."

"Good. For there's nothing we need to say to each other."

"Nor did I come here to trade witticisms."

"You didn't come here to dance, either, judging by your lack of proper attire."

"Would you have me dress as a vampire? Black cloak, tall hat, blood dripping from the corners of my mouth?"

As if considering, she glided a look over him that was every bit as thorough as the one he'd just given her. "Some men are monsters, costume or not."

The words stung. He refused to let her know it. Just as he refused to let himself take them to heart and suffer because of them. He laughed, instead. It sounded as hollow as it felt. "Some? Like me?"

"You?" Again she glided a look over him. "I am surprised that our hostess allowed you through the door."

"We are old friends." He twitched away the very notion and the memories of the woman that, each time he allowed them, twisted through him like a frowsty mist over a bog. "I have something to tell you."

Lynnette rolled her eyes. "If there's an apology on the end of that statement, sir, it is far too late for that, and besides, I do not wish to hear it. And if you're here to declare some sort of undying love—"

"No." It wasn't as if he hadn't thought of it. But each time he did, it frightened him to death. The fact that he was frightened—both by the emotion and by his own uncontrollable reaction to it—was another reason he found himself feeling as awkward as a schoolboy. It was also all the excuse he needed to deny it instantly. "No," he said again, just to emphasize the point. "No to both."

"I might have thought as much." Lynnette turned away and he had no choice but to release his hold on her.

"You left without saying goodbye." It wasn't something he'd meant to speak to her about—not here, not now—and Ravensfield cursed himself. "Back at Broadworth. The next morning. I went looking for you. Mrs. B told me that you left without—"

"Yes." She looked at him over her shoulder. "I had much to do in town."

"And much to get away from."

"If you say so."

"I didn't. I wouldn't, except that you—"

"More than wore out my welcome." She turned to him at the same time she stepped back, putting even more distance between them. "Yes, I realized that. Finally. I can only think you must have been very relieved. Just as I can only think to say that I'm sorry I did not realize it soon enough."

"Are you? Sorry, I mean?" He closed the gap between them and though he cautioned himself that it was a sure way to drive himself mad, he could not help the urgings of his body. He reached for her hand. "For I can tell you that I am—"

"Ah, I see you two have met!"

Ravensfield did not need to look to know who had come upon them unawares. He recognized the husky voice and the scent that was one part roses, one part jasmine, and three parts merciless. He clenched his jaw and gave a curt nod. "Lady Christina."

She laughed, and in spite of himself, he remembered how the sound had once made him think of the music of a stream dancing over stones. Pity it had taken him so long to realize just how icy the water was.

Ravensfield glanced her way just in time to see Christina Moore-Chastain's eyes glister behind her mask. Her blue gaze glanced down to where Ravensfield's hand was on Lynnette's, and when she looked up again, her eyes were as bright as diamonds. And just as hard.

Always masterful, she replaced the look with a merry laugh. She turned toward Lynnette and winked. "The Duke of Ravensfield is a cad, indeed. You'd be wise to remember it, my dear. He's bold enough to call me by my Christian name yet the last time I happened upon him . . ." She tapped his arm with her silk fan. "He was very bad! He called me something else entirely."

"Indeed." He wasn't in the mood for games but then Christina had never cared much about moods. Unless they were her own. Releasing Lynnette's hand, Ravensfield bent over Christina's and kissed the air an inch above her fingers. "The way I remember it, m'lady," he said, standing straight again and looking in her eyes, "the last time we had the unfortunate hazard of running into one another, what I called you had something to do with female canines."

With her typical abandon, Christina threw her head back and laughed. "And the way I remember it, you qualified even that comment and added—"

"That in order for it to be a valid comparison," Ravensfield smiled, "the female canines in question also had to have the unfortunate habit of eating their young."

Behind her mask, Lynnette's eyes went wide. Ravensfield would have liked to think it was because what they said outraged her. It took him only a moment to realize he was wrong. There were only two reasons a man and a woman spoke so to each other while they traded smiles as smooth as glass and as well honed as knives: they were either enemies. Or old lovers.

Lynnette knew Lady Christina well enough to know the former was not true. She had been at school when the air over London was blue with the scandal surrounding the older and far more sophisticated Lady Christina and the lad fresh from Oxford who was more than eager to add shine to his manhood as well as to his newly inherited title. The rumors had cooled nearly as quickly as the affair, and though Lynnette may have heard a hint of the relationship, she had clearly neither paid it any mind nor given it any credence.

Now she knew.

Awareness sparked in her eyes and she pulled her shoulders back just a bit, the gesture both defensive and so damned resolute as to make Ravensfield's heart squeeze. She managed the kind of smile that was all the go at occasions such as this: sleek, shallow, and insincere.

"Though you tease each other unmercifully, I can see that you are obviously old and dear friends," Lynnette said. "You must have a great deal to talk about. If you'll just excuse—"

"Nonsense!" Christina's smile glittered and she put a hand on Lynnette's arm, tender and insistent, the better to keep her in place. "There is nothing Ravensfield and I need to say to each other in private. Not any longer. I daresay, everything we ever said to each other in private was probably shouted about the *ton* at any rate. No, no. You stay right here, my dear, and listen to your dear mama's friend for she has much to teach you. You really must take care when you are in the company of a rogue such as this." She turned her sparkling smile on Ravensfield. "He is just the man to add a sheen of scandal to your reputation, my dear Lynnette. And I know your mother would not like that at all."

"I will remember that." Lynnette refused to meet Ravensfield's eyes and he cursed himself because of it. He sorely wished she would so that he might somehow communicate his apology—for Lady Christina's behavior as well as for the years of debauchery that meant that Lynnette would, always, be too far above his reach for hope.

"I promise to be careful," she said, keeping her attention riveted to Christina. "And I thank you for your advice. The duke and I are hardly acquainted but should he ask me for a dance this evening, I will keep your admonitions in mind."

"Should he ask you for a dance this evening or any other, you would do well to turn and run the other way!" Christina softened her warning with a silvery laugh. "He's a scoundrel and that is certain. You must have heard talk of him. The people of the *ton* call your dear cousin Somerton 'Day' because of his sparkling personality and that hair of his that glitters like the sun itself. But they have always known Ravensfield here as 'Night.' There are reasons for that. Reasons beyond his parson's clothing."

"Come, come now, Lady Christina." Keeping a check on his temper—but just barely—Ravensfield joined in the banter in the hopes of ending the conversation before it got even more intimate. And even more embarrassing. "No parson has ever paid nearly as much for a set of togs as I have."

"There! You see! It is just as I say. He is shameless. Really!" Lady Christina's laugh was as bright as the chandeliers overhead but Ravensfield knew her well enough not to be fooled. She had yet to get a rise out of Lynnette, and Christina was never happy unless she was clearly the winner. No matter what the game.

Christina stepped back and tipped her head. "You know, Lynnette, I am surprised that you and Ravensfield do not know each other better," she said. "For your darling mother and I were bosom-bows for many years and you and I have, consequently and much to my delight, always been close. As far as Ravensfield and I . . . well, it wasn't so long ago that the two of us were inseparable." She leaned in close to Ravensfield and made it look like an accident when her breasts brushed his arm. "It seems that you would have crossed paths with the duke sooner than this, considering that he was so often in my company."

She was enjoying this, damn her.

Ravensfield shot a look of warning toward Christina but, as usual, she ignored it. It wasn't as if he were ashamed of his past. Or that he had ever tried to hide it. It was just that there were better ways for Lynnette to be told the story. But then, that would not have gratified Christina at all.

Ravensfield marveled at the woman. She was as beautiful as a diamond. And just as cold. She was as fascinating as a summer storm. And just as dangerous. She was as brazen as any cyprian he had ever met. And all the more tantalizing because of it.

But she wasn't Lynnette.

The thought caught him unawares and he looked Lynnette's way. He was just in time to see her gather her composure along with her golden cloak. "You must excuse me," she said, "I see my cousin Willie across the room, and if I am not very much mistaken, she is looking for me. She may not be feeling well and . . ."

This time, she was not to be put off. Before Ravensfield could say a word, Lynnette was gone.

"I do hope, your grace, that the gleam I see in your eye is meant only for me."

He forgot Christina was there until he heard her voice, like the purr of some ferocious cat.

He pivoted his gaze to her. "The gleam in my eye is

always meant only for you, m'lady. After all, you are the one who put it there."

"Ah, yes, but I am not talking about that gleam! Really, Ravensfield, she's but a child!"

"She's older than I was when you seduced me."

"Seduced you?" Christina pouted. "And here all this time I thought I was the one who had been seduced."

"Perhaps you were."

"Perhaps I could be still." She leaned even closer, her lips no more than a breath from Ravensfield's. "It's been a long time. But we are still so alike, we two."

The very thought made him sick. Perhaps because it wasn't true. Perhaps because it was.

"Are we?" He glanced a look over her. She was still a beautiful woman.

She knew it and, pleased that he'd noticed, she sidled even closer. "Perhaps we might see each other again sometime soon."

"Perhaps . . ." Over Christina's shoulder, Ravensfield scanned the crowd, looking for any sign of Lynnette. When he didn't see her, he shifted his gaze back to Christina. "Perhaps you'd be better served to be more subtle, m'lady. Any man who sees you as the huntress cannot help but know you'd sooner shoot him through the heart than love him."

"Love?" This time, Christina's laugh came out a bit too loud, and realizing it, she pressed a finger to her lips. She backed away and studied him carefully, her expression teetering between disbelief and out-and-out cynicism. "You cannot be serious. Good heavens, man, what does love have to do with any of this?"

"This?" Ravensfield looked all around, but even before he did, he knew the answer to his question. "Nothing," he said, and the realization left him feeling oddly empty. Before he was forced to examine his reasons or his motives, he knew he'd best do what he came to do and get back to Berkshire where he could put this—all of this—behind him.

"If you'll excuse me, m'lady," he said, and bowed to Christina. Before she could say another word, he turned and walked away.

"Damnation!" The word hissed out of Ravensfield and a knot of people who stood in his pathway near the refreshment tables scattered as if by magic. The hardest thing he'd ever done in his life was to come here so that he might speak to Lynnette. The most difficult thing he'd ever *not* done was take her in his arms the moment he saw her and kiss her until her head spun. And his reward?

Not one woman to deal with but two. One more hardheaded than the other. One more bewildering. One more dangerous.

And all he had to do was figure out which was which. And why one bothered him so very much. And the other scared him even more.

"I see you have met my cousin."

For the second time that evening, Ravensfield found himself so lost in his thoughts that he wasn't paying attention to what was happening around him. He turned to find Nicholas Pryce, the Viscount Somerton, sipping a drink. If he had been feeling more like himself and less like one of the heartsick heroes out of one of his own damned books, Ravensfield might have used the opportunity to comment on Somerton's ridiculous costume. Quite obviously, some men were ruled by their wives and their wives' unfortunate whims. Rather than bothering to point it out, he looked toward the dance floor where, the last Ravensfield saw of her, Lynnette had disappeared into the crowd.

"Your cousin! Yes, indeed." The words congealed inside of Ravensfield and he somehow managed a smile that felt as stiff as it no doubt looked. "Charming girl."

"I have often thought so myself." Nick's golden hair glittered in the light. Much like his eyes. "I hope, sir, that you will remember that. She is charming and, in spite of her age, young in the ways of the world. She is also well loved by all who know her and she has a wide circle of friends." Nick's gaze flickered over Ravensfield, saying far more than his words. "She hardly needs a new acquaintance."

So, Somerton didn't know.

At the same time he told himself it hardly mattered, Ravensfield was relieved. At least he didn't have to try to explain to Somerton what he wasn't able to explain to himself. Or listen to any nonsense about pistols at dawn. What he wasn't was surprised. Lynnette was not the type who would go crying her misery and telling the story of her broken heart to her friends and relations.

Except, if Ravensfield was not very much mistaken, she did not look very miserable. And not the least bit heartbroken at all.

At the same time the thought settled inside him like a lump of lead, he saw the golden glimmer of Lynnette's gown and caught a glimpse of her winding her way in and out of the crowd.

His feet were moving that way almost before he realized it. "If you'll excuse—"

"Of course, your grace." The light pressure of Nick's hand upon his arm stopped him. "I only hope you understand when I say—"

"That your dear cousin needs no more friends. Yes, indeed. Rest assured, sir, though my mind has been muddled of late, there is one thing that I know as surely as I know my own name. The lady's friendship is not what I'm interested in."

It wasn't exactly a lie. Which was exactly why Ravensfield didn't feel guilty about saying it. He sidestepped Somerton and hurried as much as he was able through the press of the crowd and into the ballroom. A dance had just ended and he stationed himself near the French windows that led onto the veranda, watching as the couples left the floor. He saw a woman in a turban and started forward. Until he realized the hat was blue and not gold. He saw the bob of another display of feathers—no doubt attached to some outlandish headdress—but when the rest of its wearer came into sight, he saw that this woman was short and plump. Not Lynnette at all.

He was just beginning to wonder if she'd somehow

sneaked past him and out the door when he saw a soldier and Henry the Eighth standing against the far wall. If Ravensfield was not very much mistaken, the soldier had a ruddy complexion and Henry the Eighth, much in fitting with his character for the evening, did not need any padding to fill out his doublet and hose.

"Ah, Misters Hexam and Palliston." Ravensfield insinuated himself into their company, one arm around each man's shoulders. "So good to see you again. And in circumstances that are so much the better than when last we met."

Henry the Eighth's cheeks turned purple. "We were coming around to apologize," Arthur Hexam said. "We had every intention. As soon as word got to us that you were back in London. We simply hadn't heard—"

"I didn't let anyone know." Not wishing to miss an opportunity to catch another glimpse of Lynnette, Ravensfield scanned the groups of people nearby. "I was hoping you might help me. Miss Overton . . ." He took another look around.

Hexam and Palliston exchanged looks.

"I've heard she looks like a dream," Hexam said.

"Not that she doesn't always," Palliston added quickly. "It's just that tonight—"

"More of a dream, I suppose," Hexam concluded with a chuckle. He rubbed a finger under his false beard. "Heard she's in gold. Haven't seen her."

"Gold, did you say?" Palliston craned his neck. "I did see a flash of gold over that way." He pointed toward the French doors that led outside. "Perhaps if you—"

Before either Mr. Hexam or Mr. Palliston could say another word, Ravensfield was headed toward the garden.

She couldn't breathe.

Lynnette pressed a hand to her bosom and struggled to pull in a breath of air. Her heart was beating so fast she could barely contain it. Her hands were trembling. Her knees were weak.

There was a bench nearby in an alcove near a window that looked out at the garden and she hurried over and sat down. It was a good thing. She was certain her legs wouldn't hold her another second.

She bit her lower lip, barely controlling the sob that threatened to escape her. It was ridiculous, of course. Ridiculous to feel as if she'd been betrayed. She'd always known of Ravensfield's reputation. It was hardly news. Yet Ravensfield and Lady Christina . . .

She slipped a finger beneath her mask to wipe away a tear.

Doubly betrayed.

She sniffed back her disappointment and schooled her emotions. As trivial as it was, no doubt the fact that she and Ravensfield were seen talking together in the refreshment room was already news on the lips of the town gossips. She did not need to add to their arsenal or contribute to the chin-wagging, and she most certainly would should anyone see her crying.

Her mind made up, Lynnette took a careful look around. Through the rainbow sea of colorful costumes, she saw a glimpse of somber black, headed her way like a thunderstorm. There was only so long she could pretend that she could look at Ravensfield and not feel the world crumbling at her feet. Only so long that she could act as if he were nothing more than an annoyance and that every time she thought of him, her heart didn't crack a little more, just like her composure. She didn't dare take the chance of encountering him again.

She gulped in a breath for courage. There was a doorway nearby and she headed for it, not sure where it would lead and, at this point, not caring.

A few moments later, she found herself outside.

She stripped off her mask and dropped it on the ground, then hurried across the wide veranda and down the steps that led into the garden. Once she was there, she needed to stop only for a moment to get her bearings.

"Past the fountain," Lynnette told herself. "Around the fishpond." She had been to Lady Christina's home enough times to know her way around and she followed her own directions and the stone path that meandered through the grounds. Always the consummate hostess, Christina had thought of everything, even the comfort of her guests who might wish to stroll the garden. Here and there along the path, torches were lit, and Lynnette was grateful for the light for it allowed her to move quickly, each moment putting more distance between herself and the sounds of laughter and music that flowed from the house. On the other side of the rose garden she knew there was an intersecting path, one that led toward the stables. There, she would find Garvey and Garvey would take her home.

She was nearly there when a figure stepped onto the path some ten feet ahead of her.

She was some distance beyond the last torch and the man stood in shadow; it was impossible to see his face. She didn't need to. As always, Ravensfield's white linen showed like moonglow, a bright contrast to his somber clothing.

Lynnette pulled herself up short and blinked back the tears that threatened to blind her. "You have an inadequate memory, sir," she told him, her voice trembling only a little but a little more than she liked. "I thought I made myself quite clear. We have nothing to say to each other."

He didn't reply but merely took a step nearer.

Lynnette stood her ground. "If it's company you seek, you might find a more willing companion than me."

He took another step in her direction.

Lynnette raised her chin. "As a matter of fact, I am leaving. As you and she are old and obviously very dear friends, you will, no doubt, see Lady Christina again this evening. Perhaps you might extend my apologies. I am feeling unwell and—"

The man took yet another step closer, and for the first time, the light touched his face and she realized her mistake.

This wasn't Ravensfield.

But he wasn't a complete stranger. She recognized the man. The last time she'd seen him, he was outside her bedroom window at Plumley Terrace, jiggling the lock on her door.

Panic overwhelmed Lynnette and the emotions she'd been holding so tightly burst from her along with a startled cry.

"I . . ." Lynnette took a backward step. "I don't know what you want. What you think I—"

"You know exactly what it is that I'm after, my fine lady." The man's voice was gravelly, uneducated. Just as he was the last time she'd seen him, he was swathed head to toe in black but Lynnette saw a movement at his side. The torchlight glinted off the thin blade of a knife. "You 'ave the key. The one what explains them coded pages. You must."

"I don't know what you're talking about." She took another step back and considered the wisdom of running. "Keys and codes and—"

The rough sound of his laughter stopped her protest. "You know I'll get it. Sooner or later. Now be a good girl and—"

She didn't wait to hear any more. Just inside the enveloping shadows where the light of the last torch met the night, Lynnette turned and ran.

She had gone no more than a few feet when she felt a tug on her cloak. The fabric tore and the man's grip loosened. He cursed, and heartened, she ran faster, heading back to the veranda and the safety of the house. She had nearly gone as far as the next torch when his hand gripped the back of her neck.

The darkness whirled around her and the next thing she knew Lynnette felt herself falling. Her breath whooshed out of her and she found herself flat on her back with the man bent over her. His fingers were around her neck, his knife at her throat.

"The key," he said. "Tell me where I might find it. Now. Or I'll—"

"Damn it, but I really don't think so."

It was so hard to breathe, Lynnette supposed her mind must be affected. That would certainly explain why she imagined hearing Ravensfield's voice.

At the sound of it, as nonchalant as if they were at a garden party and discussing nothing more momentous than the weather, the man in black tensed and his eyes narrowed. The next thing she knew, he sprang to his feet and attacked the duke.

Lynnette struggled for breath and raised herself on her elbows. She was just in time to see Ravensfield parry an uppercut.

The man in black lost his footing, and while he was still off balance, the duke landed a punch to his jaw. The man's head snapped back and Ravensfield saw his opportunity and used it to his full advantage. He landed another blow and Lynnette's attacker staggered.

She knew he was not vanquished.

"Careful," Lynnette called out, "he has a—"

Her warning came too late.

Ravensfield grunted and fell. Lurching, the man in black escaped into the darkness.

Lynnette rolled to her side and struggled to her feet. The duke hadn't moved. Her stomach swooped and her heart thumped. Afraid of what she might see when she got there, she hurried over to where he lay.

There was a cut on Ravensfield's neck that went from his ear nearly to his chin. Fortunately, it was not deep. He was still breathing.

At the same time Lynnette fell to her knees beside him, she whispered a prayer of thanksgiving. She shook him. "Are you hurt too badly? Shall I scream for help? It was the man in black. The one who tried to steal the key to the code."

The look Ravensfield gave her was nothing short of long-suffering. "Yes, I know. I have word about it, you see, and about the Wonderlee Diamond. I told you we needed to talk."

16

"A woman should not be on these streets alone."

Lynnette wasn't surprised to see Ravensfield. She was, however, annoyed. From the moment they'd had their talk after the assault at the masquerade ball a week earlier, she suspected he would make a nuisance of himself and try to come along on this little expedition. She had done her best to sneak out of the house without being seen, but in spite of her precautions, he had followed her.

She glanced to her left where he walked between her and the street, which was noticeably dirtier than it was in the finer sections of town.

"I am not alone," she said, looking over her shoulder to where her carriage waited. "Garvey is with me. If I didn't insist that he stay with the horses, no doubt he'd be walking at my side right now."

"No doubt." The hint of a satisfied smile touched

Ravensfield's lips and Lynnette knew instantly what it meant.

"He saw you." She kept walking, her head high, her gaze straight ahead. "He saw you following us. That's why it was so easy to convince him to stay with the carriage."

"Perhaps."

She slid another look in Ravensfield's direction.

"Perhaps?" The word was as unrevealing as the enigmatic expression on the duke's face and Lynnette sniffed her opinion of it and of his resistance to telling her the truth. "I think *perhaps* . . ." She emphasized the word. "There is a possibility that Garvey did not have to look for you at all. Perhaps he knew you'd be here."

"Garvey is a good man. He only wishes to make certain that you're safe."

"As you can see . . ." She skirted the edges of a puddle. "I most certainly am. I do not need an escort."

"That's a damned fine way to treat a man who saved your life!"

"You did." She stopped so that she might look at him. "And I thank you for it. Just as I thanked you at the masquerade ball. Now . . ." She started up again. "You may leave me alone."

Ravensfield kept pace. "You know I can't do that," he said.

She sighed with annoyance. And congratulated herself. Sighing was a better alternative to what she felt like doing, and what she felt like doing was crumbling into little pieces. Just as she'd felt like doing since that night back at Broadworth. Even more so since the masquerade ball when every time she thought of all they'd done together and all she thought she meant to Ravensfield, she pictured him in the arms of Lady Christina.

Her throat tightened and Lynnette coughed away the sensation. "You are the one who told me to come here. At the masquerade ball. You are the one who said—"

"That I had made some inquiries on your behalf and that those inquiries led here. Yes, of course I remember." He sidestepped his way around a man who was lying half in and half out of the gutter, and though Lynnette was tempted to stop to see what was wrong with the poor man and how she might help, Ravensfield put a hand on her arm and hurried her along.

"Not on these streets," he said, keeping his hand on her arm even after they'd passed the man. "It isn't safe."

"I thought because you were with me, I didn't have to worry." His touch felt like the sunshine that refused to make its way through the fog and chimney smoke that clogged the sky over the tightly packed buildings and narrow streets. She could not afford to let herself luxuriate in the sensation. She twitched his hand away, preferring the cold to the light that felt like real heat and was nothing more than evanescence.

"What were you doing?" she asked him. "Watching Plumley Terrace? Guards at all the doors?"

He chuckled. “Worthy is a good man and always up for an adventure. Much to the dismay of Betty, his most recent sweetheart, he’s taken quite a liking to that kitchen maid of yours. The little blond-haired one whom you sometimes send outside to cut flowers.”

“Fern?” Lynnette was not surprised. The girl was pretty and intelligent. “Then Mr. Worthy has been guarding the back of the house.”

“And I—” A man and woman walked out of a rough-looking pub, arm in arm and none too steady on their feet, and he stopped to let them by. Rather than risk having him take hold of her again, Lynnette stopped, too. “I have had the honor of guarding the front of the house.”

“Guarding? Or spying?”

“You need ask? After the incident in the garden?”

Heat flushed Lynnette’s cheeks. It took a moment for her to realize that he was talking about the incident in Lady Christina’s garden. Not what had happened back in the garden of Broadworth Hall.

She looked at the cut on his neck, nearly healed now. “You sustained no permanent injury, I trust.”

He pressed a hand to his heart, the motion so quick as to make her think she might have imagined it. And so poignant that she wondered if, perhaps, he was thinking of the garden at Broadworth, too. Just as quickly, his hand went to his neck, his fingers feeling the edges of the wound left by the knife of her attacker.

“Nothing life-threatening,” he said. “And certainly nothing serious enough to stop me from keeping an eye on you. A man would think you'd be grateful for a little protection."

This time, the color that flushed through Lynnette's face had nothing to do with Broadworth Hall. And everything to do with embarrassment.

"Of course. I should have—" She stopped so suddenly that Ravensfield was already a couple of steps ahead when he realized she wasn't with him. He came back to where she stood. "I'm sorry. I should have thanked you properly that night. I would have. Had you given me the chance."

"My shortcoming, I'm afraid. After the attack, I thought it all the more important for you to hear what I'd come to tell you."

"And I haven't thanked you for that, either." She forced herself to look into his eyes. Bad enough that she had taken so long to express her gratitude. Worse when she let her own wayward emotions get in the way of what was proper. "Thank you for coming to my rescue back at the masquerade ball. If you hadn't been there—"

"If I hadn't been there, I daresay some other blighter would have come along and been your hero."

"I don't think so. I don't think anyone else will ever be my hero."

He glanced away.

"And thank you, too, for the inquiries you made on my behalf. It was good of you to take the service upon yourself, but really, it is my problem. I can handle it myself."

He shrugged away the compliment. "I simply wrote some letters. To people who might know what happened that weekend your mother was accused of taking the jewel. I simply asked some questions. About diamonds. And how a person might profit from them. Especially when the diamond in question is too notorious to be seen in public. You may be surprised to know that I have a wide assortment of not-so-scrupulous acquaintances. They answered my inquiries and sent me around to other unscrupulous people. Their answers led here. I thought it only right to tell you about the results of my investigation, but I did not think to give you wholesale permission to go wandering in areas of the city such as this." Before she could object, he wound an arm through hers and continued on. "When I told you what I'd learned, I hoped you might ask me to accompany you."

"You made it clear back at Broadworth that my company was not something you were interested in."

"Did I?" He hesitated before they crossed the next street. As if he were tempted to stop and face her, tempted to cup her chin in his hand and turn her face up to his. He didn't, and she was grateful. It would have been too much to bear.

"I think I have caused you a good deal of distress," he said instead. "And I'm very sorry for it. We must talk about what happened."

It was not something she looked forward to, but lest he suspect it, she forced herself to say, "Then talk."

The door to another pub swung open and a rush of

putrid air came out along with a man who staggered toward them.

"Not here," Ravensfield said. "For now . . ." He stopped at the next street and pointed. "There. I think this is the place we're looking for."

Lynnette studied the stone building with its narrow doorway, badly in need of paint, its grimy windows and its cracked stoop. The sign that hung above the entryway was old and the paint was worn and chipped. It was difficult to read and she wondered, had she been alone, if she would have found the place at all. For the first time since he'd come upon her unawares, she was glad to have Ravensfield with her.

He opened the door and the small brass bell hung above it rang. He stepped back to allow her to enter the shop first. "Don't say too much," he whispered when she was already inside.

It took a few moments for Lynnette's eyes to adjust to the dim light, and when they did, she saw that there was a long, narrow table along the far wall and behind that, a shelf on which there were clocks displayed. Each was set to its own beat, their ticking a clatter. To her left, a curtained doorway led into a back room, and beyond it, she heard the shuffled response to their arrival.

"Comin'," the voice called, and the next second, a balding man as tall as a pole and just as thin, pushed aside the curtain. His eyes were small and yellow, like a rat's. When they alighted upon his visitors, he gave a visible start. "I'm thinkin' you two 'ave got the wrong place," he said.

"Not if you are Mr. Fryer." Ravensfield stepped forward. "I've been sent by a friend."

"A friend? Is that so?" His eyes narrowed, Fryer looked them up and down. Apparently, he approved of what he saw for his face took on a kind of sheen and his yellow eyes sparked. "Here to buy, guv?" he asked. "Or to sell?"

"Perhaps a bit of both."

"Lovely." Fryer gave them a gap-toothed smile. "If it's something for the lady you're looking for—"

"It's information we're looking for, Mr. Fryer." Lynnette stepped forward. "Information about a diamond."

Ravensfield rolled his eyes. "You'll have to excuse my companion," he said, in that comfortable tone men adopt when they are trying to sound too friendly with other men they hardly know. "She sometimes does not exhibit a great deal of patience."

"I've been patient for nine years now." Lynnette turned to Mr. Fryer. "We've been told by a reliable source that you may have purchased a diamond at about that time," she said to him. "A large diamond. Very valuable and quite unique."

The glitter in Fryer's eyes dissolved to wariness. He ignored Lynnette and turned to Ravensfield. He scratched a finger behind his ear. "Diamond, eh? You can't possibly think that a 'onest businessman such as myself—"

"Nonsense, Mr. Fryer." Lynnette moved forward, the better to be seen and so, perhaps, not ignored. "From what we have heard, you are exactly the kind of businessman who—"

"Who knows how to deal wisely." Ravensfield stepped between Lynnette and Mr. Fryer. He reached into his pocket, fished out a gold sovereign and put it on the table. "We want only information. Nothing more. And we promise complete confidentiality."

"Is that so?" Fryer picked up the coin and bit it. Satisfied it was real, he tucked it in his pocket. "Information about a diamond, you say?"

Ravensfield had apparently dealt with men such as Mr. Fryer before. He took out another coin but this time he didn't set it down. With Fryer watching the whole time, he tossed it into the air and caught it.

"I have heard tell," Ravensfield said, "that there are places right here in London that deal with stolen jewels. Stones, mostly, for they are the easiest to recut and sell. Far be it from me to think you might be associated with any dealings of that sort, Mr. Fryer. But if you were . . ." He threw the coin again and this time Fryer could not control himself. He made a move to snatch it.

Ravensfield was quicker. He scooped the coin out of midair and slapped it into his palm. "If you were, I'm thinking that perhaps you might be able to tell me who brought the stone to you to be recut and sold."

Fryer weighed the value of the second sovereign against any information he might have. He ran his tongue over his lips and looked at the coin. "Some of them what I deal with, sir, are not the sorts who would take news of my prattlin' well. If it's found out that I've spoken with you—"

"It will not be."

"But if it is, I might be in some difficulties, if you get my drift." He stared at the coin. "Difficulties that, just maybe, might be eased, so to speak, by a bit o' the blunt."

"Do you know who I am?"

At Ravensfield's question, Fryer's gaze snapped to his. "I can venture a guess," he said. He cast a look over the duke's black clothing and his blacker scowl. "I have heard tell."

"Then you know I am not a man to be trifled with. You would be wise to remember that. The people you do business with might be dangerous, but I am more dangerous still. Do you have any doubt of it?"

"But—"

"If you have something to tell me, Mr. Fryer, then tell it and be done." Ravensfield slipped the coin back into his pocket. "If not, then tell me that and I will take my companion—and my sovereigns—and leave."

Fryer's gaze homed in on the duke's pocket. "I might know something," he said. "Though it was a good, long time ago and a fellow's memory tends to fade over time."

Satisfied with even that much, Ravensfield took out the coin and flipped it at the jeweler. "Perhaps that will grease the wheels of your memory."

Fryer grinned. "Indeed!" He tucked this gold coin

away with the last. "Perhaps a little more greasing—"

"You would not be wise to try and play games with me, Mr. Fryer!" His hands flat upon the table, Ravensfield leaned closer to the man, and though Mr. Fryer was taller than the duke, the rumble of annoyance in Ravensfield's voice was enough to make him shrink back against the wall.

"Of course not!" Fryer's laugh was nervous. "Whoever would have thought such a thing? It's only as how a fellow can't be sure, if you know what I mean, guv. He can't be sure of who he's dealin' with and who can be trusted like and who cannot be."

"Do you know who you dealt with then?" Lynnette moved forward. She had waited a long time to hear the real story of what had happened to the Wonderlee Diamond, and while Mr. Fryer might not have all the details, it was obvious he knew at least a part of the tale. "Do you remember who brought you the diamond?"

"Never said as how—" Fryer took another look at the duke and thought better of continuing the game. "I remember," he said.

Lynnette's heart leapt. "Do you know the man's name?"

"Man?" Fryer shook his head. His hair was long and thin and it drooped around his shoulders. "Wasn't no man what sold me that there diamond," he said. "It was a woman."

Ice flooded Lynnette's veins and for a moment she was too shocked to say a word. When her voice returned it sounded—even to her—as if it came from very far away. "A woman? Surely you must be mistaken! It couldn't have been."

"Sure as the good Lord made apples, miss. It was a woman, I remember it as well as I remember the faces of my own children. For she was not the sort of woman who is usual to these parts. I get the light-skirts in here mostly, if you take my meaning, sir." He looked toward Ravensfield and winked. "You know them, always eager to sell what they have stolen from gentlemen after they are done—" He remembered himself and Mr. Fryer's face turned scarlet. He cleared his throat.

"Beggin' your pardon, miss, for I can see you ain't of that ilk. And neither was she. The woman who brought me that there diamond."

"You didn't ask where she got it?" Ravensfield's question seemed as logical as can be yet it made Fryer chuckle.

"Ain't none of my business to ask where any of them get what it is they bring to me," he said. "And especially not this one. She was what you'd call bang up to the mark. A real lady, that one was."

Ravensfield's eyes narrowed. "What did she look like?"

"Her height," Fryer said, glancing at Lynnette. "Her coloring, though the hair . . ." He squeezed his eyes shut, thinking very hard. "Can't say I remember it. At least not for certain sure." He shook himself back to the present. "She wore a sort of bonnet. You know, sir, the way some ladies do. The way I remember it, it came low over her brow and she had the hood of her cloak pulled up over that. I couldn't rightly tell about the hair."

"Thin? Plump? Pretty? Plain?" Ravensfield peppered the man with questions. "Come on, man, there has to be more you remember about her. Especially if she was so unusual. Was she alone?"

"As near as I can remember. And you have to admit, in these parts, that takes a certain brass and no mistake." As if picturing everything that had happened that day, he looked around the room. "I do remember her standing just there, right where you are, sir. And the way the light played over her face, as it were. It were shadowed some by that hood, if you get the picture. But all the same, she was a pretty thing." Fryer pulled himself out of the reminiscence and gave Ravensfield a wary look. "Beggin' your pardon, sir, if she is some sort of relation."

The duke waved away the apology.

"Never seen anything like that cloak she was wearing, sir, if you get my drift. And I know it sounds daft, me remembering it so well, but my missus, she was in the back room that day, and hearin' a stranger's voice and a woman's at that, she peeked through the curtain." He looked toward the doorway that led to the back of the shop. "Talked about that there cloak and about how fine it was until the very day she died, she did. It was that elegant, sir. Black velvet, it was. With one of them fur collars. And not just any fur, but that what's white and dotted with black."

When Ravensfield looked Lynnette's way, there was a question in his eyes.

What did he expect her to say?

Yes, Madelaine had a black velvet cloak. Yes, it was trimmed with ermine. There weren't many women who could afford such luxury, yet Lynnette had such a cloak herself. So might a hundred other women. It meant nothing. She refused to let so small a thing condemn her mother or change her mind.

"She was as pretty a picture as I've ever seen," Fryer continued. "Beggin' your pardon, miss," he added for Lynnette's benefit when he thought he might have offended. "She was eager to sell the jewel. But she was nobody's fool. She knew what it was worth and she wasn't about to accept too little."

Ravensfield turned to her. "Was Madelaine the type who might be—"

"Fearless enough to bargain?" Lynnette had no need to hear the end of Ravensfield's question. "You would not have known it toward the end of her life, for once the world turned against her, she was timid and too often in the clutches of the blue devils. But in her prime . . . yes." She turned away, the better to hide the tears that suddenly filled her eyes. "She was bold enough to bargain and not one to back down when the bargain was not to her liking."

"And as pretty as a summer day." Fryer shook his head. "That's for certain sure."

Lynnette swiped her hands over her cheeks before

she turned around. "Would you know her? If you saw her again, would you recognize her?"

Fryer looked uncertain. "I might. I suppose. It's been a good long while, a'course, but it's hard to forget a woman such as that. Especially when she brings along a diamond the likes of which I ain't seen before or since."

When she reached into her red morocco reticule, Lynnette's hand were shaking. If Ravensfield noticed, he was kind enough not to mention it. He watched as she withdrew a golden locket. She stepped closer to the table and snapped it open. There was a miniature portrait of Madelaine inside it. Briefly, she studied the face. It was no accident that Madelaine was the toast of the town. Golden haired and blue eyed, she had skin like porcelain and features that were small and even, like those of a Roman statue.

Lynnette tipped the portrait toward Mr. Fryer. "Is this her?" she asked. "Is this the woman who brought you the Wonderlee Diamond?"

For a few seconds, Fryer did nothing but stare at the portrait and Lynnette held her breath. Finally, he nodded. "It very well could be," he said. "Very well could be, indeed."

She did not remember putting the locket away. Nor did she remember leaving Mr. Fryer's shop. But the next thing Lynnette knew, she found herself outside on the pavement. Tears stung her eyes, and though she would have sworn she hid them most effectively, the moment

Ravensfield closed the door behind him and joined her on the pavement, he held a handkerchief out to her.

Without a word, she accepted it and blotted her eyes, turning away from him as she did, the better to endure her misery alone.

Damn but he wished he knew what to do to comfort her!

Ravensfield stood staring at Lynnette's back, completely in awe of the strength it took for her to keep her composure as much as she did. Her courage only made him feel more helpless and ineffective and feeling helpless and ineffective was not something he was used to. He was not one whit happy about it.

It wasn't part of his image to be inarticulate and fumbling, damn it! It certainly was not in line with his reputation or with the devil-may-care persona he had taken so many years to build and so many more to perfect. He was known as a man of action, and certainly not as one who found himself undone by a cascade of female tears.

That man—the Ravensfield of legend—would have known exactly what to do. He would not stand here like a looby, mute and benumbed by emotions that were as foreign as they were disquieting. Now if only he could work his way through the problem of what had happened to that old Ravensfield and his legendary sangfroid. Then he might be able to understand where this new Ravensfield had come from and how, when he wasn't looking and certainly without his consent, he had turned from one man into the other.

The old Ravensfield would have made light of the

problem, perhaps offering a glass of champagne to tickle away the lady's tears, and a memorable night in his bed to make her forget her troubles completely.

He shifted from foot to foot, listening to the sounds of Lynnette's gentle sobs.

The new Ravensfield was not the man he'd ever thought to be, and finding himself face-to-face with him now, he could think of only one thing to do. For the first time in his life, he listened to a heart that, before he met Lynnette, he was not sure he even had. And before the old Ravensfield reminded him that it was inane to the extreme—not to mention weak in the way that the doleful, lovesick heroes of his books were often weak—he took Lynnette into his arms and kissed her.

17

It did nothing to solve the problem. But, la, it made her feel better!

Lynnette drank in the comfort of Ravensfield's lips, the warmth she found in his arms. It was but a moment's reprieve, she was not foolish enough to think it could ever be more. But even one moment without the grinding realization of her mother's guilt was a moment for which she was grateful.

The feel of his mouth against hers was exquisite, the touch of his hands, pyrotechnic, and a tiny moan rose from her throat. It was that, perhaps, which awakened the memories of all that had happened back at Broadworth. And all that had resulted.

"I know where this leads." Lynnette broke off the contact and moved back a step, the better to convince herself that this was utter madness. "It is cruel of you to take advantage—"

"The only thing I'm taking advantage of is the moment." Ravensfield's mouth pulled into a one-sided smile. "I certainly have no intention of taking advantage of the miss."

"So you say." Lynnette raised her chin. "Yet if our history is any indication—"

"If our history is any indication, then we are fools to let the opportunity for happiness pass us by."

Her mouth fell open. "You cannot be serious."

"I can. I am." He took her hand, and as he did, he looked around at the people passing by. Unused to seeing people of quality and most especially unused to seeing people of quality who happened to be standing in the middle of the pavement and kissing, a crowd had begun to gather and had not stopped staring.

He tipped his tall top hat to them and wound an arm through Lynnette's. "We'll send Garvey on home ahead of us and talk in my carriage," he said. "There's a great deal we need to say to each other, Miss Overton, and as much as I am tempted to say it all here and now and get it over with, I think this is neither the time nor the place."

"But I—"

"In the carriage." He pressed one finger gently to her lips and glanced from side to side. "There, at least, we will not have an audience."

It was impossible to argue with his logic. But once they were settled inside the duke's luxurious closed carriage and started on their way back to Plumley Terrace, the enormity of all that had happened washed over Lynnette like a cold wave. She shivered.

Ravensfield was seated across from her and he moved to sit at her side. "It cannot be easy to find out a truth you had not wished to hear."

"I always thought her innocent." The idea was so ingrained that thinking of it otherwise made Lynnette feel empty. As if a part of her had been removed. "All those years, I believed her when she said she had nothing to do with the theft of the Wonderlee Diamond."

"Of course you believed. You were a good daughter and you are a fine person. The very thought of such betrayal is foreign to you."

"Or perhaps I am simply a fool!" She clutched her hands together on her lap. "Could I have been so blind for so long?"

"Or so faithful."

"To what? My own dream of all a mother should be?" Before she knew it, there were tears in her eyes again, and she dabbed at them with Ravensfield's handkerchief. "I deluded myself."

"Madelaine deluded you."

"It cannot be!" Her voice vibrated with emotion. "She wouldn't have lied. Not to me. And besides, think it through. It doesn't make any sense at all. If Madeleine took the diamond, then why write part of the diary in code? Why write about the incident at all? And why is someone so anxious to get hold of the key and translate the code if all it proves is what everyone thinks to be true in the first place?"

"Good questions." Ravensfield put one hand over both of hers. "Perhaps the part of the diary that is written in code isn't about the Wonderlee Diamond at all."

It was something Lynnette had considered but she had never given it any credence. "You mean—"

"The diary may reveal the answer to some other intrigue, something Madeleine thought important enough to keep secret."

It wasn't easy to admit to the possibility and Lynnette's shoulders sagged. "All this time, I believed she was made to look culpable by some other, guilty party." She sniffed back fresh tears. Her gaze alighted on his hand over hers and her lower lips trembled. His support meant the world to her but not if it was given because he felt some obligation.

"I will learn to live with this news, just as I learned to live with the sidelong glances that are sent my way whenever Madeleine's name is mentioned in conversation," she told him. "You needn't pity me."

"Pity!" Ravensfield barked out a laugh. "If that's what you think this is, you are sorely mistaken, madam."

"Then what is it, do you suppose? You cannot have feelings for me. Not after . . ." She glanced out the window, weighing the advantage of speaking the whole truth against the possibility of spending the rest of her life wondering where they had gone wrong.

She turned to him. "What about the wager?"

He cast the thought aside with an airy wave of one hand. "I have been known to wager myself. A time or two."

It was not enough to dissuade her. "You cannot have feelings for me. I thought you did. When we made love.

But when we were finished and you treated me as if I were nothing more to you than—"

"You called me Thomas."

His voice was a rough whisper but it was as powerful as a shout. Her words dissolved and she looked at him in wonder.

"I called you—"

"Thomas." He wound his fingers through hers. "It was as intimate a thing as any woman has ever shared with me."

"Not as intimate as—"

"Yes. Truly." He looked into her eyes and she saw there a reflection of the same emotions that tore at her heart. Her longing was his. Her aching need for him was but a mirror image of what he felt for her. Her spirits soared, and as if he felt the same, a small smile touched his lips.

"I have spent my life being little more than my title," he told her. "To my friends and, yes, even to my lovers. I am Ravensfield. Always. Or 'your grace,' which is worse. I cannot say I'm surprised, for as a child I saw my grandfather treated in such a way, and when he died and my father came into the title, it was exactly what happened to him. Before I inherited . . ." He drew in a breath and let it out slowly.

"I swore things would be different for me. That I wouldn't become my title and nothing more. Unfortunately, that is not the way of the world. I learned as much once my father died and I inherited. The world perceived me as 'your grace' and 'Ravensfield' and 'the duke.' And after a while, I started acting as if it were true. As if this Ravensfield fellow were someone else altogether from me, someone who could act as he liked and do what he wished behind the mask of that title. That is why, when you spoke my name . . . When you looked upon me as a man and not just simply a title—"

"I did not mean to insult you."

"You silly, wonderful woman!" He leaned forward and brushed her lips with a fleeting kiss. A smile that was as warm and as bright as sunshine broke over his expression. "Don't you see? You were the first one. The only one."

As tempted as she was to be drawn in by the honey of his voice and her own aching need for him, she was not so easily swayed. "I am glad I touched your heart. I will not lie and say it isn't true. But I am no gull. I cannot forget how you treated me."

"And I can never begin to explain how sorry I am. It surprised me, you see. The sweetness of your love. The trust I saw there in your eyes. The honesty of the whole thing. I must tell you, my dear Lynnette, it shook me to my core. It also frightened me to death!" As if relieved to finally share the secret, he let go a long breath. "I walked the grounds all night thinking about it and all it meant. I looked for you the next morning so that I might tell you. But by then, you were already gone and I realized that I had let the best thing that ever happened to me slip from my fingers. I have another confession." He glanced at her out of the corner of his eye.

"All those emotions, they frighten me still. As does

the truth that's been staring me in the face almost since the moment I met you. I love you, Lynnette."

"Love?" It was what she'd hoped to hear but still, it made no sense. After all they'd said and done, it was as impossible to fathom as a man standing on the moon. "You cannot love a woman such as me! Why, you are the Duke of Ravensfield and I am only—"

"There, you see. Even you can get it all wrong. I'm not anything or anyone but Thomas Flander, and if I happen also to be the Duke of Ravensfield, it is but a circumstance of my birth and that alone. There's nothing I can do about it. But I can do something about the man I am and about the woman I choose to love."

Her eyes went wide. "I—"

"No, don't say anything. Not now. Not yet. I want you to think about what I've said. Before you say something you might not mean and you might later regret, I want you to look at the whole situation logically."

"Does love have anything to do with logic?"

"Not always!"

She felt a smile break through her wonderment. "You cannot be serious!"

"I am." He kissed her again. Longer this time. Harder. By the time he was finished, Lynnette struggled for breath and adjusted her bonnet where it had gone askew thanks to his enthusiasm.

"I will most gladly tell you right now what I think of your confession."

"Oh, no! There is much you need to know about me, still, and when you do, you may yet change your mind."

"You are not really a vampire?" Laughter sparkled in her voice.

"I am not a vampire." He nodded, putting the rumor to an end, once and for all. "But there are other things. Things that might embarrass you."

"Ah." Coldness crept in to smother the warmth of his affection. "You are talking about Lady Christina."

His jaw clenched and he looked surprised, as if this was not what he meant to talk about at all. He cocked his head and studied her. "Does it bother you so much to think of us together?"

"Yes, of course." The admission made her sound as unsophisticated as a schoolgirl and Lynnette wished she could call back the words. Because she couldn't, she knew her only defense was the truth. "I know it is foolish to say. We did not even know each other when you and Lady Christina were—" Perhaps she *was* as unsophisticated as a schoolgirl. She could not bring herself to say the words.

"It is not as if it were some sort of betrayal. And yet . . ." She collected her thoughts and, she hoped, the right words to explain herself. "I have always looked upon her as something of a kindly aunt."

"Your kindly aunt has a heart of glass." Ravensfield's brows dropped over his eyes. "There was no real affection between us. She saw me as a plaything. Nothing more."

"And you saw her . . ."

"As young men often see beautiful women who are older and more worldly. As a goddess. A queen. She knew things—" He leaned nearer. "Things I will most happily teach you should you give me the chance."

Her cheeks heated but even that was not enough to blunt her sudden anger. "She took advantage of your youth and your innocence!"

"I'd hardly go that far." He chuckled. "I had been up at Oxford, after all, and it is nearly impossible for a man of money and position to stay completely innocent. Even there."

"But she seduced you."

"Most assuredly. And I let myself be seduced. I was the envy of all my friends. The talk of the *ton*. It wasn't until I realized that she was just the same as all the others that I came to my senses."

"Just the same? You mean—"

"That she saw the title. And the fortune. That she never saw the man."

"And when you see her now?"

Ravensfield looked grim. "I see a woman who is so self-absorbed that she does not care about anyone but herself. She has treated other young men as she treated me. Since we parted company. She has used them and discarded them. It sickens me to think that once upon a very long time ago, I could not see past her beauty to her real character."

"You must pardon me for being so skeptical, but is it character a man wants in a woman?"

A warm smile lit his eyes. "A man wants a certain beauty in a woman. Yes, I won't deny that." He glided a finger over her cheek. "The kind of beauty I see when I look at you. He wants flash, as well. And who can blame him? A woman who is dull in bed makes for a poor companion." He touched a kiss to her lips. "I think you will agree that we are most suitable in that province."

Her smile told him she had not forgotten.

"But a man wants character in a woman, too. The kind of character I see in you. Can you forgive me for being a dolt? Will you allow me to call on you?"

The kiss she gave him was all the answer he needed.

By the time she arrived home, Lynnette's bonnet was off completely. Her hair was partly undone, one side of it hanging around her shoulder in a tumble of curls. Her clothing was in disarray. Ravensfield's kisses still warm upon her lips, she climbed down from his carriage and wished him a good night. She was already inside the front door of Plumley Terrace before she realized she had a visitor.

"Christina!" It was foolish to feel as if she'd been caught in the act, like a child apprehended with a taste of forbidden sweets still on his lips. Yet Lynnette could hardly help herself. Lady Christina stepped out of the morning room where she'd been waiting and skimmed a look over her mussed hair, her wrinkled clothing, her swollen lips.

In spite of the fact that she knew she had nothing to be ashamed of, Lynnette felt her face get hot. She smoothed a hand over her pelisse, fighting the temptation to check and see if she'd remembered to fasten the buttons that Ravensfield had gone to a great deal of trouble to unfasten so that he might caress her.

"You really must learn to be more discreet." Christina looked over her shoulder toward the windows of the morning room that looked out over the street. "And to choose your companions with more care."

"I can't imagine what you mean." Though she always greeted Lady Christina with a peck on the cheek, this time Lynnette refrained. It would feel odd and be too insincere, and rather than risk either, she kept her place.

If Christina was surprised, she didn't show it. She looked down her well-shaped nose at Lynnette. "If you are to continue down this path, you must also learn to be a better liar."

Lynnette was saved from giving a reply when Mrs. Wilcox appeared—as she always did—as if out of nowhere. She handed her housekeeper her pelisse and gloves. "Lady Christina has been offered tea?" she asked.

"She was offered it, ma'am, and she refused."

"Then perhaps a glass of sherry?" Lynnette forced herself to smile and led the way into the morning room. She went to the sideboard. "You may need some refreshment if you've been waiting long."

"Too long." Christina tossed her beaded reticule onto the sofa and strolled over to where Lynnette filled two crystal aperitif glasses. "Had I known you were with Ravensfield—"

When Lynnette turned to her in wonder, Christina smiled. "My, my child. You do have a great deal to learn if you pay no mind to what is so very obvious." She accepted the glass that Lynnette handed her and took a tiny sip. "His coat of arms is painted on the side of his carriage, of course," she said. "I do hope you haven't done anything foolish, Lynnette dear."

"Do you?" Lynnette took a sip, too. She was not in the habit of drinking sherry. She wasn't even sure she liked sherry. But she needed something to do with her hands lest Lady Christina detect how upended she'd been by all that had happened to her in the past hours. "You must excuse me for asking, Christina dear, but why in the world do you think it is any of your business?"

Christina threw back her head and laughed. "What would your mother say if she heard you speaking like this?"

The reminder of all she'd learned that afternoon was still too fresh and Lynnette refused to consider it. "My mother is not here," she said. "And though you were her true friend, I wonder if the things you say to me mean that you are mine."

Still smiling, Christina set down her glass. She strolled about the room, her head tipped to one side, her face serene. Lynnette had left her copy of *Greystone Castle* there in the morning and Christina picked it up and cradled it in her arms. When she'd returned to London, Lynnette had removed the precious paper from inside the cover. It was sewn into the hem of her gown, safely with her at all times. Still, it did not keep her from thinking how, once, she would have done anything to keep Madelaine's code from falling into the wrong hands. Now, it did not seem to matter so very much.

Except that someone was still willing to do her harm to possess it.

Thinking through the problem, Lynnette watched Christina finger the book.

"Let's play a bit of a game." Christina skimmed a hand over the leather cover of *Greystone Castle*. She opened it and flipped through the pages as if doing nothing more than passing the time. "I will tell you what Ravensfield has told you about the relationship between the two of us."

"There's no need for that." Lynnette put down her glass. "I can see nothing to be gained from—"

"Don't be ridiculous!" Christina's gaze snapped to her. "There's everything to be gained. You see, I have no doubt that he lied."

"And I have no doubt that he didn't."

"Of course." The smile was back, as smooth as ice and just as cold. "He told you I initiated the affair."

"Didn't you?"

"Really!" Christina tossed her head. "Do you think I needed to? That I didn't—that I don't—always have enough men around me? I can pick and choose whichever I wish."

"Which doesn't explain why you tried to seduce Ravensfield again as recently as the masquerade ball."

Christina drew in a sharp breath. "Did he tell you that? Of course, he would. He wants to wheedle his way into your drawers. He hasn't yet, has he?" She gave Lynnette a careful look. "I have no doubt that if he wants it badly enough, he will succeed. He always does. Just like he did with me."

"Are you telling me you were the innocent?"

"Innocent? Hardly!" Christina's face glowed. "But I did not set my sights upon a schoolboy, either." She made the kind of pretty pout Lynnette had seen her use a thousand times in a thousand social situations. "At first I simply felt sorry for the lad. But he was sweet. He rather grew on me. And my, my, he did have a tender way about him when he was pleasuring me. He was skilled for someone so young, and altogether delectable!"

It was more than enough. Lynnette moved across the room. "So kind of you to come and see me," she said, opening the door that led into the passageway and hoping it was warning enough. She stepped aside to allow Christina to leave. "Perhaps we'll see each other again soon."

"Perhaps you would be better served to hear what I have come here to say to you."

"Really?" When Christina drew near, Lynnette plucked *Greystone Castle* out of her hands. "I thought I'd already heard it."

"Don't be ridiculous, darling." When Christina made a move to pat her cheek, Lynnette moved aside. This time, the message was too clear for Christina to ignore. The light in her sapphire eyes hardened. "Very well. If that's the way you wish things to be. I only wanted to talk to you. Woman to woman and friend to friend."

"You've done that. And in the event you did not understand my response clearly, let me tell you that I believe Thomas—"

"Thomas?" Christina's brows rose just as her voice did. "It's gone that far, has it?" she hissed. "Honestly, I cannot for the life of me fancy why I've come here to do you a favor when you treat me so poorly, Lynnette. If you would put aside thoughts of your schoolgirl calf love for just a moment, you might realize that I am here to discuss something far more important than Ravensfield. I heard what happened, you see. At the masquerade party. I heard about the fight Ravensfield had with someone in my garden. I heard that someone attacked you."

"It matters little. I'm fine."

"I can see that. But it doesn't change a thing. As hostess for the night, I bear the culpability for the incident and I wanted you to know that I am very sorry, indeed. I left that very night for my home in Brighton. Rather suddenly and with a rather delectable fellow I had not had the opportunity to meet until that night," she added as an afterthought. "I did not hear what happened until today when I returned, otherwise you can be sure I would have been here sooner to check on your welfare. I hope . . ." As if barely able to understand the indiscretions of youth, Christina shook her head sadly. "I sincerely hope the disturbance had nothing to do with Madelaine's diary."

"Her diary!" The blood drained from Lynnette's face, and before she knew it, she found herself clutching the door, as if that might help her keep her grip on reality. "How do you know about Madelaine's diary?"

Christina's silvery laugh echoed in the high-ceilinged room. "Don't be ridiculous, my dear. I was your mother's dearest friend. I've always known about her diary. As a matter of fact, I have it in my possession."

18

When the Blades heard that Ravensfield was back in London, they planned a supper in his honor.

He was not happy about it.

"Damn it, Worthy. I don't see why I have to—"

"Because it is expected of you, your grace." Ravensfield was standing in front of his cheval mirror while Worthy brushed the shoulders of his coat. "You know that right enough. Your friends have heard that you are back in town and if you do not participate—"

"Rumors will fly. Yes, I know that, as well." The duke found himself thinking about his friends. They were fine fellows all, but for the first time, he thought an evening of their companionship would pall in comparison with going around to see Lynnette.

"What do you think they would say, do you suppose, Worthy? If they found out the true identity of Mrs. Mordefi? The Blades and the Dashers? The dandies and the diamonds of the first water? What would they all say?"

Worthy whistled low under his breath. "Can't imagine it myself. Not sure I want to. There would be a great to-do and no mistake, sir."

"Indeed! It is the reason I've never shared my little secret with anyone but you."

"And it is the reason I would never breathe a word of it, not to a living soul."

"Not even to Fern?"

At the mention of the yellow-haired maid who worked at Plumley Terrace, Worthy's cheeks got dusky. "Beggin' your pardon for sayin' it so straight as it were, sir, but no, not even to Fern. She's a sweet little thing and as pretty as a summer day. But she don't pay my wages, if you get my meanin', sir!"

"Does that mean, Worthy, that you value your position and the money you earn more than you value Fern's affection?"

"Can't say I value my money more than her, sir." Worthy went over to the dressing table on the other side of the room. He returned with a bottle of the bay rum scent that Ravensfield purchased from Yardley of London on Old Bond Street. "But I do realize that without that bit o' the blunt, I'd no more have a chance with Fern than I would with the man in the moon." The valet's nose wrinkled. "If you get my meanin', sir, as I wouldn't be interested. Not in the *man* in the moon."

Ravensfield splashed on the scent. "So do you think, then, that sweet little Fern is interested in you only because she knows I pay you an ungodly amount of money?"

"I may have mentioned it, sir." Worthy grinned. "A man needs a leg up, if you get my meanin'."

"I do." Ravensfield nodded. "And if Fern discovered you had a secret, Worthy, how might she react?"

Worthy considered the question. "Somethin' tells me, sir, that the young lady in question is not Fern but another young lady of our acquaintance, and if you are intending what I think you're intending with that young lady of our acquaintance . . ." He hauled in a breath. "I must say, sir, that I am as pleased as can be. But, beggin' your pardon for bein' so forward . . ." Worthy waited to see if the duke would take him to task for the promised forwardness, and when he did not, the valet continued.

"I think we both know that you don't want to start into it with a secret hanging over your head, your grace. Not a secret between the two of you."

"I've told myself the same things a hundred times." Ravensfield sighed and regretted it instantly. Sighing was not for a man of his caliber. "Yet I must admit, there is a certain comfort in the thought of not telling her. Of never telling her."

"Oh, but you know she's bound to find out, sir! Sooner or later. Sooner or later. And when she does finally discover the truth of the thing, that you write them books and earn your money from them . . ." A shiver cascaded over Worthy's slim shoulders. His curls twitched. "It won't be pretty, if you don't mind my sayin' so."

There was no use denying the logic of Worthy's argument. Ravensfield drummed his fingers against a nearby table. "I am not a man who is often unsure of himself, Worthy."

"Right enough!" Worthy smiled. "Never known you to be timid, that's for certain sure!"

"Then perhaps you can explain why I'm feeling that way now."

Worthy's smile melted. "You don't mean—"

"About Miss Overton?" The very thought made Ravensfield feel as if he were filled with pins and needles. He thought about having Worthy get him a claret but decided against it. He wasn't thirsty, and besides, he did not think the liquor would make its way past the uncharacteristic lump in his throat. "I'm as sure of Lynnette as I ever have been of anything and anyone," he said. The truth of the statement and of all he was feeling settled him a bit. "But I am not so sure that once she learns the truth about me . . ."

It was not Worthy's place to analyze and certainly he would never be so brazen as to second-guess his employer. Yet they had known each other a very long time. "You're worried she'll give you the mitten." He nodded, sure he was right in his assessment. "You're afraid she'll throw you over."

"Wouldn't you be worried?" Ravensfield scrubbed one hand along his chin. "It would be bad enough if I were in some sort of trade, but this . . ." He glanced at the slim sheaf of papers he'd brought along from Broadworth, all there was of the newest book that was supposed to be to his publisher as soon as possible. "I wouldn't care a fig if I scandalized the *ton* and no one ever invited me to another boring musicale or another ho-hum soiree. But if Lynnette should learn the truth and think me common or dishonorable . . ." He dropped into a chair near the window. "What would I do, Worthy?"

Worthy didn't have an answer. Ravensfield didn't expect that he would. It was unfair to even ask.

"Yes, you're right." The duke shook away the dismals. "There's not a thing either of us can say. If she's a woman like every other woman I've ever known . . ." The very thought was enough to fill him with a cold chill. "If she's like every other woman I know, I will, no doubt, get exactly the kind of reaction I expect to get."

"But something tells me, sir, as how you're thinking she is *not* like all the others. What if it's true? What if she isn't?"

"If she isn't, Worthy . . ." Just thinking of the possibility lifted Ravensfield's spirits and the chill melted in a rush of heat. "Then I have been right about her all along. I could spend the rest of my life with a woman such as that."

"Your mother was not the paragon you believed her to be."

Still clutching tight to her copy of *Greystone Castle,* Lynnette dropped into the seat opposite the one where Lady Christina had ensconced herself. Had she been less surprised by Christina's revelation about the diary and more sure of herself and her memories now that the truth of her mother's past had been revealed by Mr. Fryer, she might have been able to offer at least some sort of argument in defense of Madelaine's character. As it was, she simply stared at Christina.

"Yes, I can see it would come as something of a shock." Christina leaned forward and patted Lynnette's hand. It was a well-meaning gesture, sympathetic and not at all threatening, yet something about it coupled with all she had learned from Ravensfield snapped Lynnette back to reality. She pulled her hand out of Christina's reach.

"I knew my mother's character well enough," Lynnette said, ignoring the voice that reminded her that until that afternoon, even she had not known the full extent of Madelaine's shortcomings. "You're not telling me anything that surprises me."

"Oh, but I think the diary would."

"The diary!" Lynnette's eyes narrowed. "You took it. And it did not belong to you."

"I had hoped you would understand." Christina sat back, her shoulders rigid, her head high. She was dressed in pale silk, a gown that would have made most women with her fair skin and light-colored hair look dull. Christina looked anything but. She was as regal as a queen and she knew it. It was no wonder so many men fell under her spell. No wonder Ravensfield had been one of them.

Lynnette cast the thought aside. "How could you have treated my mother and me so badly?"

"Badly? Do you think so?" Christina smiled. "And

here I thought I was doing you a favor. I thought that once you were ready—"

"Ready? For what?"

"For the truth, of course. My, my, Lynnette. You are testy." Christina's laugh reminded Lynnette of glass. Clear and trenchant. Ready to shatter and dangerous if it did. "I would think a woman in love would be a bit more amiable."

She did not want to hear about love. Not from Christina. Not when the heat of Ravensfield's kisses was still warm upon her lips and the anticipation of his sweet promises still sung through her veins.

"We are not talking about me," Lynnette told the older woman. "Or about the fact that I may or may not be in love. We are talking about Madelaine. About her diary. You said—"

"That I have it. Yes, of course." Christina toyed with the length of perfectly matched pearls she wore at her throat. "Let us be frank with each other as old friends should always be. There is much in your mother's diary that would be a scandal to her memory should it be made public."

"It is difficult to imagine her memory being more defamed than it already is."

"If only you knew! You haven't read her diary, have you?" Christina saw the truth in Lynnette's eyes and looked at her in wonder. "Imagine that! You have! So you know some of what her life was all about. The lovers. The intrigues. And still you defend Madelaine as if she were some saint. She was a beauty, to be sure, and as dear to me as any sister. But as much as I loved her—as much as I love her still—I have never lied to myself about her true character. She betrayed your father a dozen different times with a dozen different men."

"I know all that." Lynnette rose and walked to the fireplace. "Papa knew it, as well. He and Mother had an understanding. From the moment they met. His family had the name and the prestige. Hers had the money. It was, from the first, a business arrangement." She glanced at her guest. "From what I've heard, your marriage was much the same."

Christina's shoulders went back and her eyes turned as frosty as the color of her gown. "It would do you well to remember that my husband died soon after we were married. I had no great love for him when we were parsoned. I had no time afterward to develop any sort of feelings for him. I have none now. But that makes my situation very different from your mother's. I am a widow and thus not beholden to my vows."

"I doubt it would have made any difference. You see what you like and you take it. You don't care who you hurt."

"Good lord, he has spun your head, hasn't he?" There was no rancor in Christina's voice, only a note of sympathy and an edge of mocking amusement. "The Lynnette I remember of old would never think so poorly of me as to accuse me of being heartless. At least not before Ravensfield insinuated himself between us. What has happened to our friendship?"

As much as Lynnette hated to admit it, Lady Christina

was right. They had been friends for many years and what happened in the past was over. Ravensfield loved Lynnette now. He had said as much with words and deeds in the carriage on the way home. Instead of worrying about the past, she should celebrate the promise of her future. It was a future that did not include Christina. It never would. She did not feel so much triumphant as she did sorry for Christina.

She turned to her guest. "I'm sorry. It is wrong of me to pass judgment so quickly. You have always been a true friend to me just as you were to my mother. I shouldn't allow any feelings I might have for Ravensfield to get in the way of that friendship. But I will not tolerate hearing you speak poorly of him. I know he wouldn't lie. Not to me."

"Of course." It was as much of a surrender as she would ever get from Christina and Lynnette knew it. "There was a time I would have said the same. I cannot blame you. It would be wrong of me to even try to think of all that might be in your head or in your heart. It is a fault you share with your dear mother. Poor little fool! She actually believed she had feelings for her lovers. Every single one of them."

"And you never do."

Christina's smile was lean and predatory. "I might have. Once." She did not say who that one man might have been. She didn't need to. She sloughed away the very idea with a lift of her shoulders. "Unlike your mother, I came to my senses long ago. She thought love could last forever. But one by one, her lovers tired of her.

They left her. After the affair with the Wonderlee Diamond, I think she actually thought that at least one of them might come back. One man to be her hero, her knight in shining armor, who would stand at her side when all the rest had abandoned her. But of course, none of them did. Why would they, and risk their own reputations? In the end . . . well, I think that's when she realized that I was her only true friend."

Christina's words were heartfelt but they didn't make any sense. "Is that why you stole her diary, then? Because you were her friend?"

"Exactly!" Christina rose from her seat and strolled across the room to where Lynnette stood. "Her friend and yours. You see, I didn't know you'd read the diary. I thought to save you the pain of knowing the whole truth of your mother's scandalous past. I thought that someday, when you were ready to understand and forgive her many weaknesses, I would return it to you. Should even half of what's in her diary come to light, I knew you would be devastated. And the *ton* . . . they would have even more to prattle about."

"But I would never—"

"Of course not! Not you! You wouldn't want dear Madelaine's past dished out along with the scandal broth. But there are others. Others who are not as kind as you. You know them. Those who live on the bits and scraps of other peoples' lives. They would like nothing better than to get their hands on the diary. And where would be the most logical place for them to look?" Christina glanced all around. "Plumley Terrace, of course! I simply thought to save you the worry. I was here visiting Madelaine one morning near the end of her days." Her smile faded, and curbing her emotions, she pressed a hand to her heart. "You left the room for a few minutes and I—"

"Helped yourself to what didn't belong to you."

Christina's expression fell. "Yes. I admit it. It was too cruel of me and I should have told you sooner. But I had to do something. Before someone else did. We couldn't risk a scandal."

"It is too late for that."

Christina shook her head sadly. "Poor Madelaine just couldn't resist. It was one of the reasons I stood by her, don't you see. She was so deluded as to think she could actually get away with stealing the diamond. That no one would ever find out."

Another wave of realization washed over Lynnette. In spite of what she'd learned from Mr. Fryer, the news was like a punch and she sucked in a breath. "You knew?"

"Knew? From the beginning? No, not for certain. But I suspected. After all, there is no smoke without fire. And the jewel case that had once contained the diamond was found in Madelaine's room. Poor darling! She'd already sold the diamond long before she told me that she was, indeed, the one who'd taken it. And stealing it in the first place . . . well, honestly, I don't think she meant anything malicious by it. But you know how she was. So much like you are yourself. She could not resist an adventure." Christina watched Lynnette closely.

"She did it to pay the gambling debts of one of her

lovers, you know. She thought to buy his love, but it made no difference. He still left her. Just like all the others did. By then, the diamond was sold. The money she'd garnered from it was spent to salvage his reputation. There was nothing she could do to make recompense and she could not turn herself in to the authorities without the risk of losing your devotion." She spun away and walked across the room, her voice drifting with her.

"I think it was that realization, that feeling of being trapped by her own actions, that simply ate away at her, day after day after day. You saw as much for yourself. You saw the way she deteriorated."

"Yes." Lynnette brushed away a tear.

"Society meant a great deal to Madelaine. But it wasn't the misery of being banished from it that broke her heart and robbed her of her reason in the end. It was the guilt."

Everything Christina said only made Lynnette feel even more miserable. "And you knew? All this time, you knew she really was the one—"

"I'm sorry. I know it isn't easy to hear." Christina turned to her. She was on the far side of the room and the afternoon shadows made it impossible to see her face. Her voice, though, was choked with anguish. "It hasn't been easy for me to live with the truth all these years. If only I had been able to help her somehow! If only I had been a better friend! She could have come to me for the money, you see. She should have known that all she had to do was ask. Even now, I wish there was some way I could have helped."

After all Lynnette had learned, she knew there was not. "I have felt the same way," she said. "I thought that if I could but get the diary back and use the code to translate it—"

"Code?" Christina hurried back across the room. "What on earth on you talking about?"

"The coded message. At the back of the diary. I thought if I had both the diary and the key, I might find out what it means. I had the notion that it would somehow vindicate her."

"Do you mean to tell me that gibberish at the end of the diary is a code of some sort? That there is meaning to it?" Christina was incredulous. "I thought it nothing but the scribblings of Madelaine's poor, afflicted mind."

"I think not." Lynnette pictured the sheet of paper sewn into her garment. Though she could easily have retrieved it and used it to illustrate her argument, her instincts told her it was not the time to reveal it. "If you could see the code, you would know. It is clearly drawn and, as far as I can see, just as clearly logical. No. Madelaine definitely knew what she was doing when she created the cipher. Think about it, if it made no sense, if it was nothing but gibberish, the man in your garden wouldn't have attacked me to get it."

Christina's mouth dropped open. "Good heavens! You're right, of course. But if that is true, it means . . . It means you have seen it. That you actually have the code!"

"Yes, I have it in my possession. And someone has been trying to steal it from me for months."

Christina's eyes widened. "I told you! I told you there is further scandal in poor Madelaine's diary. There must surely be or someone wouldn't be so anxious to get hold of the code. We must examine it together." When Lynnette did not readily agree, Christina's expectant smile faded. Her eyes narrowed. "You say you are my friend but you still don't trust me."

"I don't trust anyone. Not about this."

Christina's eyes narrowed. "Not even Ravensfield?"

"He knows. About the cipher. About the diary."

"That is fine, Lynnette." She tossed her head. "To trust a man who is practically a stranger more than you trust me."

"I did not know what to think." Her voice choked over the words and the feeling of remorse that brought tears to her eyes. "Until today, I always believed my mother to be innocent."

Lady Christina laughed. "You are as deluded as Madelaine!"

Perhaps she was. The truth settled in Lynnette, made all the more razor-sharp by the cutting edge of Christina's laughter. She shook her head, clearing it of the thoughts that had taken up residence there ever since the moment Mr. Fryer identified Madelaine as the lady who had sold him the diamond.

"You're absolutely right," she told Christina. "I realize that now. I have been deluding myself. For a long time, I thought my mother innocent simply because she was my mother. Now I hear from you and others that she was not so innocent at all. But I must tell you, Christina,

I am not convinced. I think, perhaps, you might be lying to me."

Christina's voice rose. "She took the diamond!"

"Then let us find out, once and for all." Lynnette raised her chin and looked Christina in the eye. "You said it yourself, Christina. You said you planned to return the diary to me when I could understand all it contained. When I was ready to forgive. Well . . ."

Lynnette went to the door. Her message was clear. "I am ready to forgive Madelaine now," she said. "Whether the code proves my mother's innocence or is damning evidence, I am ready to know the truth. I've waited long enough. I will come around in an hour's time to collect the diary."

19

Lynnette sent a message to Ravensfield telling him what she had learned from Lady Christina. By the time she traveled to Christina's, recovered the diary, and arrived back home with it, he was waiting for her at Plumley Terrace.

She had not asked him to come for she suspected that now that he was back in London, his schedule was full. The simple fact that he had put aside more entertaining pursuits in favor of her little mystery warmed her through to her bones.

Side by side, they went up to the room that had once been her father's study. It was little used now, though Mrs. Wilcox made sure it was kept spotless. Upon Lynnette's request before she left for Lady Christina's, the housekeeper had ordered a fire to be laid. There were candles lit on the tables and on the desk near the windows. Though she was certain there was no need for intrigue inside her own home, Lynnette closed the door behind them as soon as they were inside. The diary itself was wrapped in a length of midnight blue velvet, just as Madelaine had always done and just as Lady Christina had given it to her. She laid the book on the table and unfolded the cloth.

The leather-bound book was no more than eight inches tall and contained perhaps two hundred pages. Such a small thing to have caused such a great fuss!

"After all this time! I can't believe it is as simple as all that." It was as if Ravensfield were reading her mind, for he said exactly what Lynnette was thinking. He came up behind her and leaned over her shoulder to take a look at the book. His arms went around her waist. "Chased by mysterious men in black, attacked at the masquerade ball, rooms ransacked . . . all for this? And now to have it dropped in your lap this way. It seems a great to-do to have ended with so little pomp and circumstance."

"We do not know that yet. We have yet to see what is inside." Lynnette drew in a long breath. She had dreamed of this moment since the day she first came upon Madelaine's diary and saw the coded message at its end. Now that it was upon her, she found herself strangely hesitant. "What if it doesn't answer my questions?"

"You'll never know until you open it and find out." As if he could feel the excitement that vibrated through her and caused her knees to feel weak and her insides to flutter as if there were a family of butterflies inside her, he gave her a reassuring squeeze. "Besides, I thought you were convinced. Mr. Fryer—"

"When I first heard all Mr. Fryer had to say, I was

overwhelmed. But upon thinking of it, he did not strike me as the most reliable of men." She looked over her shoulder at Ravensfield and when he smiled she felt the tension inside her ease. "He may have been mistaken. Or I . . ." She thought back to everything Lady Christina had said. "Perhaps I am merely deluded. Just as Madelaine was in her last days. Perhaps I have been trying too hard to believe."

"Is it such an awful failing of character, then?" Ravensfield kissed her neck. "I for one see it as quite admirable."

"That's not what Christina said." The fact that Lynnette could mention her name in Ravensfield's company was not so surprising, she realized. There was peace in the circle of his arms. "Yet as much as she thought I am cork-brained for trying to prove my mother's innocence, Christina herself is just as much a fool. To think that all this time, she has been trying to shelter Madelaine's memory. Her intentions were kind, even if the fact that she stole the diary was cruel. I hate to confess that in return, I was less than generous in my feelings toward Lady Christina. I will admit as much to you because then you will know that I can be small-minded and—"

Ravensfield's laughter cut her short. "You are not small-minded or ungenerous." He propped his chin on her shoulder. "If you thought little of Lady Christina, I would say that you are a very good judge of character, indeed."

She did not want to think of everything Christina had told her. Not when they were so close to finding out the answer to the mystery that had plagued her all these months. Yet there were some things it was impossible to ignore.

One of them was the physical sensation that burst through her every time Ravensfield was near. Another was the way her heart responded. But like it or not, the third was his veracity and the problem would always stand between them if she didn't deal with it. Now was not a good time, but it was as good a time as any.

She turned in his arms and linked her fingers at the back of his neck, looking into Ravensfield's coal-dark eyes. "She has given me a much different version of the story," Lynnette told him. "Not the story of Madelaine's diary and the Wonderlee Diamond. The tale about the young man and the older, more sophisticated woman. In her telling of it, she was more the innocent party and you the rake."

His expression hardened. Not as a man's might when he's angry, but in the way it does when he sees something he wants very much drift from his reach. "Do you believe her?"

"I do not wish to believe her."

He loosened his hold. "That doesn't answer my question."

With no choice, Lynnette brought her hands back down to her sides. She held them there, close against her body. "I am not jealous of her if that's what you think."

"If you were, you would be little more than a paperskull."

"And if you were not telling me the truth?"

He turned away from her. "The truth is a fluid thing."

A drumming started up inside Lynnette's chest. She pressed a hand there in an effort to ease the pain. "Not this truth. It cannot be changeable. Not between us."

Ravensfield cursed his bad luck. When the message arrived from Lynnette that told of how she'd discovered the whereabouts of her mother's diary and how she was planning to retrieve it, he had started for Plumley Terrace immediately. He was not disappointed at the prospect of forsaking the company of the Blades for the evening. Time spent with them did not compare to passing the hours with Lynnette. He had come in the hope of offering his support and, though he had yet to suggest it to her, with the thought that before the night was out, they might spend it as only lovers do, up in her bed and lost in the pleasure of each other's bodies.

He had not meant to find himself on the horns of a proverbial dilemma or stuck in the untenable spot told of in the tongue-in-cheek proverb: "no good deed goes unpunished."

This was the perfect example. In exchange for the good deed of coming to offer his encouragement, his punishment was a heart-to-heart discussion of the truth. The very thing he'd been avoiding telling her practically from the moment they met.

"I never lied," he said. "Not about Christina. She seduced me. She used me. She spent a good deal of my money buying herself jewels and a little cottage in Brighton that was then and is now where she goes to rendezvous with the paramours her London paramours know nothing about. Then she threw me over. I never lied about being an unwitting victim, either. For I was not and I have never pretended to be. She was a temptress and I was more than eager to be tempted." He turned back to her, eager to see her response because it was vital to know what she was thinking. "If you would rather believe her version of the story—"

"I would rather believe you. Above all. Above everything." Her remarkable eyes shone with conviction. Her face was bathed in candlelight. "But if you think there are instances where you cannot tell me the whole of the truth . . ."

For a moment, he wondered what she knew. How much she guessed. Was there any chance that she knew his fortune was gained through Mrs. Mordefi's glory?

He dismissed the idea with a twitch of his shoulders. And if another idea pricked his conscience? One that reminded him that if this was the moment for the truth to be told, it would be best to tell the whole of it?

He cast that thought aside, too. There were some things that were more important even than the truth. Holding on to Lynnette was one of them. He didn't dare take the chance of losing her.

He closed the distance between them, one careful step at a time. "Do you believe I'm telling you the truth when I tell you I love you?"

"I want to."

A slow smile lifted the corners of his mouth. "Would you be more inclined to believe me, Miss Overton, if rather than expounding on them, I demonstrated the intensity of my feelings?"

"Here? Now?" She offered all the right protests but he could not fail to see the spark of interest that flared in her eyes.

"We are alone." She was near enough now to touch and he found it impossible to wait a moment longer. With one hand, he traced the shape of her jaw, the length of her neck. She had removed her pelisse the moment she was inside the door and she was dressed tonight in green silk. He skimmed his hand along her bosom. "Here and now is as good a time and place as any I can think of," he said. "The night is spread out before us and we have little else to do."

She glanced a look toward the desk. "There is the diary to examine."

"It will wait." Ravensfield could not. He crushed her to his chest and kissed her and when he felt her respond instantly—her head titling back, her back arching, her hips tipping to meet his—it only made him want her all the more.

"Last time we hurried," he said, scooping her up into his arms and carrying her to the fire. "This time, we will take our time."

He laid her on the Persian carpet in front of the fireplace, and Lynnette stretched contentedly. She looked up at Ravensfield, still smiling. "Lay with me." Though she was sure he had every intention of doing it, she could no more wait than she could fail to take her next breath. Reaching for him, she pulled him down beside her. He lay on his side, propped on one elbow, and ran his fingers lightly over the green silk that hugged her breasts.

Lynnette purred with pleasure. She was not, however, about to be put off. "You promised a leisurely pace," she reminded him. "And I intend to make you keep the promise."

"Indeed!" Ravensfield's eyes sparkled in the firelight. "What exactly did you have in mind?"

"For one thing . . ." She slid her hands across his chest and up to his shoulders. "If I recall correctly, your grace," she teased him with the title, "last time, you removed neither your coat nor your shirt. This time, I think, we must be more thorough."

He obliged her, slipping out of his coat and unfastening his shirt. But when he would have undone his splendid neckcloth, Lynnette pushed his hands aside. "Mr. Worthy is skilled and quite artistic. We must do his knots justice. This one . . ." She tugged and one end of the neckcloth loosened. "And this one . . ." She tugged again and another bit of the linen came free. "This one . . ."

She pulled at the neckcloth slowly, releasing one of Mr. Worthy's byzantine knots as she drew herself nearer to Ravensfield. She slipped the cloth from around his neck at the same time she kissed him.

For a moment, he was startled by her brazenness. The next moment, all surprise forgotten, Ravensfield deepened the kiss, nudging her lips open with his tongue and gasping with delight when she brought her own tongue to meet his. One kiss was not enough, just as one touch would never be enough to satisfy her. Lynnette tugged at the front of his shirt, eager for him to discard it, eager to feel his body pressed against hers. He sat up and sat back on his heels. He pulled the shirt out of his trousers and shrugged out of it.

"Better?" He smiled down at her.

Lynnette's gaze traveled from his broad shoulders to the sprinkle of dark hairs across his chest. She itched to touch him and, raising herself on one elbow, she reached out and brushed a hand across his chest. She marveled at the hardened muscle beneath the thatch of hair and smiling, kissed the skin above his heart.

He reached for her hand and brought it to his lips, kissing each finger in turn. When he was finished, he kissed her palm, her wrist, the tender skin inside her elbow. He touched a hand to the lace that edged the short, puffed sleeve of her gown. "And you will let me take this off?"

Rather than answer, she sat up and turned around so that he might undo her gown.

He unfastened the top button and planted a kiss on the skin it exposed. With each unfastened button, he bestowed a kiss, down her spine to the top of her corset, and when he was done, he pushed the gown off her shoulders.

Lynnette shivered with anticipation. Still, Ravensfield was not done. This time he started at the top of her corset. But he did not kiss each bit of skin as he had done before. He flicked it lightly with his tongue. Up her spine and to the back of her neck.

Lynnette's longing grew. It pulsed through her until her whole being was focused on the slow, aching need that rose through her like the fire that sparked only a few feet away. The touch of Ravensfield's lips, the feel of his hands, only deepend the burning, until it was as real as the throbbing of her heart where it pounded against her ribs.

His tongue skimmed her neck and Lynnette moaned with pleasure. Impatient to lie beside him, skin to skin, she twisted, eager to discard the rest of her clothing.

"Oh, no!" Ravensfield laughed and held her in place. "I promised we would take our time."

"That is really very thoughtful of you, but I don't think I can wait. I don't want to wait. I want more."

"And you shall have it," he promised. "More kisses." His mouth covered hers. "More touching." One hand on either side of her neck, he stroked downward, outlining her body.

His eyes hooded, Ravensfield watched Lynnette's face flush with desire. Her tongue darted from between her teeth and dipped to moisten her lower lip. Her arms went around him and she pulled him nearer.

He had mastered himself as long as he could. With a groan torn from deep inside, Ravensfield untied her corset and cast it aside, exposing Lynnette's breasts to the soft light of the fire. For a second, he could do no more than stare. Back in the garden at Broadworth, he had been too eager to be surrounded by her, too eager to feel his own release, to pay too much attention to how she looked. Now, he saw that she was as flawless as he had imagined. Her breasts were small and round. Her skin was as dewy as morning roses. It glowed pink and beautiful in the light of the fire.

He was not sure how long he sat, a man transfixed. He knew only that when he came to his senses, she was watching him.

Ravensfield smiled. "You're lovely." With one finger, he circled each breast. His tongue followed where his finger led and he traced the outline of both breasts before he caught one nipple, then the other, in his teeth. He suckled her until her nipples were hard, like jewels.

"Thomas!" Lynnette heard her own voice vibrate with longing. It sounded as urgent as the need she felt inside. She basked in the admiration she saw in Ravensfield's eyes. It heated her through and when he brought his mouth to hers again, and pressed her back against the carpet, she pulled him down beside her. She did not stay still long. She rolled to her side and unfastened the button on Ravensfield's trousers. When she was done, she tugged them down as far as she was able and waited impatiently while he hauled them off.

She felt no embarrassment when she looked at him.

"You're as bold as a cyprian." Ravensfield did not seem put off by the assessment. He slipped his hands inside her drawers and smiled when he skimmed them down over her hips and tossed them aside. He kissed her long and hard before he knelt above her and eased his weight onto her. "Just lay back. And let me love you."

Lynnette opened herself to the union of bodies and minds and wills that made her heart swell with joy while her blood pounded desire through her veins.

She moaned with pleasure, her voice an echo of

Ravensfield's as they moved in perfect rhythm. Faster and faster, the cadence increased, far beyond the leisurely rate the duke had promised. She heard Ravensfield call her name and at the same time the world came to a halt. It stopped and she with it, teetering on the brink of an abyss so deep, she could not begin to fathom it.

When it started again, it was with an astonishing jolt. Lynnette gasped and held Ravensfield tighter. He trembled, his body still thrusting against hers. Faster and harder. Harder and longer, her name on his lips.

The next second, his mouth was on hers. He kissed her lips and her neck and her eyelids.

He held her close against him as if he were afraid she might disappear. He found her mouth again and covered it with his, his kiss desperate and urgent and grateful. He held her close, her breasts pressed against his chest, her heart only inches away from his, and he breathed a long sigh of satisfaction and relief.

At last, he had found himself.

And peace.

If Lynnette knew nothing else about Ravensfield, she knew he was as good as his word. They spent the better part of an hour tangled together in front of the fire. He was both gentle and urgent, achingly sweet, and so comfortable with his own body that it was natural for her to feel at ease with hers.

"You're beautiful." Ravensfield straddled her. He brushed a series of soft kisses against her mouth and her breasts and her belly.

They had just finished their lovemaking yet Lynnette felt herself tighten again with need. She wondered if it was so easy for men to be stirred again so quickly, and she caressed him so that she might hurry him along.

"Upon my honor!" Ravensfield smiled. "You are a quick study and no mistake. Not thinking of the diary now?"

"I should be." Lynnette's voice was as dreamy as her mood. "I will be. As soon as I am done here."

He kissed his way back up again, from her belly to her breasts to her mouth, stopping along the way to outline her nipples with his tongue. "And that will be . . ."

"Sometime soon, I think, Thomas." She watched him carefully as she spoke the name, and seeing the flare of warmth in his eyes, she smiled her delight. "There will be time for the diary," she said. "A great deal of time. Just a little later."

It was, in fact, much later by the time they were dressed again and seated at the desk. The candles had burned to stumps and Ravensfield gathered them from around the room and brought them all to the desk, the better to see the diary and read everything in it. When she returned from Lady Christina's, Lynnette had retrieved the copy of the key from the hem of her gown. She unfolded the page and opened Madelaine's diary on the desk next to it.

"It is just as I remember," she told him, skimming a finger over the first page where Madelaine had written her name in her flowing, intricate hand. "It isn't the only volume of her diary, you know. She kept a journal since she was a girl. I have the other volumes in the library. Even as a child, I remember her writing every day. But after what happened with the diamond, well, her nerves were too overstrung for her to continue the routine. See!" She flipped through the pages, promising herself that when she could devote the whole of her attention to it, she would reread the diary thoroughly and with an impassioned eye.

"This is the last entry." She stopped at the page. "I remember reading it. In it, she talks about getting ready for the country weekend, how excited she was to have been included in the party and how she thought it would be great fun. And then here . . ." She turned all the way to the back of the book to the place where the cursive ended and the code began.

The pages weren't there.

For what seemed an age, Lynnette sat staring at the diary, and though she didn't say a word, Ravensfield sensed that something was wrong. He put a hand over hers.

"The pages?" As if it would somehow make the truth that was staring them in the face easier to understand, he leaned closer. "The pages are—"

"Missing." The realization was hollow. So was Lynnette's voice. She tipped her head, the better to see the book's binding. From this angle, she could see where the pages had been cut out of the diary. Lynnette's voice rose over the sound of her own pounding heart. "Lady Christina! It must be her. For certainly, when last I saw the diary, it was intact. And now the pages that contain the coded message are gone."

Ravensfield's expression hardened. His jaw looked as if it might snap. "There must be something in those pages that she wishes to protect."

The realization seeped through Lynnette like ice water. "Then we will never know the truth. For she will already have destroyed them."

"I think not." Ravensfield curled one hand into a fist and tapped it fitfully against the desktop. "She is far too clever for that. And too devious. If there is a chance that there is something in those pages that concerns her or that might, in any way, profit her, she will go through hell and high water to discover what it is."

"Then she is the one who's been trying to steal the code!" This was a new thought and it took a good deal of time to get used to. Lynnette wrinkled her nose and narrowed her eyes. "But why?" she asked.

"I cannot say." Ravensfield shook his head. His hair was tousled and a curl of it drooped over his forehead. "But you can be sure that if Christina is behind the thing, there is a villainous reason."

"And that she is looking to get her hands on the code still!" Instinctively, Lynnette dragged the page with the cipher closer. "We must keep it safe at all costs. We cannot let her have it."

"Or perhaps we can use her desire for the code for our own purposes." He slid his hand over hers where it protected the cipher. "Do you trust me?" he asked her.

She glanced toward the fireplace and he knew what

she was thinking. "I trust you with my heart," she said.

"And with Lady Christina's?"

When her mouth fell open, he laughed. "If you trust me now," he said, "we can find the missing pages. I have an idea."

"But I—"

He didn't wait to hear her objection. He silenced her words with a kiss.

It was the only argument she needed.

Lady Christina was a creature of habit. At least that is what Ravensfield claimed. Rather than think about all he knew of the woman and how he knew it, Lynnette put her faith in him.

Just as he predicted, Christina was not at all surprised when, the very day after Lynnette had retrieved the diary, she received a note from the duke saying that he knew about the key to the code and that he was sure he could obtain it easily from Lynnette. The information could not have come at a more opportune time, he told her. He was tired of Lynnette, and if Lady Christina was serious about reinitiating their relationship, he would most assuredly like to discuss the key to the code with her. He would call on her the next evening.

Christina was used to having her own way in all things and this, Lynnette supposed, was just another of them. Christina wanted Ravensfield. She had made that clear on the night of the masquerade ball. She was certain that if she waited long enough, he would come back to her.

A prickle of jealousy made Lynnette uncomfortable and she shifted in her seat and peeked out the window of Ravensfield's closed carriage, stopped in front of Christina's home. Tonight, most of the house was dark. But on the first floor, lights sparkled from the parlor window.

"Thirty minutes," Ravensfield had told Lynnette. "Wait until I go inside and then wait thirty minutes."

She wondered if he realized how interminable thirty minutes could feel.

Lynnette picked at a loose thread on one of her gloves while she reminded herself of Ravensfield's plan. Two nights ago back at Plumley Terrace, it had, at first, seemed daft. And strangely familiar, like something she had read in one of Mrs. Mordefi's books.

"Why can't we simply wait until she is out?" Lynnette had asked him, uneasy from the first.

He must have sensed her discomfort for he had been looking out the window and he crossed the room to stand at her side. He slipped an arm around her waist and smiled down at her, his eyes soft in the last of the candlelight. "Because when she is out, her servants will be doing whatever it is servants do when their mistress is not at home. Cleaning. Dusting. Polishing. Christina refuses to let her servants have so much as a free evening when she is away. She keeps them busy. They will be everywhere in the house, as thick as flies around a meat wagon."

"And when Christina is at home and entertaining a gentleman?"

"Then the servants are sent up to their rooms and told to stay there."

"Which means—"

"That while I keep Lady Christina occupied, Worthy—who could be waiting outside or in my carriage—can slip inside and have free access to the lady's bedchamber."

"Unless she is busy trying to lure you into it."

He had kissed the tip of her nose, and in the grand scheme of things, she thought it better than she deserved. Surely he knew what she was thinking. The very thought of Ravensfield alone with Christina made her heart ache. It wasn't that he couldn't take care of himself. It was simply that Lady Christina—

It was a warm night and the windows of Christina's parlor were open. Even from down in the carriage, Lynnette heard the silvery sounds of the lady's laughter.

She felt as peevish and as childish now as she had the night Ravensfield had suggested the plan.

"She may try to lure all she wants," he'd told her. "It will not happen."

"I know." She turned, the better to let him take her into his arms. "It's simply that I know—"

His smile brightened and just thinking of it now warmed her through. "You know what, Miss Overton?"

"I love you so very much!" The declaration had slipped out, as naturally as breath.

"And I have never thought myself worthy of such love." Ravensfield had tightened his arms around her. "Or so lucky."

"Which is exactly why . . ." She stood on her toes and

pressed a kiss to his lips. "You will leave Worthy at home where he belongs. I will go to Lady Christina's with you."

His muscles bunched. "Don't be ridiculous! You can't—"

"Burglarize Lady Christina's home? Certainly I can. It will be just like that scene from *Great Holloway Palace,* one of Mrs. Mordefi's earliest works."

"And in that work?"

"Julia, the heroine, does exactly this. While her good friend, Patrice, keeps the wicked earl occupied, Julia steals into his secret study and—"

"You don't think that's real, do you?" There wasn't so much laughter in Ravensfield's voice as there was a note of incredulity. "You don't think that you can take what happens in a book and translate it to real life?"

"It seems to be exactly what you have done."

"I—"

"Spare me your excuses, sir." Lynnette held up one hand as a barrier to the protest she knew to be forthcoming. "You thought of it. Completely independent of Mrs. Mordefi's influence. You thought of it, so obviously you think it will work for Worthy. If you think it will work, then it follows quite logically that it will work just as well for me as it would for Worthy."

"You cannot afford to get apprehended."

"Neither can Worthy."

"No." The glower that went along with the single word had, no doubt, worked in Ravensfield's favor any number of times. It was, after all, a formidable expression and it must have stopped any number of protests from any number of people.

Fortunately for Lynnette, she was not just another of those people.

She had never been one to play the kinds of games she saw other women engage in. But this was important. She could not trust Ravensfield's fate to chance. Or the safety of the coded diary pages to the duke's valet.

"Worthy may be a perfectly capable man," she'd told Ravensfield.

"He is."

"But Worthy does not know his way around Lady Christina's town house. Not the way I do."

It was impossible for him to argue. That, of course, did not keep him from trying.

"You simply can't go crawling through some window—"

"I have no intention of doing any such thing." Lynnette pulled back her shoulders and lifted her chin. "You see, your grace, I know some things about Lady Christina's household that even you cannot possibly know. Her lady's maid, Florence, happens to be quite madly in love with one of my footmen, John, the tall boy with the crooked teeth. They meet whenever they are able. I have no doubt that should I give John a free evening, Florence will be sure to see that the kitchen door is left open for him."

Lynnette had given him a small, triumphant smile. "It is simply impossible for Worthy to find his way from the kitchen up to Lady Christina's room. At least not quickly. And perhaps not quietly. I, on the other hand, know my way around her home with my eyes closed."

"But—"

She silenced his objections with a quick kiss. "It is my mother's diary, after all," she'd told him. "And my responsibility to get it back."

"But—"

It was no hardship to have to silence him again. "If I do not go, you do not go. And if you try to go without me—"

"God help me!" Ravensfield surrendered. "If I have learned nothing else about you, madam, it is that you will have your own way. No matter what. Are you sure you are ready for such an adventure?"

At the time, she had assured him that she was.

Now, she was not so certain.

Lynnette's hands trembled and she clutched them together and took a deep breath. With one last look at the light that sparkled from the parlor windows, she glanced around to make sure that no one was about and alighted from the carriage. Quickly, she made her way around to the side of the house and the garden where, on the night of the masquerade ball, the man in black had lain in wait to ambush her.

At the garden gate, Lynnette swallowed the panic that threatened to dampen her determination. Carefully, she threaded her way through the dark garden, stopping now and again when the path turned and she was not sure what—or who—she might find waiting for her when she turned the corner. Once, she thought she heard footsteps behind her but when she whirled around there was no one there. Another time, she swore she heard the rustle of leaves, and when she investigated, she found nothing more threatening than a cat that had come in over the garden wall.

She took a false turn near the fountain and had to come back around but soon she found herself at the kitchen door.

Rather than stand and consider the consequences, she remembered Julia in Mrs. Mordefi's book. Julia did not let fear stop her, and she had more to worry about than simply being discovered by the unscrupulous earl. For Great Halloway Palace was haunted by the hideous ghost of an equally cruel ancestor and—

Casting the thought aside, Lynnette opened the door and slipped inside. The house was dark and that, she thought, was a very good sign. It was not, however, quiet. Just as she expected, John was visiting Florence. From the room where the dishes were stored, she heard the unmistakable sounds of their impassioned coupling.

As reluctant to interrupt as she was to be discovered, she made her way through the kitchen and on toward the front of the house, gliding up the staircase as quietly as she was able. At the top of the stairs, she paused for a moment, her gaze on the closed parlor doors.

"La, sir!" She heard Christina's voice and the ripple of her laughter, but what Ravensfield said in response, Lynnette could not tell. She could hear no more than the rumble of his voice and Christina's murmured reply.

She thought about John and Florence down in the kitchen and wondered—

No.

If she could not trust Ravensfield, then they could never have a future together. And if they never had a future together, she knew now that she would never find happiness. Rather than even consider it, she continued up the stairs.

She had visited Christina here enough times to know which room was her bedchamber and Lynnette opened the door and went inside.

"A carved wooden box," Ravensfield had told her. "It is very plain. Not the sort of thing you'd expect Christina to prize. Yet if I were a betting man, I would say that is where she keeps the pages torn from your mother's diary. Though she would never let anyone know it, she is a foolishly sentimental woman and she found the box in a little shop in Brighton. It is her treasure chest."

Though she was tempted, Lynnette did not ask how he knew all that. It didn't matter.

Just as he predicted, she found the box in Christina's dressing room, mixed in with the jewels, the cinnamon breath sweeteners and the face powders. Holding her breath, she opened it.

20

"Empty."

Lynnette could hardly believe her eyes. Though she knew it would do no good, she turned the box over and shook it. Of course, when she turned it back around again, nothing had changed.

This was something they hadn't discussed, something they hadn't even considered, and faced with the prospect, her spirits sank and her stomach bunched. Ravensfield was so sure of where Christina would keep the precious pages, they had not thought what Lynnette might do should she not find what she was looking for.

And now she must think on her own. And think fast.

She set the box back down where she found it and glanced around Christina's room. She had been in the chamber before, and then as now, she found it a riot of overindulgence. From the midnight blue silk curtains on the windows to the furniture with its elaborate carvings and the murals of classical scenes painted on the ceilings and walls, the room was much like Christina herself. Both elegant and intimidating.

It held no end of hiding places.

Lynnette had just convinced herself that if she didn't start her search, she would never finish it, when she heard a voice outside the door.

"So what I told the mistress . . ." It sounded like a young girl. Like one of the maids. "I told her I would wait so that I might dress her hair before bedtime."

The voice stopped just outside the door.

"And let me guess what she told you, Gwen." This was another voice, a maid who sounded even younger than the first and far more taken with her mistress's renown. She giggled. "She said as how she had a gentleman calling tonight. And he would take care of all the dressing—and undressing—that she needed!"

"Exactly so!" Gwen squealed her delight. "And such a gentleman he is! Did you see him, Tess?" The two women moved closer to the door and panic overtook Lynnette. She looked around for a place of concealment and found it close by. She darted behind the draperies.

Just as she did, Tess and Gwen came into the room.

"I saw him right enough." The burr of excitement in Tess's voice told Lynnette the maid knew full well what her mistress had planned for the evening. She peeked around the edge of the drapery just in time to see Tess give Gwen a knowing wink. "We'd best get the bed turned down and the room ready for her. Knowing Lady

Christina, she will have him up here and out of his clothes before another hour is over."

"If she waits that long!" Gwen laughed.

The two maids went about their business. Fortunately, the room was large and Lynnette was concealed at the far end of it, next to the cheval mirror where, more than once, she had seen Christina preen. She chanced another look to see what the maids were doing.

They were turning back blankets and plumping pillows, and rather than watch and think of what it meant—or at least of what Christina hoped for—Lynnette slid a look to her left. From this angle, she could see the back of the mirror and, to her surprise, there was something fastened to it with two nubs of sealing wax.

Something that looked like papers.

Lynnette's heartbeat sped up but she forced herself to keep her place. No sooner had Tess and Gwen finished and the door closed behind them than she darted from her hiding place and grabbed for the papers.

She looked at them briefly. They were filled with line after line of Madelaine's code. Lynnette breathed a sigh of relief. She tucked the pages into her reticule and carefully slipped into the passageway and down the stairs.

It was very quiet in the parlor.

She did not have the luxury of considering all it meant. From somewhere belowstairs, Lynnette heard a door close. She hurried to the ground floor and did not dare risk the chance of going back through the kitchen. The front door was not locked and slowly, so as not to make any noise, she opened it and fled outside.

Her color high, her eyes bright, Lynnette stared at the papers scattered over her father's desk. She had been working side by side with Ravensfield for a little more than four hours. The coded pages from Madelaine's diary, the sheet of paper that contained the key, and the papers they had used to write the message that was revealed were spread out before them.

It was late and the long night was slowly dissolving into morning. Ravensfield had no doubt that Lynnette was exhausted. Still, though her shoulder muscles must have ached as much as his, though her head was probably pounding just as his was, and though the redness that streaked her eyes said that they were burning, she was not about to give up. Not when they were this close to solving the mystery. He had watched her excitement mount, little by little, as they started into the translation. Now that they were nearing the end, he knew she would find no peace and accept no rest until they were finished.

Madelaine's account of the affair of the Wonderlee Diamond was remarkably detailed, and though they had both heard the story told dozens of times by dozens of people who had been there and just as many who had not, it was also surprisingly riveting. Madelaine was a dab hand at description, and had a wit as sharp as a rapier when it came to describing the appearance and actions of those who had spent the weekend at the house party.

There was a good deal of gossip mixed among the facts. Some of it more than a little surprising. Like the line Lynnette was in the midst of translating.

"Lady Christina! In bed with Lord Charlesworth!" She read the words as she deciphered them.

Ravensfield slid the paper out from in front of her and used the key to make out the rest of the text. "That may be what she'd like to see kept quiet," he said. "He is now a respected member of Parliament."

"And may not be, if the truth were known. See here!" Lynnette pointed to another line of the diary. "He had both Lady Christina and one of the chambermaids. At the same time!"

Glancing at the look of utter astonishment on Lynnette's face, Ravensfield chuckled. "You are wonderfully innocent! It is as refreshing as a summer breeze and I do love you for it. Almost as much as I love you for not asking what happened between Christina and myself this night."

She waved away the thought as inconsequential. "I do not have time for such things. Besides, I do not have to ask. I assume that after a good deal of small talk and a few glasses of champagne, you told her that you could provide her the key to the code. Just as you'd promised in your note to her."

"I did better than that. I told her I would sell it to her!"

"You are remarkably devious." A smile lit Lynnette's face. "Did she agree?"

"She had her own thoughts on the matter. She

thought that rather than exchange the key for money, she would pay me in other ways."

"Yes." Lynnette's lips puckered. "I saw her maids turning down the bed."

"Well, I hope she was comfortable in it all alone. I know she was surprised when I wished her an early good night and left." Ravensfield kissed Lynnette's cheek.

Even that was not enough to distract her. They were too near the end and soon they were back again to the text. Piece by piece, Madelaine told the tale and Ravensfield found himself admiring the way she set the stage and described the characters who inhabited it.

It was interesting work but tedious, and more than once, Ravensfield suggested they put it aside and pick up again after they had rested. Lynnette refused. They were this close, she told him. She would not stop now.

They had translated more than thirty pages, symbol by symbol, by the time the sun came up. The story was nearly complete. Madelaine recounted how she had still been abed that morning when her host and hostess came to her door, asking to search her room. They found the jewel case there, just as a note slipped under their chamber door told them they might, and feeling both humiliated and betrayed, Madelaine had left and come back to London immediately. Just as quickly, the rumors started to fly.

Watching a tear slip down Lynnette's cheek, Ravensfield put his arm around her shoulders. "You're sure you want to continue? It seems as if the whole of the story has been told. I'm sorry, my darling, but the truth seems clear enough. She has not come out and said she took the jewel. But she has not said that she didn't take it, either. And she hasn't accused anyone else. Are you certain you—"

"There are but a few more pages. See. Here . . ." By now, they were both familiar enough with the code to be able to decipher a string of letters at a time. Lynnette pointed to the diary page. "This is a word we have not run across before now. It starts a new section. "*L-Y*— It is my name, surely."

The realization gave Lynnette new energy and she worked over the words. "See here, it is a message for me. 'Lynnette, I end the telling of my tale now and leave the rest of this message for you. I know that someday you will find both my diary and the code. I'm glad of it for I want you to know the truth. You see, my darling, you are the reason I invented the code. You are the reason I cannot say a thing about what I've learned since the day of the theft. For you see, though my friends have turned their backs on me and my lovers abandoned me, there are still those who will do a service for a woman with the wherewithal to make it worth their time.

" 'I have made inquiries, Lynnette. I have learned the truth. I know who stole the Wonderlee Diamond.' "

"Good heavens!" Ravensfield rubbed his eyes. "Are you sure that's what it says?" He peered over Lynnette's shoulder and hurriedly deciphered the lines again. His results were the same. "See here . . ." He continued with the line.

" 'I have confronted her and she has confessed. Little good it does me! For I cannot prove a thing; she has already sold the jewel and she swears that if I tell anyone, you will suffer for it, my dear Lynnette. She vows that she will keep you from all the things I wish for you, a good marriage, a family, being presented at court. Thus the code. We must keep this our secret. Forever.

" 'This is the price of my silence. My banishment. My shame. Do not feel sorry for me. My reputation is beyond redemption. All I can wish for now is that which she promises she will do for you in return for my silence. She swears she will ease your acceptance into Society. For all her faults, she is a woman of her word.' "

That was the last of the diary. Madelaine didn't say who had stolen the Wonderlee Diamond.

She didn't have to.

"It will not work."

"Of course it will." Ravensfield pressed a kiss to Lynnette's forehead. "After all, it is your plan."

She was too nervous to keep still. She paced to the other side of the room and back. "It is my plan, yes. But it is a bad plan. What makes you think—"

"She will come." He was as steady as she was agitated, and as much as she was grateful for it and for his unwavering support, it did little to soothe her nerves. "Thanks to a cheerful message I sent her this morning, she has discovered that the diary pages are missing. She knows that you have the key. Oh, she'll come, right enough." He smiled and Lynnette wondered how he could look so calm. "Much like you, my darling, Christina cannot resist a mystery."

Lynnette took another turn around the room. "Yes, but even if she does come, we can tell her what the diary reveals. We can tell her we know the truth. But we, like poor, dear Madelaine, have no proof!"

"Leave that to me." When they heard a carriage pull up to the front of Plumley Terrace, Ravensfield headed for the door. "I will be right here," he said, pointing to the room directly across the passageway. "If you need anything—"

"I will call you. Yes. Certainly." Because she did not like the idea of him leaving and thinking her less than grateful for all he'd done, she hurried over and kissed him.

"It's going to be fine," he told her, and when they heard the butler downstairs greeting Lady Christina, he went into the room across from the parlor and tilted the door.

By the time Lady Christina was escorted up, Lynnette was more in control than she expected to be. "Christina! How good to see you."

"Really, Lynnette, I have told you before. You are a terrible liar." Christina was dressed in a gown the color of sunshine. It matched her hair perfectly. She did not remove her hat or gloves. Clearly, she was not planning a long visit. "Apparently, your friend Ravensfield does not have the same problem. In case you have yet to discover it for yourself, let me tell you. He is a very practiced liar."

"Do you think so?" Lynnette smiled. "I thought you might have figured that out from the beginning. He sent you a note saying he was coming around to call, but you don't really think he was there just to see you, do you?"

Christina's shoulders shot back. "And you don't really know what happened between us while you were skulking through my house like a thief."

"But I do!" Lynnette seated herself in the upholstered chair pulled up to the windows. It was a fine early summer day and she wanted to enjoy the sun as much as she was able. "I know exactly what happened."

Christina snorted. "You don't believe him, do you?"

"I haven't even asked him what happened. I don't need to."

This was clearly a surprise, and Christina crossed the room to stand in front of Lynnette. "Let us stop playing games. You took the pages."

"I did, indeed." There was no use denying it. As a matter of fact, the simple admission made Lynnette feel giddy. "I took them because they belong to me, not to you. Thanks to the code, I translated them, as well."

The older woman's eyes sparked. "And what," she asked, "did your poor, mad mother say in those pages?"

"She was hardly mad." There was a certain pleasure to be found from dragging out the suspense. Lynnette smoothed a hand over the skirt of her apple green muslin gown sprigged with white embroidery. "It seems that all along, Madelaine was telling the truth."

"Impossible!" Christina's mouth thinned. "If she said she didn't take the diamond—"

Lynnette stood. "You did."

The color in Christina's cheeks paled but she kept her shoulders steady and her head high. "Madelaine was brainsick! You know that as well as I do. She invented stories!"

"Do you think so? Perhaps you can help clarify what she says. For instance, she tells one story in particular in great detail. A little something about Lord Charlesworth."

"That is hardly news!" Christina sloughed off the statement with an elegant little lift of her shoulders and a laugh to match. "Lord Charlesworth and I were once lovers. Everyone in London knows that."

"But I daresay they do not know that it was not just you and Lord Charlesworth in that bed. There is some mention of a chambermaid."

Christina's mouth fell open. "She couldn't have said that. How did she know?"

"Know? It seems my mother knew a great deal about what happened that weekend. And you called yourself her friend!"

"And you really believe all this?"

"I do. Just as I believe it is why you stood by my mother through her illness. You were there to remind her, weren't you? You were there so she would never forget that you were the one who pulled her down from the pedestal where the *ton* had raised her. You always have been greedy, Christina. And I have no doubt you were jealous. It was the perfect way for you to solve both problems."

Christina smiled. Her teeth glinted in the sunlight. "I will tell you what I told her. Prove it!"

Lynnette shrugged. "I cannot."

"But I can."

When Ravensfield walked into the room, Christina spun around, startled.

Lynnette was surprised when she saw that he wasn't alone.

"I do believe you've met." Ravensfield motioned to the man who stood at his shoulder. It was Mr. Fryer.

The jeweler and Christina recognized each other instantly. He nodded vigorously. "Right as rain, that one is." He looked across the room at Lynnette. "When you showed me that there portrait of the other lady, I thought it looked enough like the woman I saw in my shop that day. But this is her and no doubt. Alive and in the flesh."

"And let me guess . . ." Lynnette turned to Lady Christina. "You even thought to borrow my mother's velvet cloak the day you visited Mr. Fryer."

"I've never seen this man before." Christina's words were brave but her face was the color of ashes. "I don't know what you're talking about."

"About that diamond. That is what we are talking about." Mr. Fryer was apparently not shy or averse to stating his case to his betters. "I gave you a right fair price for it, I did. And to think you could forget me completely after so little time—"

"This is insane!" Christina's shoulders shot back. Her jaw was rigid. "You cannot prove a thing and don't think you can. Not with this . . ." Her top lip curled and she gave Fryer a look that was nothing short of astringent. "Not with this man. Not with anyone."

"What about him?" Ravensfield motioned to someone standing out in the passageway. The moment the man stepped into the room, Lynnette's throat closed over a lump of panic. For she would recognize him anywhere. He was the man who had tried to steal into her bedchamber, the one who had accosted her at the masquerade ball.

The man in black didn't say a word. He didn't need to. No sooner had Christina clapped eyes on him than she scrambled for the door. "Whatever he's told you, it isn't true." She shot a look at the man, another at Ravensfield. "If he says I paid him to retrieve the code—"

"You did pay him to retrieve the code." Ravensfield bowed her out. "Just as I have paid him for the truth."

By the time she got to the door, Christina's hands were shaking. She turned and aimed a look at Lynnette and at Ravensfield, who had come to stand at Lynnette's side. "You may spread your rumors all you like. No one will ever believe this man . . ." She cast a scathing look at the man in black. "Or this one." She sent another in Fryer's direction. "You will never prove a thing."

She was gone and Ravensfield paid both Mr. Fryer and the man in black for their time before Lynnette turned to him.

"However did you—"

"I have friends," he told her. "People who know things. All it took was a little research. And a bit of the blunt. It wasn't really hard."

Lynnette did not know if she should laugh or cry. She was delighted that they had proved Madelaine's innocence and dismayed that, because there was no proof except for the testimony of a known burglar and a less-than-honest jeweler, no one would ever know. "She is right, you know. There's nothing we can do to clear Madelaine's name."

"We can try." He gave her a reassuring squeeze. "We can make further inquiries, delve further into the story now that we know this piece of it. Why, we might even—" Ravensfield's dark eyes lit with something so like inspiration, Lynnette wondered what was going on inside his head. He raced for the door. "I have to go," he told her.

"Go? Where?"

"Berkshire."

"Berkshire?" She followed him as far as the passageway but it was clear from the start that there was no holding him back. "Why? And how long will you be gone?"

"Not long." He kissed her quickly. "A few months at the most. I will write to you. I'll let you know how things are progressing."

"But I—"

He kissed her again to stop her questions. Harder this time. Longer. By the time he was finished, Lynnette's head was spinning.

"There you go, my love." He gave her one last kiss. "Something to remember me by."

It has been many years since all that I have told you has passed. I am older now, more experienced. Less likely to see phantoms where none exist. But this I can tell you: all I have recounted here in these pages is true. The guilty party has been found out. My innocence is proved once and for all. This is the end of the Affair of the Waverly Diamond.

Lynnette closed her book and set it down. She had not even realized that while she was reading, her heartbeat had sped up, and now it throttled back, bit by bit. She pressed a hand to her heart.

"It is . . ." She looked at Willie who, now that her confinement was near, was resting on a couch in the parlor at Somerton House. It was evening and the windows were closed against an autumn rainstorm. Thunder rumbled in the distance. Rain beat against the walls and made patterns against the windows. "It is most remarkable. It is surely the story of—"

"The Wonderlee Diamond. Yes! Can you believe anything so marvelous!" Nick had gotten up to pour Willie a glass of water and he crossed the room to hand it to her. "It's the most incredible thing," he said. "And the talk of the town."

"Even I have heard as much!" Willie grinned. "And I have been out little of late."

"But the details are all there!" Lynnette turned the newest of Mrs. Mordefi's works over in her hands. She had had little inclination to read since Ravensfield's hasty departure from London some months before and would not have picked up the book at all except that Willie and Nick insisted. Now, she saw why. "It is just as the story is told in Madelaine's diary. I do believe someone must have told the tale to Mrs. Mordefi and I know it wasn't me. It is all there except that the names have been changed."

"And certainly not to protect the innocent!" Nick laughed. "There's no mistake at all who your Mrs. Mordefi is talking about. Madelaine, the poor maligned heroine, is now known as Magdalene. And is there any doubt that the cruel beauty with the sparkling blue eyes who Mrs. Mordefi calls Lady Christian is other than our Lady Christina? Imagine the way the news has gone through the *ton* in seven-league boots!"

"As if Christina would care." Lynnette plunked *The Affair of the Waverly Diamond* down on the table next to the chair where she sat. She had been reading for some hours and she stretched and rubbed a hand to the small of her back. "As remarkable as the whole thing is, no one will ever believe it more than anything but coincidence. No one will think that Lady Christina is guilty."

"Will they not?" As if he couldn't wait to impart the latest news, Nick beamed. "I was at my club this afternoon. It seems that Christina has read the book, as well. Word has it that she's closed up her house. She's fled to the Continent. That alone must surely prove your mother's innocence. And Christina's guilt."

It was remarkable, surely, and Lynnette wished she could enjoy the news more. If only—

"You miss him very much." Willie's words broke through Lynnette's blue mood. "I have told you not to worry."

"And I can hardly help myself." Lynnette rose from her chair. It was late and she must be getting home. She looked out the window and saw that the rain was beating down harder than ever. Lightning flashed through the sky. "It has been months, Willie. Months since Ravensfield disappeared."

"No word from him?" Nick's question was as gentle as the look in his eyes.

"I've received some letters." The memory should have warmed Lynnette but instead it only made her feel worse. "He promises he will return but . . ." She hardly dared speak her worries. "Perhaps he is the one who located Mrs. Mordefi and told her the story of the diamond. Perhaps he believes that now that he's helped me clear Madelaine's name, any allegiance he owes me is settled. Do you suppose he's gone for good?"

Willie and Nick exchanged looks.

It was not an answer but it confirmed what Lynnette was thinking. However much it did not correspond with the actions of the Ravensfield who had won her heart, it did tally with his past. However much she did not wish to consider it, there was a possibility.

Rather than upset Willie at this delicate time, Lynnette headed back to Plumley Terrace. Mrs. Wilcox greeted her at the door and took her pelisse, glancing as she did at the rain and the lightning that now was so frequent and so bright that it lit the evening sky as bright as day.

"You've heard, haven't you?"

It took Lynnette a moment to realize what her housekeeper was talking about. "Do you mean about the book?"

"I do, indeed!" Mrs. Wilcox was so excited, she shifted from foot to foot. She was a short, round woman and the effect was not unlike a ball rolling about the floor. "I'm so happy for you. And for your mother, may she rest in peace."

"And I am happy, too."

Now all Lynnette had to do was remind herself that she was. A task that might be far easier if she could shrug away the misery that sat upon her shoulders like a weight. Slowly, she started up to her room.

When she got there, she closed the door behind her and thought of the night she'd locked it, the night the man had appeared on her veranda, intent on stealing the code. Things had turned out well, she reminded herself.

"If only . . ." Another growl of thunder crashed overhead, drowning out the sound of Lynnette's sigh. There was a fire in the grate and she crossed the room to warm her hands at it. That was when another bolt of lightning flashed.

And she saw the man on her veranda.

Lynnette's heart stopped. Her hand went to her chest. Frozen by surprise, she watched as the French doors opened and the figure, cloaked in black and dripping with rain, stepped inside.

"It's about bloody time!" Ravensfield shook the rain from his shoulders. "How is it a man is supposed to surprise the woman he loves when the woman he loves takes such a damned, long bloody time getting home!"

"Thomas?" Lynnette clutched a hand at her throat. It did little to relieve the lump of emotion there. "Is it really you?"

His smile flashed through the gloom. "Really me," he said. He slipped off his cape and left it on the floor near the door. "And I have really missed you."

It was all she could do not to run to him. She forced herself to keep her place. "You've been gone a devilishly long time."

"I have been devilishly busy."

"Indeed. You are—"

"Wet and tired." He stepped nearer. "And wanting to kiss you so damned much, I can almost taste it."

"Almost?"

He tossed aside his tall top hat and crossed the room in three long strides. He had her in his arms before she knew it, her chest pressed to his. "I've missed you!"

"And I have missed you. But—" When he bent to kiss her, she stopped him, one finger on his lips. "There is surely something you need to tell me. You have kept a secret. Though you belittle her talents and disparage her books, you are acquainted with Mrs. Mordefi!"

"I—" He grinned, the expression almost sheepish in the firelight. He took her hand and led her closer to the fire. There was a chair set in front of it and he sat and pulled her into his lap. "It is a little more complicated than that," he told her. "You see, when I inherited my title, I learned that my dear father was not as prudent as I thought. I had estates. I had homes. I had more titles than I knew what to do with. What I did not have was money."

"In the suds?" It seemed impossible to imagine. "What did you do?"

Now that the moment was here, he found himself more nervous than he had ever been. If she didn't believe him, he might be able to address the problem. But if she did . . . if she thought less of him because of it . . . if she couldn't love him because of his scandalous secret—

It was the one thing that had kept him from returning to London as soon as his newest book was finished. He was a coward. Plain and simple. A coward who feared losing the most precious thing in his life.

Ravensfield swallowed down his misgivings.

"I have always been told I have something of a way with words. I thought if I could put that talent to use, I might be able to save the family name and increase the family fortunes."

"And so you—"

"Well, you see, I didn't have much of a choice. It was that or sell myself to the highest bidder. It's ridiculously romantic, I know, but I had always thought to marry for love rather than money."

A smile tickled her lips. "Ridiculously romantic? Do you think so?"

He rested his arms more comfortably around her waist. "I've always thought so. Now I am not so sure."

"Ah! A revelation! Just as the heroes of Mrs. Mordefi's books so often have."

"Yes . . . Well . . . Mrs. Mordefi's books." He harrumphed his opinion. "They are foolish in the extreme. As are the people who populate them. But they are remarkably popular and they have kept the wolf from the door." He loosened his hold. "You see, my love, I am Mrs. Mordefi and she is me. There. So now you know the truth. And there isn't another person aside from Worthy who does, for he is my emissary, so to speak, the person my publisher deals with, the only connection Mrs. Mordefi has to the real world. If the truth were known—"

"It would surely ruin you!" There was a sparkle in Lynnette's eyes that told him that while it might be true, it would never matter to her.

"Would you care very much?" he asked her.

She kissed him.

"Will you marry me?"

She kissed him yet again.

"As simple as that?" Ravensfield chuckled.

"Mrs. Mordefi has long been my favorite author," she told him. "To think that I might have a look at the stories before they are even printed!"

"If that is the only reason you have agreed to my proposal . . ." He laughed and tightened his hold, cupping her bottom so that he might settle her more comfortably on his lap. His clothes were damp and they scratched the delicate skin of her arms and neck.

"It is not the only reason." She skimmed a finger along his cheek. "There is the part about wanting to spend the rest of my life with you. The part about being in love."

"And the part about the scandal?"

Lynnette smiled and wound her arms around his neck. "I say, your grace, you should know me better than that. You know I can never resist an adventure. And a life with you, I think, will be the greatest adventure of them all!"